13 Moons: Legacy of the Guardians

• A YA Paranormal Fantasy of Magic, Legacy, and Love

Donald J. Wright, Stephen Walker

Blurbs

After three years, sixteen-year-old Sean Murphy thought the worst was behind him. After banishing an ancient malevolent spirit and becoming the leader of his teenage coven, he spent the past three years building a life of balance—between magic and school, between duty and love. But when his beloved grandfather passes away and global supernatural attacks begin surfacing, Sean is thrust into a deeper mystery that reveals a terrifying truth: the spirit he once fought was merely a harbinger.

From the ruins of Peru to the shadows of the Black Forest, magical nexuses are being activated by different spectral predators—each with unique, horrifying powers. And the final ritual, one that could rip the veil between worlds, will unfold at the very nexus Sean's family has guarded for generations.

As the new Guardian of the Keystone, Sean must unite his coven, confront his estranged uncle's magical legacy, and delve into the Sanctuary's buried knowledge. But the spirits are watching, waiting—and this time, they are Legion.

Set against the backdrop of love, loss, and legacy, **13 Moons:** Legacy of **the Guardians** is a gripping young adult fantasy that explores the cost of power, the strength of found family, and the courage it takes to stand when the darkness calls.

Also by Donald J. Wright

Lilith's Garden
The Golden Book
The Terraforming Protocol
The Prometheus Protocol (Book I)
The Codex Protocol (Book II)

THE Quantum Schism (Book III)

13th Moon (Book I)
Killer Ice
The Codex Protocol
The Ghost Code (Book I)
The Quantum Echo (Book II)
The Quantum Heart (Book III)

Nonfiction
Diamonds Under Fire (Revised)
The Handbook of Lab-Created Diamonds
Eternal Shine
Globe Treasure Hunting

Beyond Climate Debates

Contents

Chapter 1: The Coven's Confidence

The air in the clearing by Goose Creek crackled, not with the familiar humidity of a Carolina afternoon but with focused, thrumming power. Three years had passed since the battle in the cellar, three years that had transformed Sean Murphy from a frightened, newly awakened warlock into a confident, sixteen-year-old coven leader. He stood in the center of a circle of seven other teenagers, his hazel eyes scanning each face, his posture radiating an authority that came as naturally to him now as breathing.

But something felt different today. A subtle wrongness in the air that made the hair on the back of his neck stand on end. He pushed the feeling aside—they had work to do.

"Hold the shield," Sean commanded, his voice calm but resonant. "Kim, anchor it to the earth. Matthew, reinforce the eastern arc. Don't just see the energy; feel it. Let it become a part of you."

Kim pressed her palms to the ground, her connection to the earth sending roots of green energy deep into the soil. The grass beneath her hands grew an inch taller, responding to her magic with eager life. Matthew's kinetic energy hummed as he strengthened the shield's weakest point, his magic manifesting as ripples of compressed air.

Across the circle, Katie met his gaze, a playful smirk dancing on her lips. At sixteen, her beauty had sharpened from youthful prettiness into something more striking. The crystal Sean had given her years ago rested against her collarbone, but it was her own power that now made the air around her hum. She'd grown into her magic with a grace that still took his breath away.

With a graceful, almost dismissive flick of her wrist, she sent a shimmering wave of turquoise energy to bolster a weakening section of the protective dome they had collectively cast over the clearing. The gesture was casual, but Sean could sense the precise control behind it—the years of practice that made such displays look effortless.

Show-off, Sean sent the thought directly to her mind, a private channel they had perfected over years of practice.

Her mental reply was instantaneous, laced with laughter. Just making sure you're paying attention, farm boy. You were staring again.

He was. He couldn't help it. The way the dappled sunlight caught in her blonde hair, the fierce concentration in her blue eyes as she wove intricate spells—it all still made his heart skip a beat. They were a unit, two halves of a whole, and the entire coven knew it.

Their magical bond had deepened over the years into something profound and rare. When they cast together, their power didn't just combine—it multiplied, creating effects that neither could achieve alone. Sam had called it "magical resonance," but to Sean and Katie, it was simply how things were meant to be.

Sam, now a poised young woman of twenty-three, stood beside Katie, her own sea-green eyes focused as she channeled a steady stream of protective energy into the dome. Her magic had a different quality than the others—older, more refined, touched by experiences she rarely spoke about. "It's holding steady, Sean," she called out. "But I feel a probe at the southern edge. Faint, but it's there."

Sean closed his eyes, extending his senses. He felt it too—a minor woodland spirit, curious about the sudden surge of power. But there was something else, something that made his stomach tighten with unease. A whisper of wrongness, like a single discordant note in an otherwise perfect harmony.

He sent out a gentle, non-verbal command to the woodland spirit: Peace. We mean no harm. The probing sensation vanished, but the underlying wrongness remained, subtle as a shadow at noon.

"Alright," Sean said, opening his eyes. "Let it drop."

As one, the coven released their focus. The shimmering dome dissolved into a thousand motes of light that danced in the afternoon air before winking out. A collective sigh of relief and exhaustion went through the group.

"Good work, everyone," Katie said, stepping forward. "Your coordination is getting better. Remember, it's not about raw power; it's about harmony. Like a choir, not a shouting match." She playfully punched Matthew on the arm. "That includes you, Mr. 'I-can-carve-a-rune-into-anything.'"

The young warlock grinned. "Hey, it works."

"Speaking of which," Jake, one of the younger members, piped up, "Matthew, can you help me with those protection runes later? My bedroom window's been rattling at night. Probably just the wind, but..."

"But nothing's ever 'just' anything anymore," Matthew finished, his grin fading slightly. "Yeah, I'll come by after dinner."

As the other coven members gathered their things, chatting about school and weekend plans, Sean and Katie hung back, the familiar comfort of their shared silence settling between them. The routine was now second nature: school, chores, coven practice, and the constant, underlying vigilance for any sign of the Malevolent Spirit's return.

"You're thinking about it, aren't you?" Katie asked softly, her fingers finding his.

"Always," Sean admitted. "It's been quiet for three years. Too quiet."

"Maybe Uncle Joe was right. Maybe we drove it off for good," she said, though her tone lacked conviction.

"Maybe," Sean squeezed her hand. "But 'maybe' isn't good enough. That's why we practice." He paused, then added quietly, "And that's why I can't shake the feeling that something's watching us. Even now."

Katie's eyes sharpened, scanning the tree line. "I don't sense anything."

"Neither do I. Not exactly. It's just..." He struggled to find the words. "You know how the air feels before a storm? That electric charge that makes everything feel alive and dangerous at the same time?"

She nodded slowly. "The farm's been feeling like that all week. I thought it was just me being paranoid."

They started the walk back towards the farmhouse, the path worn smooth by their countless trips to the cave and clearing. The farm was thriving. With the money from the sale of the Pilgrim's Progress book, Tom had paid off the loan and even invested in some new equipment before officially handing the reins of the day-to-day work over to Sean. Life had settled into a rhythm that was demanding but deeply satisfying.

As they walked, Sean noticed things that would have been invisible to him three years ago. The way certain shadows seemed too dark for the angle of the sun. The unnatural stillness of birds that should have been singing. The faint, acrid scent on the breeze reminded him of burned electronics, though there was nothing mechanical for miles.

"Don't forget we have that history test on Monday," Katie reminded him, pulling him from his dark thoughts. "And I saw the look on Mrs. Brim's face today. You're in for another lecture about not applying for the state science fair."

Sean groaned. "I don't have time for the science fair. Between Grandpa's new obsession with daytime television and that leaky trough in the north pasture, my plate is full."

"Your plate is full because you're a sixteen-year-old running a farm, a coven, and maintaining a perfect GPA. I think you're allowed to be busy," she said, bumping her shoulder against his. "Besides, you have me to help."

They stopped at the edge of the woods, the setting sun casting long shadows that stretched toward the familiar silhouette of the farmhouse. In the distance, Sean could see his grandfather sitting in his favorite rocker on the porch, a small, frail figure against the vast backdrop of the land he so loved. A wave of deep affection washed over Sean mingled with a persistent, gnawing worry about Tom's health.

"He looks tired today," Sean whispered.

Katie followed his gaze, her expression softening. "He's 84, Sean. He's allowed to be tired. He's happy. That's what matters." She turned to face him, her hands resting on his chest. "We've done good here. We've built something safe. Something strong."

"We are strong," Sean corrected her, his hands coming up to cup her face. He leaned in and kissed her, a kiss that was no longer the tentative, exploratory press of their first years but one filled with the deep, confident love of two souls intrinsically bound. It was a kiss that tasted of sunshine, magic, and shared history.

When they pulled apart, Katie was smiling. "See? Strong."

Sean grinned, feeling the weight on his shoulders lighten, as it always did when she was near. "Alright, you powerful, beautiful witch. I've got chores to do before Grandpa decides to do them himself."

"Wait," Katie said suddenly, catching his arm. "Before you go... walk with me? Just for a few more minutes?"

Something in her tone made Sean pause. He studied her face, seeing a flicker of vulnerability beneath her usual confidence. "Of course."

She led him down a side path that wound along Goose Creek, away from the house and prying eyes. They found their spot—a fallen oak that had created a natural bench overlooking a bend in the creek. The water caught the dying light, turning it into liquid gold. Katie settled against him, but he could feel the tension in her shoulders.

"Talk to me," he said softly.

Katie was quiet for a long moment, organizing her thoughts. "Do you ever think about the future? I mean, really think about it. Not just tomorrow or next week, but... years from now?"

"Sometimes," Sean admitted. "Why?"

"Everyone at school is talking about college applications, SATs, campus visits. Jessica Matthews got early acceptance to Duke. Tommy Chen is being recruited by three different schools for football." She turned to look at him. "What are we going to do, Sean? We can't exactly put 'saved the world from an ancient evil spirit' on our college applications."

Sean felt the weight of the question settles over him. It was something they'd both been avoiding —the looming reality that their magical lives and mundane futures might not be compatible.

"I used to think I'd just take over the farm full-time," he said slowly. "Maybe take some agriculture courses at the community college. Simple. Normal." He met her eyes. "But that was before."

"Before the magic."

"Before you," he corrected gently. "Before I understood what we could be together. Our power, when we combine it... Katie, we could do so much good. Real good. Not just protecting this place, but learning, growing stronger."

"So... magical college?" she asked, a small smile playing at her lips.

"Maybe. Sam mentioned there are universities with... unofficial programs. Places where people like us can learn alongside regular students. Harvard has a whole occult library that's officially just for 'historical research.'" He took her hands. "We could go together. Study by day, research wards and protection spells by night."

"In Boston?" Katie's voice was carefully neutral.

"Or wherever you want," Sean said quickly. "Duke has a parapsychology program. UNC-Chapel Hill has those medieval manuscripts Sam's always talking about. We could go to California if you'd like. Berkeley's supposed to be crawling with hedgewitches."

Katie laughed, the sound bright and surprised. "You've really thought about this."

"Of course I have." He cupped her face gently. "Katie, I can't imagine a future that doesn't have you in it. Whatever we do, wherever we go... we do it together."

"Even if I wanted to go to Scotland? Study at the ancient sites?"

"I'll learn to love haggis."

"Paris? For their esoteric archives?"

"My French is terrible, but I'll manage."

"What about here?" Her voice dropped to a whisper. "What if I wanted to stay right here, help you run the farm, raise the next generation of guardians in the same place that made us who we are?"

Sean's heart stuttered. "Is that what you want?"

"I want you," Katie said simply. "Everything else is just geography. But Sean... the thought of having a normal life, a magical life, a life where we wake up together every morning and protect this place side by side... yeah. I want that."

He kissed her then, pouring all his hopes and dreams into the connection. When they broke apart, both were breathless.

"Marry me," he whispered against her lips.

Katie pulled back, eyes wide. "What?"

"Not now," he clarified quickly, though his heart was racing. "After graduation. Or college. Or whenever you're ready. But Katie... I know you're it for me. You're my anchor, my partner, my everything. So yeah. Someday. Marry me."

She stared at him for a long moment, then burst into tears. "You absolute idiot," she managed through her sobs. "Of course I will."

They held each other as full darkness fell, making promises they believed they'd have a lifetime to keep. But as they finally made their way back to the farmhouse, Sean couldn't shake the feeling that something in the darkness was listening, watching, waiting.

The feeling followed him as they parted at Katie's house. It lingered as he completed his evening chores, as he helped his grandfather to bed, as he lay in his own room staring at the ceiling.

Something was coming. The three years of peace hadn't been a victory—they'd been a preparation. The enemy was out there, gathering strength, making plans. And somehow, Sean knew with a cold certainty that settled in his bones like ice their quiet life was about to shatter.

As he finally drifted off to sleep, he thought he heard something on the wind—a sound like distant laughter, cold and patient and older than memory. But when he startled awake, heart pounding, there was only the familiar creak of the old house settling and the distant bark of a dog.

Still, he reached out with his mind, finding Katie's sleeping consciousness and wrapping it in a protective embrace. Whatever was coming, whatever darkness was gathering just beyond their perception, they would face it together.

They had to. Everything they'd just promised each other depended on it.

In the corner of his room, a shadow moved independently of any light source, and for just a moment, the temperature dropped twenty degrees. Then everything was still again, peaceful and quiet.

But the peace was a lie, and somewhere in the darkness, ancient eyes had turned their attention to a small farm in South Carolina, where two young people in love had just painted targets on their backs by daring to dream of a future.

The game was about to begin again. And this time, the stakes would be infinitely higher.

Chapter 2: A Fading Light

The late afternoon sun bled gold across the fields, painting the rows of corn in brilliant, fiery strokes. Sean drove the last fence post into the soft earth with a final, satisfying thud of the mallet. The familiar ache blooming in his shoulders and back was a good one. This kind spoke of honest work and tangible accomplishment. Wiping a sleeve across his sweat-beaded brow, he stood back to admire the newly repaired section of fencing along the north pasture. It was a mundane task, one of a hundred he performed each week, yet it grounded him in a way that even the most powerful magic could not. This land was real, its needs simple and direct. It was an anchor in the swirling currents of his extraordinary life.

He gathered his tools, the clang of metal a familiar tune against the backdrop of the farm as it wound down for the day. The cicadas had begun their evening chorus, a sound as constant and comforting as the beat of his own heart. As he rounded the corner of the big red barn, its flank still bearing the faint, ghostly scorch marks of a battle long past, he saw his grandfather.

Tom Murphy wasn't in his usual rocker, the one whose gentle creak had been the soundtrack to Sean's entire childhood. Instead, he was sitting on the top step of the porch, his back resting against the familiar white post, his gaze fixed on the horizon where the sky was beginning its slow burn from blue to orange. At eighty-four, Tom seemed smaller, as if the years were slowly whittling him away, leaving behind something more essential, yet more fragile. A pang of love and worry, so sharp it was almost painful, shot through Sean's chest.

He quietly set the tools by the porch steps and went inside, returning a moment later with two tall glasses of sweet tea, ice clinking against the sides. He handed one to his grandfather, whose gnarled fingers accepted it with a grateful nod.

"Figured you could use this," Sean said, settling onto the step beside him. The old wood groaned softly, a familiar sound of welcome.

"Appreciate it, son," Tom said, his voice a low, gravelly rumble. He took a slow sip, his eyes never leaving the fields. "Fence looks good. Straight and tight."

"It'll hold," Sean confirmed.

"Knew it would." Tom fell silent again, a comfortable quiet that had defined their relationship for years. Sean had learned more from his grandfather in these shared silences than he had from most books.

"I remember when you were no bigger than a field mouse," Tom said suddenly, a faint, raspy chuckle in his voice. "Tried to help me with that same stretch of fence. You couldn't even lift the mallet, but you insisted. Swung it with all your might and ended up flat on your back in the dirt, staring at the sky like you'd just discovered it."

Sean smiled at the memory. "I remember. You didn't laugh. You just told me I had a good swing and that the ground needed softening up, anyway."

"Well, you've still got a good swing," Tom said, turning to look at him fully. His pale blue eyes, though clouded with age, held a sharp, clear intensity that saw right through Sean, past the powerful warlock, and straight to the boy he'd raised. "You're doing good with the land, son. Better than I did at your age. Your father... he was a builder, always looking to improve things and make them better. Your mother had a gentle touch; she knew just what a struggling plant needed to thrive. You've got the best of both of 'em in you. They would've been so proud."

Sean's throat tightened. "I hope so, Grandpa."

"No hoping to it. It's a fact." Tom's expression grew serious, his brief smile fading like the day's light. "You've grown into your power, too. Faster and stronger than any of us ever did. You and that girl of yours... you two are a force of nature."

Sean waited, sensing this was more than just praise. It was a preamble.

"But you gotta remember something," his grandfather's voice lowered, becoming more deliberate. "Power calls to power, son. Always. Like moths to a flame, but not all of 'em come to admire the light. Some come to snuff it out, and some just want to burn in it."

He gestured out at the peaceful landscape, a sweep of his hand that encompassed everything they could see. "These quiet times... they're precious. But they're just the world taking a breath before the next storm. There's always another storm." He fixed Sean with his piercing gaze. "And when it comes, you trust your heart, Sean, not just your strength. Your magic, it's a tool. It can do amazing things, but it can also deceive you, making you think you're stronger than you're, and causing you to see enemies where there are actually friends. Your heart, though... a good, true heart like yours won't ever lead you astray."

Sean nodded slowly, the familiar unease stirring within him again. It was the same disquiet he'd felt on the wind the other day—a sense that their peaceful interlude was built on borrowed time.

With a slight tremor in his hand, Tom reached into the deep pocket of his worn overalls and pulled out a small, soft leather pouch, its surface darkened and softened by age. He carefully untied the drawstring and tipped the contents into his palm. It was a bird, no bigger than Sean's thumb, intricately carved from a dark, smooth wood he didn't recognize. Its wings were swept back as if in mid-flight, and along their edges were tiny, almost microscopic runes etched with impossible precision. They seemed to pulse with a light of their own in the fading twilight.

Tom pressed it into Sean's hand. The wood was strangely warm, smoothed by what must have been the hands of generations, and Sean could swear he felt it hum with a faint, dormant energy.

"My grandad gave this to me when I was your age," Tom whispered, his voice thick with memory. "Called it a 'Wayfinder.' He was a Murphy from the old country, came over with more secrets than luggage. He said this little fella gets warm when great magic is near." He looked at Sean, his expression heavy with unspoken meaning. "Good or bad. It's a warning. A guide. It's been quiet in my pocket for sixty years. But I've felt it stirring lately. Just a little. It's waking up."

Sean closed his fingers around the small carving, the weight of it in his palm feeling immense. This was more than a gift; it was a mantle being passed. A legacy of guardianship he was only just beginning to understand. He looked at his grandfather's hand, now resting on his own knee—at the papery, translucent skin stretched over gnarled knuckles, at the faint, blue web of veins that looked like rivers on an old map. He noticed, for the first time, how shallow his grandfather's breathing was, how each inhalation seemed to require a deliberate, rattling effort. The setting sun wasn't just ending the day; it was heralding the end of an era.

"Grandpa..." Sean started, the word catching in his throat. What was there to say? *Don't go? Stay forever?* The words were useless, childish pleas against the unstoppable tide of time.

Tom simply nodded, a silent acknowledgment of the truth that lay between them, as vast and profound as the darkening sky. He patted Sean's knee, his touch surprisingly firm, a final reassurance. "Just you be ready, son. That's all a man can be."

That evening, after Tom had retired early—his breathing more labored than he'd admit—Sean found himself restless. The weight of their conversation, of his grandfather's failing health, pressed down on him like a physical thing. He sent a thought to Katie through their mental link: Can you come over?

Already on my way, came her immediate response.

He met her at the edge of the property, where the old stone wall marked the boundary between their families' lands. She was wearing one of his hoodies, the blue one she'd claimed months ago, and her hair was pulled back in a messy bun. She looked like home.

"How is he?" she asked without preamble.

"Tired. More tired than I've ever seen him." Sean's voice cracked. "Katie, I think... I think he's getting ready to let go."

She pulled him into a fierce hug, holding him as his shoulders shook. They stood there in the darkness, surrounded by the night sounds of the farm and a familiar symphony.

"I'm scared," he admitted into her shoulder. "Not of the Spirit, not of the magic. I'm scared of losing him. Of not being ready. Of failing everyone."

Katie pulled back enough to look at him, her hands framing his face. "Listen to me, Sean Murphy. You are the strongest person I know. Not because of your magic but because of your heart. Your grandfather knows that. We all know that."

"What if I'm not enough?"

"Then we'll be enough together," she said firmly. "That's what you taught me, remember? The first time we linked our power? You said magic wasn't about individual strength—it was about connection."

They walked hand in hand to the old barn, climbing up to the hayloft where they'd shared so many conversations over the years. The space was filled with the sweet scent of dried hay and memories.

"Tell me about the future," Katie said, settling beside him. "Not the Spirit, not the danger. Tell me about after. When we win."

Sean was quiet for a moment, then began to speak. "We'll strengthen the wards until nothing can threaten this place again. We'll teach the younger kids—Jake's showing real promise with elemental work. We'll expand the sanctuary, add our own knowledge to Mary's collection."

"And us?" Katie prompted softly.

"We'll build a house," Sean said, warming to the subject. "Right there, on the hill overlooking the creek. Close enough to help with the farm, far enough for privacy. Big kitchen, because you actually know how to cook. A library for all your books. A workshop where I can experiment with new protection charms."

"Kids?" The question was barely a whisper.

"If you want them." He turned to look at her. "Can you imagine? Little witches and warlocks running around, driving us crazy with accidental magic?"

"Your grandfather would love that," Katie said, then froze. "I mean—"

"No, you're right." Sean managed a small smile. "He would. He'd spoil them rotten, tell them all his stories, teach them the old ways before they could even walk properly."

They fell silent, the unspoken truth hanging between them—Tom wouldn't be there to see those hypothetical grandchildren. But somehow, speaking the dream aloud made it feel more possible, more worth fighting for.

"I love you," Katie said suddenly. "I know we say it, but I need you to really hear it right now. I love you, Sean Murphy. Not just the powerful warlock, not just the coven leader. You. The boy who talks to plants when he thinks no one's listening. Who still tears up at the end of Old Yeller. Who makes the worst pancakes in existence but keeps trying anyway."

"They're not that bad," Sean protested weakly.

"They're terrible," Katie said, laughing through her tears. "And I love you for every burned, lumpy one of them."

He kissed her then, soft and sweet and full of promise. "When this is over," he whispered, "I'm going to give you the life we dream about. All of it."

"We'll give it to each other," Katie corrected. "Partners, remember?"

"Always," Sean confirmed.

They stayed in the loft until the sky began to lighten, planning a future they desperately hoped they'd live to see.

They sat in silence as the last sliver of the sun dipped below the horizon, plunging the world into the soft, purple hues of dusk. The air grew cooler, carrying the scent of damp earth and the promise of fall's chill. The first star of the evening pricked the darkening canvas above, a lone diamond in a sea of velvet.

Sean didn't move. He sat beside his grandfather, the man who had been his rock, his guide, his entire world, and felt the profound, aching certainty of change. He clutched the wooden bird in his pocket, its latent power a heavy, tangible promise of the future. He felt the weight of his grandfather's words settling over him, understanding with a clarity that was both terrifying and absolute that the greatest challenges of his life were not behind him, but waiting just beyond the encroaching shadows. The light was fading, and soon, he would have to be strong enough to face the darkness on his own.

Chapter 3: The Unthinkable

- -

Sean woke to a world washed in the gentle gray light of predawn, but something was wrong. The silence was too complete, too absolute. Even in the deepest hours of the night, the old farmhouse was never truly quiet. There was always the soft creak of settling wood, the whisper of wind through the eaves, and the distant hum of the refrigerator downstairs. But now, the house held its breath like a living thing in hiding.

For a moment, he lay still in the familiar cocoon of his childhood bed, adrift in that liminal space between sleep and awareness. The weight of his grandfather's words from the evening before settled back over him like a heavy quilt. *Trust your heart. There's always another storm.* The Wayfinder felt cold and lifeless in the pocket of his jeans, draped over the chair where he'd left them. Even the small wooden bird seemed to sense that something fundamental had shifted in the night.

He reached for his phone to check the time—5:47 AM. Earlier than he usually woke, but not unusually so. The farm demanded early risers, and his internal clock had been set by years of pre-dawn chores and the rhythms of the land. What was unusual was the quality of the silence, the way it seemed to press against his eardrums like deep water.

Something's wrong.

The thought came unbidden, a cold certainty that made his stomach clench. He'd learned to trust these instincts over the past few years—his magical awakening had sharpened his intuition to a razor's edge, and right now, every instinct he possessed was screaming danger.

He swung his legs out of bed, his bare feet finding the familiar grooves worn smooth in the wooden floor by generations of Murphy men. The floorboards, which had creaked under his weight since childhood, were silent now as if the house itself was holding its breath. He pulled on yesterday's jeans and a faded t-shirt, moving with the careful quiet of someone who didn't want to disturb whatever fragile equilibrium had settled over the world.

The hallway stretched before him, longer than it should have been, filled with a gray twilight that seemed to swallow the weak light from the window at the far end. Family photographs lined the walls—three generations of Murphys staring down with familiar eyes—but their faces seemed watchful now, expectant. Waiting for something he couldn't name.

Trust your heart, his grandfather had said. And his heart was hammering against his ribs with a terror he didn't want to acknowledge.

The door to his grandfather's room stood slightly ajar, just as it had been when he'd passed it the night before. But now, in the pre-dawn gloom, it looked like a mouth hanging open in surprise. Sean approached it with the reluctant steps of a man walking to his own execution, each footfall echoing in the oppressive quiet despite the carpet runner beneath his feet.

He paused at the threshold, raised his hand to knock, and listened. Nothing. Not even the sound of breathing. The absence of sound was so complete it felt like a physical presence, a void that pulled at his consciousness.

"Grandpa?" His voice came out as barely a whisper, swallowed by the hungry silence. He cleared his throat and tried again, louder this time. "Grandpa, it's Sean. I... I thought I'd make us some breakfast before we start on the north fence."

The lie felt bitter on his tongue. He hadn't been thinking about fence repairs. He'd been thinking about the weight in his grandfather's words the night before, the finality in his voice when he'd said *be ready.* As if he'd been saying goodbye.

Still no answer. Sean pushed the door open with fingers that trembled despite his efforts to steady them.

The room was exactly as it had always been—the worn quilt his grandmother had made spread neatly over the bed, the ancient dresser with its collection of framed photographs, the straight-backed chair by the window where Tom would sit to watch the sunrise. Everything was normal, peaceful, undisturbed.

Except for the figure lying motionless on the bed.

For a split second, hope flared in Sean's chest. His grandfather was simply sleeping in, tired from the emotional weight of their conversation the night before. Old men needed their rest. It was natural. Normal. Nothing to worry about.

But even as he clung to that desperate hope, Sean knew it was a lie. The stillness was too complete, too profound. There was no gentle rise and fall of breathing, no soft snores, no small movements that spoke of dreams and life. Tom Murphy lay on his back, his hands folded peacefully over his chest, his head turned slightly on the pillow as if he were gazing out the window at the fields he'd loved so deeply.

His face was serene, almost smiling, as if he'd finally found the answer to a question that had been troubling him for years. But his chest was still. His lips were blue. And when Sean reached out with trembling fingers to touch his grandfather's forehead, the skin was cold as winter stone.

"No." The word escaped Sean's lips as barely a breath. "No, no, no. Not yet. We were supposed to have more time."

He sank to his knees beside the bed, his legs suddenly unable to support his weight. The familiar bedroom tilted and swayed around him as if he were at sea in a storm. This couldn't be happening. Not now. Not after everything they'd been through together. Not when he still had so many questions, so many things he needed to know.

Tom Murphy had been the one constant in Sean's chaotic life, the steady lighthouse that had guided him through the dark waters of adolescence and the magical awakening that followed. He'd been father, mentor, friend, and protector, all rolled into one weathered, stubborn package. And now he was gone, slipped away in the quiet hours of the night while Sean slept peacefully in the next room, unaware that the most important person in his world was taking his final breath.

The grief hit him like a physical blow, driving the air from his lungs in a harsh sob. It wasn't the clean, noble sorrow of books and movies. It was messy and raw and consuming, a black hole that threatened to swallow everything good and bright in his world. He pressed his face against the familiar quilt, breathing in the lingering scents of Old Spice and pipe tobacco, as well as the indefinable essence that had been uniquely his grandfather's.

"I'm sorry," he whispered into silence. "I'm so sorry, Grandpa. I should have known something was wrong. I should have checked on you. I should have been here."

But even as the words poured out of him, he knew they were meaningless. Tom Murphy had lived his life on his own terms, and he'd chosen to die the same way—quietly, with dignity, in the place he loved most. He'd waited until after their conversation, until after he'd passed on his final warnings and gifts. He'd held on just long enough to say goodbye, even if Sean hadn't understood it at the time.

The thought brought a fresh wave of anguish. Their last conversation replayed in his mind with brutal clarity: *Power calls power, son. Always. These quiet times... they're precious. But they're just the world taking a breath before the next storm. Trust your heart, Sean, not just your strength.*

His grandfather had known. Somehow, he'd known this would be their final conversation, their last chance to share the wisdom of generations. And instead of clinging to life, instead of fighting the inevitable, he'd used his remaining time to prepare Sean for what was coming. Even in death, Tom Murphy had been thinking of others, sacrificing his own desires for the greater good.

The realization made Sean's grief even sharper, cutting through him like a blade. He'd lost not just his grandfather but his teacher, his guide, his connection to the long line of guardians who had protected this land. He was alone now, the last Murphy, to stand watch over their ancient responsibilities.

No, he corrected himself, remembering Katie's fierce loyalty, the bond that connected him to his coven. *Not alone. Never alone.*

The thought was enough to give him the strength to push himself up from the floor. His legs shook with the aftermath of shock, but he managed to stand to look down at his grandfather's peaceful face one more time. Tom looked younger in death; the deep lines of worry and responsibility smoothed away, leaving behind the ghost of the young man he'd once been.

On the nightstand beside the bed, Sean noticed something that made his breath catch. The Wayfinder—the other Wayfinder, the one his grandfather had kept locked away for decades—sat beside a glass of water and Tom's reading glasses. But this wasn't the same wooden bird Sean carried. This one was carved from a different wood, darker and heavier, and it was warm to the touch, pulsing with a gentle inner light.

Beside it lay an envelope, yellowed with age, with Sean's name written across it in his grandfather's familiar, spidery handwriting. Sean picked it up with shaking hands, already knowing that this was Tom's final gift, his last attempt to prepare his grandson for the battles ahead.

But before he could bring himself to open it, he needed to call Katie. He needed to hear her voice, to anchor himself in the present before he lost himself entirely to grief. His phone felt impossibly heavy in his hands as he scrolled to her contact, but the moment he heard her sleepy "Hello?" he broke down completely.

"Katie," he managed through his tears. "I need you. He's... Grandpa's gone."

The silence on the other end of the line stretched for an eternity before Katie's voice came back, sharp with sudden alertness. "I'm coming. Right now. Don't move, don't do anything. I'll be there in five minutes."

Sean sank into the chair by the window, still clutching the phone, and stared out at the fields his grandfather had loved so much. The sun was rising now, painting the sky in shades of gold and rose, and the familiar landscape stretched out before him like a promise. Whatever came next, whatever storms were gathering on the horizon, this place would endure. The land would remember Tom Murphy's love, his sacrifice, and his unwavering dedication to protecting what mattered most.

The sound of a car door slamming broke through his reverie, followed by running footsteps on the front porch. Katie burst through the bedroom door like an avenging angel, her hair wild from sleep, her eyes blazing with protective fury and grief. She took in the scene at a glance—Sean hunched in the chair, Tom's still form on the bed—and without a word, she crossed the room and pulled Sean into her arms.

He collapsed against her, all his strength finally deserting him. She held him as he sobbed, her own tears falling silently into his hair, her presence a warm anchor in the storm of his grief. She didn't offer empty platitudes or try to make sense of the senseless. She simply held him, sharing his pain, letting him know that he wasn't alone in his sorrow.

"He knew," Sean whispered against her shoulder when the worst of the storm had passed. "Last night, when we talked... he knew this was goodbye. He was trying to prepare me."

Katie's arms tightened around him. "Then he succeeded," she said fiercely. "Look at you, Sean. You're not broken. You're not lost. You're exactly who he raised you to be—strong enough to carry on his legacy, wise enough to know that love is the greatest magic of all."

The envelope on the nightstand seemed to pulse with its own inner light, and Sean knew that his grandfather's final lesson was waiting for him. But for now, in the circle of Katie's arms, with the morning sun painting the world in gold, he allowed himself a few more moments of simple human grief.

Tom Murphy was gone, but his love remained, written into every board of the old farmhouse, every stone of the ancient walls, every blade of grass that grew on the land he'd protected for so long. And in Sean's heart, where it would burn like an eternal flame, guiding him through whatever darkness lay ahead.

The storm his grandfather had warned him about was coming. But Tom Murphy had done his job—he'd raised a guardian worthy of the name, surrounded him with love and allies, and given him the tools he'd need to protect what mattered most.

The last lesson could wait a little longer. Right now, Sean just needed to mourn the man who'd been his whole world and to remember that even in the depths of loss, love endured.

Outside, the farm awakened to another day, eternal and patient, carrying the memory of its guardian in every whisper of wind through the corn.

Chapter 4: The Unexpected Guardian

The air in the lawyer's office was thick with the scent of old paper, lemon polish, and the kind of stale grief that clings to places of official loss. A grandfather clock stood sentinel in the corner, its heavy, metronomic pendulum slicing time into precise, indifferent seconds. Each tick felt like a stone dropping into the vast, silent well of Sean's sorrow. He sat stiffly in a leather chair that was far too large for him, the polished mahogany of the enormous desk in front of him reflecting a distorted, pale version of his own face.

Three days had passed since his grandfather's death. Three days of a hollow ache in his chest, of well-meaning neighbors bringing casseroles, of phone calls that blurred into a meaningless hum. Now came the bureaucracy of death, a ritual colder and stranger than any he'd ever practiced in the woods.

Katie sat beside him, her presence a small, warm anchor in the disorienting sea of legal jargon. She wasn't holding his hand—that would have felt too conspicuous here—but her knee was pressed firmly against his. A constant, silent message: *I'm here. You're not alone.* Across the desk, her parents, the Becketts, looked on with expressions of gentle concern. They had been his bedrock, handling the cascade of logistics with a quiet grace that Sean was too numb to muster.

The lawyer, Mr. Abernathy, a man whose frame seemed constructed entirely of sharp, disapproving angles, cleared his throat. "So, to summarize," he said, peering at them over his spectacles. "Thomas Murphy's will is quite clear. The farm, all assets, and all responsibilities are left to you, Sean. However, as you are a minor, the court requires the appointment of a legal guardian." He turned his gaze to the Becketts. "You have graciously offered to assume this role. We just need to sign the requisite petitions..."

He slid a formidable stack of papers across the desk. It all seemed so logical, so right. The Becketts were family in every way that mattered. Sean should have felt a sense of relief, of things being settled. Instead, a strange, powerful unease coiled in his gut. It felt like walking down a path that was safe and well-lit while his instincts screamed at him to look to the woods.

Mrs. Beckett reached for a pen, her smile soft and reassuring. "We'll take good care of you, Sean. Always."

It was at that precise moment that the heavy oak door to the office swung open without a preceding knock.

Every head turned. A man stood framed in the doorway, and the quiet, stuffy air in the room instantly shifted, becoming charged and electric. He was in his mid-thirties, dressed in dark, well-fitted jeans and a simple gray jacket that spoke of quiet quality. He wasn't handsome in a conventional way, but his face was striking, with the same strong Murphy jawline as Sean's, but where Sean's features were still rounding with youth, this man's were honed by a weariness that seemed to go soul-deep. His eyes, a shade of blue paler than Tom's but just as piercing, scanned the room and landed on Sean.

For a heartbeat, Sean felt a jolt of recognition, so profoundly it was like looking into a distorted mirror of his own future. He felt the Wayfinder, tucked safely in his pocket, give off a single, faint pulse of warmth.

Mr. Abernathy was the first to recover. "Can I help you?" he asked, his tone laced with the sharp annoyance of a man whose tidy schedule had been disrupted. "This is a private meeting."

The man stepped fully into the room, closing the door softly behind him. His movements were fluid and contained, holding a stillness that commanded attention. "I apologize for the intrusion," he said, his voice quiet but carrying easily through the room. "My name is Todd Murphy. Tom was my father."

A collective, sharp intake of breath. Katie's hand flew to Sean's, her grip tight and protective. The Becketts exchanged a look of stunned confusion. This was the uncle from the stories, the source of his grandfather's deepest, oldest pain. Sean's own feelings were a tangled mess of defensive anger on his grandfather's behalf and that same strange, inexplicable pull of kinship.

Todd's gaze remained fixed on Sean, and his weary expression softened with a profound sadness. "I didn't know about the meeting," he explained, his voice laced with regret. "I... felt it. When he passed. It was like a bright light going out in the world, one I'd been pretending not to see for a long time. I had to come."

Felt it. The word hung in the air, meaningless to the lawyer but a thunderclap to Sean and Katie.

"Mr. Murphy," Mr. Beckett said, recovering his composure with the practiced calm of a judge. "This is... unexpected. Your father's will made no mention..."

"I know," Todd cut him off gently. "I wouldn't expect it to." He finally broke his gaze from Sean and looked at the Becketts, his eyes filled with gratitude that seemed entirely genuine. "Thank you for being here for him. For both of them. More than I ever was." He then looked back to Sean, and it felt as if the rest of the room faded away.

"Sean," he said, and the name was both an introduction and an apology. "Your grandfather and I... we were two sides of the same stubborn coin. We saw the world differently. Especially... the parts of the world most people don't see." He took a slow breath as if the admission cost him something. "I can't weave spells or command the elements like I suspect you can. I never learned. For me, it was always just... a hum in my blood. A knowledge of things I shouldn't know. A sense of a world layered just behind our own."

He ran a hand through his dark hair, the gesture weary and deeply human. "It scared me. I wanted to be normal, to shut it out. Your father and your grandfather... they ran toward it. They embraced it. That was the heart of everything. He was terrified for me, and I was terrified of him, of what he represented. I was a stupid, angry kid, Sean. And he was a proud, scared father. We both said things... things that couldn't be unsaid." His voice cracked on the last words, and he looked down, the mask of composure finally failing. "I should have called. God, I should have been here."

The raw, undisguised pain in his voice dissolved the last of Sean's resentment. This wasn't the monster from his grandfather's pained memories. This was a man haunted by his own choices, by a magic he had tried to deny.

Todd looked up again, his expression now set with a quiet determination. "I know you've offered to be his guardian," he said to the Becketts. "And I have no doubt you would be wonderful. But he's a Murphy. This farm, this... legacy... it's in his blood. It needs to be guided by someone who understands it, even someone who spent half his life running from it."

He took a step closer to the desk, his focus entirely on Sean now. "I want to be your guardian, Sean. Not to control you or tell you what to do. Lord knows I'm not qualified for that. But to protect your right to choose your own path. To give you the space and support to become who you're meant to be without interference. I won't interfere with your practice or your coven. I just want to... hold the line. For you. For him."

The air was thick with tension. Mrs. Beckett, her maternal instincts on high alert, spoke first. "Mr. Murphy... Todd. Forgive me, but you've been gone for fifteen years. Sean needs stability. He needs people he knows and trusts."

"I understand that ma'am. And I don't deserve his trust. Not yet," Todd admitted, his honesty disarming. "But I'm his only blood. And I'm the only one in this room besides Sean and Katie, who knows that the chill you sometimes feel on a sunny day isn't always the wind."

The decision fell to Sean. The room was silent save for the merciless ticking of the clock. He looked at the Becketts, his heart swelling with gratitude so immense it was painful. They were his haven, his unwavering support. Then he looked at his uncle, this stranger who was also a family member. In his weary eyes, he saw a reflection of his own struggle, of the push and pull between the ordinary world and the magical one. He felt the solid weight of the Wayfinder in his pocket, a link to the past and a guide to the future. It was what his grandfather had given him. A legacy. And Todd, for all his flaws, was a part of that legacy.

"Okay," Sean said, his voice quiet but firm. The single word seemed to echo in the silent office. He looked at his uncle. "Okay."

The drive back to the farm was a long, quiet affair. The legal papers had been amended, the Becketts gracious and understanding in the face of Sean's decision, promising to be just next door, always. Now, Sean sat in the passenger seat of his uncle's car, a vehicle that was clean and, practical and anonymous, just like the man beside him. The silence wasn't awkward, but it was heavy, laden with fifteen years of unspoken words, of shared grief.

As they turned onto the long dirt road leading to the farmhouse, Todd slowed the car to a crawl. He stared at the familiar silhouette of the house and barn against the afternoon sky, his hands gripping the steering wheel.

"Haven't seen this place in over fifteen years," he murmured, his voice thick. He stopped the car a hundred yards from the house and killed the engine. The only sound was the wind rustling the cornstalks. "It feels... louder than I remember."

Sean understood immediately. He didn't mean the cicadas or the distant lowing of a cow. He meant the thrum of magic, the energy that radiated from the cave, the wards, the very soil itself.

"It is," Sean said.

Todd nodded slowly, his gaze distant and troubled. "That's what I was afraid of."

They got out of the car and stood there for a moment, two generations of a magical family, united by a profound loss and now bound by a mysterious and uncertain future. The sadness of his grandfather's absence was a physical ache in Sean's chest, but it was now intertwined with a new, sharp thread of tension. Why was his uncle afraid? What did the "louder" magic of the farm signify?

The storm Tom had predicted was no longer a distant threat on the horizon. Sean had the distinct, chilling feeling that it had already made landfall.

Chapter 5: Whispers on the Wind

The day after the funeral, the world returned to its normal rhythms, a cruel indifference that felt like a personal betrayal. The sun rose, the birds sang, and the life of the farm demanded its due. But inside the old house, a profound silence had taken root, a quiet so deep and heavy it seemed to absorb all sound. It was the silence of an empty chair at the head of the kitchen table, the silence of a porch swing that no longer creaked under a familiar weight, the silence of a voice that would never again call out, "Come and get it, or I'll feed it to the chickens!"

Sean moved through the quiet like a ghost in his own home. He felt hollowed out, his grief a vast, echoing chamber inside him. He went through the motions of his morning chores—feeding the chickens, checking the troughs, mucking out the stalls—. Still, the familiar tasks brought him no comfort. Every corner of the farm was a memory; every tool he picked up and held the faint, phantom impression of his grandfather's hands. The world felt muted; its colors leached away, leaving only shades of gray.

He found Katie in the kitchen when he came back inside. She wasn't bustling around, trying to fill the silence with forced cheerfulness. She was just there, methodically washing the mountain of casserole dishes and plates that had been left by well-meaning neighbors. Her presence was as quiet and steady as the running water, a silent act of companionship that was more comforting than any words could be.

He took a dish towel and began to dry, standing beside her, their shoulders occasionally brushing against each other. They worked without speaking, the simple, shared task of a small raft in the overwhelming ocean of their sorrow.

"I can't be here right now," Sean said finally, his voice raspy. He stacked the last plate and turned to her. "The quiet is too loud."

Katie's eyes, full of wisdom that belied her sixteen years, met his. She simply nodded. "The sanctuary?"

"Yeah."

The walk to the cave felt different today. The familiar path through the woods, usually a place of peace and burgeoning power, seemed to mourn with him. The leaves underfoot whispered of endings, and the air, though crisp and clean, felt heavy with unspoken loss. When they reached the hidden stone entrance, Sean spoke the incantation, his voice flat and devoid of its usual energy. "NEPO ECNARTNE."

The stone door slid aside, revealing the dark passage. They descended the stairs into the earth, and as they stepped into the first chamber, the magical sanctuary beyond seemed to sense their sorrow. It came to life not with a burst of joyous light but with a soft, gentle glow, the color of a hazy dawn. The air warmed around them, carrying the mingled, comforting scents of his grandfather's favorite lilacs and Katie's roses. The very magic of the place seemed to envelop them like a comforting embrace.

They didn't speak or practice. They collapsed onto the familiar, overstuffed sofa that had been there for centuries, a silent testament to the long line of guardians who had come before. Sean leaned his head back, closing his eyes, letting the ambient magic of the room try to soothe the raw edges of his grief. Beside him, Katie pulled out her tablet, its modern glow a stark contrast to the ancient chamber. She wasn't looking for anything in particular, just scrolling, seeking a mindless distraction from the ache in her heart.

For a long time, the only sound was the faint, mystical hum of the room itself. Then Katie made a slight noise, a soft intake of breath.

"What is it?" Sean asked, not opening his eyes.

"Nothing, it's just... weird," she murmured. "Some story from Germany. A hiker found in the Black Forest... Police are baffled. They're saying it looks like some kind of bizarre animal attack, but there are no tracks."

Sean remained silent, lost in his own thoughts. It was a strange story, but the world was full of bizarre stories.

He must have dozed off, because the next thing he knew, Katie was gently shaking his shoulder. Her face was pale, her brow furrowed with a new and unfamiliar tension.

"Sean," she said, her voice tight. "I think you need to see this."

He sat up, rubbing the sleep from his eyes. She handed him the tablet. The article she had pulled up was from a Peruvian news agency, which had been poorly translated into English. It detailed a series of recent disappearances near an ancient Incan ruin. Local authorities were blaming opportunistic bandits, but the villagers had their own theories. They spoke of a *sombra que bebe la vida*—a shadow that drinks life—and of finding livestock left behind, nothing but husks, completely drained of blood.

A cold finger of dread traced its way down Sean's spine. "Drained...?"

"That's not all," Katie said, her voice barely whispering. She took the tablet back and, with a few quick taps, brought up a map of the world. "I started searching. For anything similar. Ritualistic markings, victims drained of blood or life force, unexplained disappearances near places of old power."

Her finger tapped on the map. A pin appeared over Peru. Then another over Germany.

"Look," she said, her voice trembling slightly. "Hong Kong. A high-profile banker was found in his locked penthouse. The coroner said it was like every drop of fluid had been desiccated from his body. They called it 'spontaneous dehydration.'" She tapped again. "Egypt. A geologist on a dig near Giza vanishes from his tent. His colleagues found his research notes scattered, covered in what they thought was dried mud. Still, they was later identified as a strange, organic residue they couldn't identify."

Another tap. "A librarian in a small town in the Scottish Highlands, found in the archives, surrounded by books on local folklore about the *baobhan sith*. Cause of death? Massive, unexplainable organ failure."

With each new report, the air in the sanctuary grew colder, the magical warmth of the room receding as if frightened by the darkness they were uncovering. The stories were disparate, spanning continents and cultures, the methods of death bizarrely different. But beneath the surface, a horrifying pattern began to emerge. Each incident was an echo, a variation of the same terrifying theme: a supernatural entity feeding on human life.

"It's not just one," Sean breathed, the words feeling like shards of ice in his throat. The hollow ache of his grief was being filled with a new, sharp emotion: fear. A cold, creeping terror that was vast and absolute.

"They're different," Katie theorized, her mind working furiously, her intelligence a sharp blade cutting through the horror. "The one in Germany leaves claw marks. The one in Peru is a shadow. The one in Hong Kong is like a psychic vampire. They're... specialists."

Sean suddenly shot to his feet, his mind racing back to his uncle's arrival. *It feels louder than I remember.* He ran to one of the scroll tubes in the corner of the room and pulled out the ancient map of ley lines his uncle had shown him. He spread it across the wide wooden table, its surface covered in a complex web of glowing lines that crisscrossed the globe.

"The locations, Katie," he said, his hands shaking as he pointed to the map. "Where were the attacks?"

One by one, she called them out, and he found the corresponding points on the map. The Black Forest. The Andes. Giza. The Scottish Highlands. Each one was a nexus. A major intersection where the earth's magical energies converge, places of immense power.

A final pinprick of dread entered his heart. "Is there... is there one near here?"

Katie's eyes met his wide with dawning horror. She pointed to a spot on the map. In this place, several major ley lines intersected, glowing with a brighter intensity than almost any other on the continent. A place deep in the swamps and forests of the Carolinas. A place less than two hundred miles away. It was, as of yet, untouched.

The truth crashed down on Sean with the force of a physical blow. He stumbled back, gripping the edge of the table for support. The Malevolent Spirit he had fought, the creature he had unleashed and barely managed to banish, wasn't just a random monster. It was a scout. A harbinger. The quiet of the last three years hadn't been a reprieve. It had been a period of preparation. It had been claiming its territory, fortifying its own nexus, and waiting. Waiting for its brethren to begin their own harvest, all leading to some terrible, unknown purpose.

Sean's grief for his grandfather suddenly twisted, transforming into something new. It wasn't just a sad, natural end. His grandfather had felt this coming. *Power calls to power.* The world's magic was growing louder because a war was brewing in the shadows, and their little farm, their sanctuary, was sitting on the front lines. Tom's death wasn't the end of the story. It was the prologue.

Sean looked at Katie, the profound sadness in his eyes now forged into a grim, hard resolve. The weight of his legacy, of the cold wooden bird in his pocket, of the open journal on his grandfather's nightstand, settled onto his shoulders. For the first time, he didn't buckle.

"He told me to be ready for the storm," Sean said, his voice low and steady, the voice of a leader accepting his charge. He looked at the glowing map, at the web of darkness spreading across the world, and at the single, angry point of light that pulsed in their own backyard. "He knew. The storm is already here."

Chapter 6: The Sanctuary's Secrets

The farmhouse kitchen, usually a place of warmth and comfort, felt like a command center for a war no one had signed up for. The air was thick with the scent of day-old coffee and the electric hum of fear. Sean had called an emergency meeting of the coven, and they were all gathered around the large oak table, their faces pale in the harsh light of the overhead fixture. In the center of the table, the ancient ley line map was spread out, its glowing lines a beautiful and terrifying spiderweb. Sean had used small colored pins to mark the locations of the attacks Katie had discovered online. The result was a constellation of darkness spreading across the globe.

Sam, ever the calmest, traced a line connecting Peru and Germany with a slender finger. "The patterns are too similar to be a coincidence, but the methods are too different to be a single entity."

"Katie called them specialists," Sean said, his voice low. He looked around the table at the faces of his friends, his coven. He saw Kim, whose connection to the earth usually made her a grounding presence, twisting a napkin in her hands. He saw Matthew, usually quick with a joke, staring at the map with a grim intensity. This was their reality now. The weight of it threatened to suffocate him.

"So, what are we supposed to do?" Matthew asked, finally breaking the tense silence. "Fly to Egypt and take on a mummy? This is... this is global. We're seven teenagers on a farm in South Carolina."

"Eight," Katie corrected softly, but the fear in his voice was contagious. Sean could feel the doubt rippling through the small group. He had to stop it before it took root.

"He's right," Sean said, and all eyes snapped to him, surprised. "We can't fight a war on ten fronts. We don't even know what we're fighting. That's why we're not going to panic." He met each of their gazes, his own projecting a confidence he didn't entirely feel. "We have a resource no one else does. We have the sanctuary. Mary and the others who came before her fought against these things. The answers have to be in there. We're not going in blind; we're going in to get armed."

His words, filled with a resolve forged from his grief, settled the room. The panic subsided, giving way to a grim determination. They were scared, yes, but they were a coven. They were together.

They moved as a unit to the cave, the cool night air doing little to quell the anxiety that followed them. The sanctuary greeted them with its gentle, responsive magic; the light was a soft, soothing blue, and the air smelled of lilacs and roses. But tonight, the chamber's peace felt fragile, like a thin pane of glass separating them from a howling storm.

"Okay," Katie said, her voice taking on a practical, commanding tone that Sean was endlessly grateful for. She was his partner in every sense of the word, her sharp, organizational mind the perfect complement to his intuitive power. "We need a system. Wading in randomly will get us nowhere."

She quickly assigned tasks. "Sam, you're the best with ancient languages. Take the European codices and any text that appears to be in Latin or Old German. Matthew, you, and Kim start with the scrolls. They're more likely to be personal accounts battle reports. Look for illustrations, such as those depicting shadowy creatures or symbols, like the ones on the map. Sean and I will take the oldest texts—the Egyptian and Incan ones. We're looking for a name, a weakness, a history. Anything."

The library, a repository of millennia of magical knowledge, became their new battlefield. The scent of ancient parchment and dry ink filled the air as they carefully opened fragile books and unrolled brittle scrolls. The sheer scope of the task was daunting. Generations of witches and warlocks had stored their wisdom here, a silent accumulation of power and secrets.

Hours bled into one another. The only sounds were the soft rustle of turning pages and the occasional sharp intake of breath as someone discovered something new and disturbing. The illustrations they found were the stuff of nightmares. They saw depictions of creatures made of pure shadow, their forms vaguely humanoid but twisted, as if the concept of a physical body was an insult to them. There were entries describing entities that could peel a person's soul from their body, leaving behind a breathing but empty shell. They found frighteningly detailed anatomical drawings of beasts with too many joints and teeth like obsidian shards.

"Listen to this," Sam said, her voice hushed. She was poring over a massive, iron-bound book. "It's a text from a 15th-century warlock in the Carpathian Mountains. He calls them the *Vatra Sângelui*—the Blood Fire. He says they don't just drink blood for sustenance; they weave it into their clothing. They can use it to create illusions, to control the minds of the weak-willed, even to scry on their enemies."

"That matches a pictograph I found," Sean said, looking up from a heavy stone tablet. "The Incans called them the *Yawar-Machaq*. The Serpent of Blood. The legends say they could command a whole village to walk off a cliff just by whispering on the wind."

A chilling picture began to form. These weren't just monsters. They were ancient, intelligent houses of spirits, each with its own culture of horror, its own unique and terrible magic. They were the hidden predators of humanity, the truth behind a thousand terrifying myths.

Matthew unrolled a long scroll, his face paling as he scanned it. "Guys... this is an account from a coven in Alexandria, around 30 BC. They tried to stop a ritual. They mention a 'Convergence of Worlds' and a 'Chorus of the Damned.' They...

they failed." His voice dropped. "The scroll ends there. The script just... stops. The witch who was writing it never finished."

The implication hung in the air, heavy and suffocating. An entire coven was wiped out.

By the time the first hints of dawn threatened the sky outside, they were exhausted, overwhelmed, and no closer to a viable plan. They had a mountain of horrifying lore but no clear strategy. The texts were fragmented, the languages obscure. They spoke of complex banishment rituals that required ingredients no longer existing—the dust of a fallen star, the tear of a gryphon, the heart of a mountain.

"This is impossible," Kim said, her voice trembling with fatigue and fear. "It's too much. The books say trapping even one of them requires the power of a full coven in a month-long ritual. How are we supposed to stop a dozen of them at once?"

Sean felt the hope that had buoyed him earlier, beginning to fray. She was right. He slammed a heavy book shut, the sound echoing the finality of their failure. Dust motes danced in the candlelight. He had to get some air.

"I'll be back," he muttered, leaving the heavy silence of the library behind.

He half-expected to find his uncle in the house, but the kitchen was empty. Sean walked out onto the porch, the cool, pre-dawn air a shock to his system. And there he was. Todd was sitting in his father's rocker, a steaming mug cradled in his hands, staring out into the darkness as if he'd been waiting.

"Tough night?" Todd asked, his voice quiet. He didn't look at Sean, just kept his gaze fixed on the lightening horizon.

Sean slumped onto the porch steps, the frustration and fear of the long night finally boiling over. "You knew," he said, the words less an accusation and more a statement of weary fact. "When you got here, you said the farm felt 'louder.' You knew something was coming."

Todd took a slow sip from his mug before answering. "I didn't know what, Sean. Not for sure." He finally turned, his pale eyes reflecting the gray morning light. "I told you, I'm not a warlock. I don't see visions or read futures. I just feel... the pressure in the air. Like the barometer dropping before a hurricane. The magic on this land, the sanctuary, it's a beacon. And something big and dark has been turning its eye this way for a while now."

Wordlessly, Sean went back inside and returned with the ley line map. He spread it out on the porch floor between them, the magical lines glowing faintly in the dim light. He pointed to the pins, explaining everything they had discovered, the different types of spirits, the global attacks, the nexus points. The terrible, impossible scale of it all.

Todd stared at the map, and for the first time, Sean saw genuine fear in his uncle's eyes. He traced the line leading to the nexus in the Carolinas, his finger hovering over the glowing point. "The Keystone," he breathed, the word a ghost of a memory.

"What?" Sean asked, leaning in. "What's Keystone?"

"It was just a story," Todd said, shaking his head as if to clear it. "A story my father told me and your dad when we were kids, trying to scare us into behaving. He called it the 'Conjunction of Thirteen.' We thought he meant witches." He looked at Sean, his eyes wide with a terrible, dawning comprehension. "God, he wasn't talking about witches. He was talking about *them*."

He explained, his voice low and urgent, drawing on the family lore he had spent a lifetime trying to forget. The Conjunction wasn't a gathering; it was a catastrophic ritual. Thirteen powerful spirits, each anchored to a central ley line nexus, could pool their collective power during a celestial event—like a solar eclipse—to shatter the ancient prisons holding their brethren. The spirit Sean had fought, the one native to this region, was the Keystone. Its job was to establish a beachhead, to prepare the nexus, and to act as the primary anchor and conduit for the entire horrifying ritual.

"It's not just about freeing the others, Sean," Todd said, his voice cracking with the weight of the revelation. "The power required for something like that... it doesn't just open doors. It rips a hole. If they succeed, the magical barriers between worlds at that nexus point will be shredded. It won't just be their kind we'll have to worry about. That place... it'll become a permanent, open wound. A gateway for things much, much worse." Before Sean leaves, the Guardians perform an ancient ceremony:

"Kneel, Sean Murphy," Lyralei commanded, her voice resonating with ceremonial power.

Sean knelt in the center of the Guardian circle. Each Guardian extended a translucent hand, and streams of different colored light flowed from them—silver from Lyralei, star-deep blue from Thaddeus, green-gold from Seraphina, geometric patterns of light from Khalil, and shifting, temporal energy from Temporis.

"By the authority of those who came before," Lyralei intoned, "we recognize you not just as a guardian by blood but as a Guardian by choice. You carry our knowledge, our hope, and our trust. May you prove worthy of all three."

The energies merged above Sean's head, then descended, sinking into his skin like warm rain. For a moment, he felt their collective experiences—battles won and lost, loves found and sacrificed, the weight of centuries of vigilance. Then, it settled into his bones, becoming part of him.

When he stood, he was subtly changed. Not more powerful, but more aware. He could feel the sanctuary's heartbeat, sense the flow of its protections, and understand its moods and needs.

"You are truly one of us now," Mary said, pride evident in her ghostly features. "The sanctuary will respond to you as it does to us. Its deepest secrets will open to your touch. But remember—with this gift comes responsibility. You are not just protecting a place but a legacy that stretches back to the dawn of human magic."

He buried his face in his hands, his shoulders slumping. "Your grandfather tried to prepare you for this. He spoke of his own grandfather's journals, of prophecies of a 'Time of Thinning Veils.' I called him a crazy old man. I told him he was obsessed with fairy tales." He looked up, his face a mask of profound regret. "I ran away from this, Sean. I left him and your father to stand the watch alone. And now... now you're the one left holding the line I abandoned."

Sean listened, his own sorrow momentarily eclipsed by the sheer, terrifying scale of what his uncle was describing. He looked from the map on the floor to his uncle's anguished face and then back to the quiet, sleeping farmhouse.

His grief was still a raw wound, but now it had a purpose. His fear was still present, but now it had a target. He couldn't fight a global war. He couldn't save the world. But the Keystone... the anchor... that was here. That was on his soil.

He stood up, his exhaustion replaced by a cold, sharp clarity. He walked back into the kitchen, the coven looking up at him, their faces etched with fatigue and despair.

He laid the map back on the table. "I know what we have to do," he said, his voice ringing with a newfound, terrible authority. He pointed to the bright, angry nexus point pulsing in their own backyard.

"We can't stop all of them," he said, meeting each of their eyes. "But we can stop the Keystone. We cut off the snake's head. We have to prevent that ritual from happening right here. Whatever it takes."

A heavy silence descended on the kitchen. The mission was no longer a vague, impossible notion of fighting monsters; it had become a tangible goal. It was precise. It was focused. And it was suicide. A small group of teenagers standing against an ancient, world-ending power. The weight of it all settled on their shoulders, immense and crushing. But as they looked at each other, a flicker of something new passed between them. Not hope, not yet. But the grim, unbreakable resolve of those with nothing left to lose.

Chapter 7: The Guardians of Memory

The day after Sean's first full exploration of Mary's sanctuary,

Sean approached the cave entrance with a mixture of excitement and trepidation that had become familiar over the past week. Each visit to the sanctuary revealed new wonders, new mysteries, and new responsibilities that seemed to grow heavier with each discovery. The familiar weight of protective crystals in his pocket provided comfort as he whispered the opening words and descended into the cave's depths. But today felt different somehow, charged with possibility and ancient purpose.

The outer chamber responded to his presence like a living thing awakening. The air hummed with an energy that seemed to recognize him now, welcoming him as more than just a visitor. Tiny symbols carved into the stone walls glowed with soft, pulsing light as he passed, and the very dust motes in the air seemed to dance in patterns too deliberate to be random, forming brief, cryptic messages in languages he didn't recognize but somehow understood.

When he reached the sanctuary door, Sean hesitated. Over the past several visits, he'd grown accustomed to Mary's gentle presence and her patient guidance as he learned to navigate the vast collection of magical knowledge. But today, something felt different about the space beyond the threshold—fuller somehow, as if the chamber held more than just books and memories.

"Mary?" he called softly. "May I enter?"

The door swung open without his touch, but instead of the familiar blue light, the sanctuary was filled with a soft, multi-hued radiance that seemed to shift and change like the aurora borealis. As Sean stepped across the threshold, the air itself shimmered, and suddenly he wasn't alone.

Translucent figures materialized around him—not solid like living people but more substantial than mere ghosts. They appeared to be from different periods, their clothing spanning centuries of magical tradition. A tall woman in medieval robes stood beside a man whose Renaissance-era doublet was embroidered with astronomical symbols. Near them, a figure in what looked like ancient Egyptian garments gestured toward shelves that held scrolls Sean had never seen before.

"Welcome, young guardian," said the medieval woman, her voice carrying the quality of wind chimes in a gentle breeze. Her silver hair was braided with what looked like moonbeams, and her eyes held the deep wisdom of someone who had seen the rise and fall of kingdoms. "I am Lyralei, keeper of the ancient ways. We have been waiting for you."

Sean stood before the assembled Guardians, their translucent forms creating a semicircle of ancient power around him. The sanctuary's light dimmed, replaced by a silvery radiance that seemed to emanate from the Guardians themselves.

"Before we share our deepest knowledge," Lyralei said, her voice carrying the weight of centuries, "you must prove you understand the true nature of guardianship. Tell us, young Sean—what makes a guardian?"

Sean felt the weight of their collective gaze, thousands of years of experience judging his worth. He thought of his grandfather, of the quiet way Tom had tended the farm, protected the town, and raised him with patient love.

"A guardian isn't defined by their power," Sean said slowly, finding the words as he spoke them. "It's not about being the strongest or knowing the most spells. A guardian is someone who stands between the darkness and the people they love, not because they have to, but because they choose to. Every day. Even when it costs them everything."

The Guardians exchanged glances, and Sean caught glimpses of their own memories—Lyralei standing alone against a demon horde while her village evacuated; Thaddeus spending decades in isolation to perfect a ward that would protect future generations; Seraphina choosing to bind her life force to a dying forest to save it.

"And what of sacrifice?" Temporis asked, her ageless eyes boring into his. "What would you give up to protect your world?"

Sean touched the spot where the Wayfinder rested in his pocket, already feeling its hungry pull. "Whatever is asked of me. Time, power, life—they're all just currency. What matters is what you buy with them."

A profound silence fell over the gathering. Then, one by one, the Guardians began to glow brighter, their approval manifesting as warm, golden light.

"You understand," Lyralei said, and for the first time, she smiled. "Not all who find this sanctuary grasp this truth. Many seek power for its own sake. But you... you understand that power without purpose is meaningless."

Sean's eyes widened as he took in the assembled figures. There was something unmistakably powerful about each of them—a presence that spoke of lives devoted to magic, to knowledge, to the protection of things greater than themselves. The surrounding air thrummed with residual energy as if their very existence was a spell made manifest.

"You're all... witches?" Sean asked, his voice barely above a whisper.

"We are the Guardians of Memory," replied the man in the astronomical doublet, his voice carrying the authority of ages. His dark hair was streaked with silver, and his eyes sparkled with the light of distant stars. "I am Thaddeus Nightwhisper, and we are the accumulated wisdom of those who came before. When a witch or warlock of true power passes on, they may choose to leave their essence here, in this sanctuary, to guide future generations."

Mary's familiar presence made itself known as her translucent form stepped forward from the group. But seeing her now, surrounded by these other figures,

Sean realized that she was part of something much larger than he'd understood. "Sean, these are my predecessors and successors—the greatest magical minds who have contributed to this sanctuary over the millennia. They have much to teach you, and given what's coming, you'll need every advantage they can provide."

An elegant woman, dressed in what appeared to be a Renaissance gown, approached, her gown seeming to be woven from fallen leaves that rustled musically as she moved. Despite her ethereal nature, she radiated warmth and the kind of nurturing energy Sean associated with his grandfather's gardens. "I am Seraphina Goldleaf, and I lived during what you call the Renaissance. I specialized in the magic of growing things, of life itself—knowledge that will serve you well in the battles ahead."

She gestured toward a corner of the sanctuary that Sean now noticed had been transformed into an incredible garden. Plants from every climate and season flourished together in impossible harmony—Arctic lichens growing beside tropical orchids, desert cacti sharing space with temperate ferns. Their leaves glowed with inner light, and the air around them hummed with vital energy.

"How is this possible?" Sean asked, reaching toward a flower that seemed to be made of crystallized starlight.

"Magic is not bound by the laws of your physical world," Seraphina explained with a gentle smile that reminded Sean of his grandmother's patient teaching. "In this sanctuary, we exist in a space between worlds, where thought and will shape reality more than physics. Here, the impossible becomes merely improbable, and the improbable becomes inevitable for those with sufficient understanding." Seraphina's Garden Wisdom: She led Sean to a corner of the sanctuary where impossible plants grew—flowers that bloomed with starlight, trees that bore fruit of crystallized memory.

"Every guardian needs something that grounds them to life," she explained, plucking a small silver seed. "Plant this at your farm. It will grow into a Sentinel Tree—its roots will strengthen your wards, and its blossoms will bloom as a warning when dark magic approaches. But more importantly, it will remind you what you're fighting for. Life. Growth. The future."

Khalil's Mathematical Mysteries: The mathematician pulled Sean aside to a wall covered in equations that seemed to move and shift.

"Your grandfather understood this intuitively," Khalil said, "but you must learn it consciously. Magic follows patterns. See here." He traced a spiraling equation. "This is the mathematical signature of your family's magic. Every Murphy guardian has this at their core. Learn to recognize it, and you'll be able to identify threats that specifically target your bloodline."

Thaddeus's Star Maps: In a chamber with a ceiling of living constellations, Thaddeus showed Sean configurations of stars that didn't exist in Earth's sky.

"These are the Navigator Stars," he explained. "They exist in the spaces between dimensions. When you're lost—whether in the physical world or the astral plane—look for these patterns. They will always guide you home. Your grandfather used them once when he was trapped in a pocket dimension for three days. Remember their shapes."

A shorter figure stepped forward—a man of Middle Eastern origin, his robes decorated with geometric patterns that seemed to shift and change as Sean watched. The designs were mesmerizing, forming mathematical relationships that spoke to something deep in Sean's mind, a part of him that understood the underlying order beneath magical chaos.

"I am Khalil ibn Sinan," the man said, his voice carrying the precision of a master mathematician, "and I mastered the magic of numbers and patterns during the Golden Age of Baghdad. Observe."

He gestured, and the air filled with geometric shapes made of pure light—hexagons, spirals, and complex fractals that were painful to look at directly but filled Sean with a profound sense of understanding. The shapes moved in perfect harmony, demonstrating relationships between energy, matter, and consciousness that modern physics was only beginning to glimpse.

"Each spell you cast," Khalil continued, his voice filled with the passion of a true teacher, "follows mathematical principles older than civilization itself. The more you understand these patterns, the more precise your magic becomes. Power without understanding is chaos. Understanding without wisdom is destruction.

But when all three are united..." The geometric display suddenly coalesced into a single, perfect mandala that pulsed with harmonious energy. "Then you approach the true art."

Sean felt overwhelmed by the wealth of knowledge surrounding him, but also deeply honored. These weren't just historical figures; they were the accumulated wisdom of his magical heritage, the greatest minds who had ever walked the path he was now following. "Why are you showing me this now? I'm still learning the basics."

Lyralei's expression grew serious, and the warm light in the chamber seemed to dim slightly. "Because dark times are coming, young guardian. We sense the growing shadow, the ancient evil that stirs in the depths of the world's foundations. The enemy you will soon face is not the first of its kind we have encountered. Our combined knowledge represents centuries of battles against such creatures—victories and defeats, triumphs and tragedies, all preserved here for those who come after."

Thaddeus nodded gravely, his star-filled eyes reflecting depths of sorrow that spoke of losses beyond counting. "Each of us faced similar challenges in our lifetimes. We made mistakes, learned hard lessons, and paid a price that left scars on our souls. We're here to ensure you don't have to face them alone and, more importantly, to help you avoid the errors that cost us so dearly."

"And to help you understand," Mary added, her voice filled with a mixture of pride and concern, "that being chosen as a guardian isn't just about power or knowledge. It's about making choices that others cannot or will not make, about standing between the darkness and the light even when—especially when—the cost seems too high to bear."

A new figure emerged from the group—a woman whose appearance seemed to flicker between youth and age, her hair shifting from golden to silver and back again like the phases of the moon. Her eyes held the weight of eternity, and when she looked at Sean, he had the unsettling feeling that she was seeing not just who he was but who he could become.

"I am Temporis, the Timekeeper," she said, her voice carrying harmonics that seemed to echo from both past and future. "I have seen the threads of possibility, the paths your future might take. Some lead to triumph, others to tragedy. Many lead to sacrifices that will test the very core of who you are."

She waved her hand, and the air before Sean filled with swirling images—glimpses of possible futures that flashed by too quickly to fully comprehend. He saw himself standing victorious over a defeated enemy, light blazing from his hands. But he also saw darker visions: Katie's face twisted with an agony he couldn't bear to witness, his grandfather's grave marker standing alone in a devastated landscape, himself aged beyond his years, silver-haired and hollow-eyed with the weight of impossible choices.

"The future is not fixed," Temporis said as the visions faded, leaving Sean shaken and pale. "Every choice creates new possibilities, new paths, new potential outcomes. But knowledge of what might come can help you prepare for what will come. The question is: are you ready to know the price of the path you're walking?"

Sean's throat felt dry, but he managed to nod. "Tell me."

"The greatest battles are not fought with fire and lightning," she said softly. "They are fought in the quiet moments, when you must choose between what you want and what is needed, between saving one life and saving many, between holding onto your own humanity and doing what must be done to protect others."

"And sometimes," Lyralei added, her voice filled with ancient sadness, "the greatest victory requires the greatest sacrifice. We have all faced that choice, Sean. We have all paid that price. The question is not whether you will face it too, but the question is whether you will be ready when the moment comes."

The chamber fell into a contemplative silence, and Sean felt the weight of their words settling into his bones. This wasn't just about learning magic or even about fighting monsters. This was about becoming the kind of person who could make the hardest choices, who could stand firm when everything else was falling apart.

"There's something else you should know," Seraphina said softly, her voice breaking the silence. "This sanctuary exists in multiple dimensions simultaneously. What you see here is just one layer of reality. As your power grows, as your understanding deepens, you'll perceive other levels, other rooms, other collections of knowledge that exist in the spaces between worlds."

To demonstrate, she gestured toward what Sean had thought was a simple bookshelf. Suddenly, he could see through it to another room beyond—a vast library that stretched impossibly far, its shelves reaching toward a star-filled sky that couldn't exist in any earthly architecture. Books flew through the air like birds, their pages glowing with inner light, while scholars from a dozen different time periods studied at tables that floated in midair.

"The Infinite Archive," Thaddeus said, following Sean's gaze with a smile. "Every book that has ever been written, every scroll that has ever been penned, every tablet that has ever been carved. In time, when you're ready, you'll learn to navigate its corridors, to find the knowledge you need when you need it most."

"And beyond that," Khalil added, "are the Workshop Realms, where magical items are forged from pure intention and crystallized will. The Meditation Gardens, where the soul can find peace even in the midst of chaos. The War Rooms, where strategies are planned, and battles are fought on levels of reality that most minds cannot even conceive."

Sean's head spun with the implications. The sanctuary wasn't just a library; it was an entire universe of knowledge and power, a place where the accumulated wisdom of ages had been preserved and protected. And somehow, impossibly, he was being offered access to all of it.

"Why me?" he asked, the question torn from his heart. "I'm just a kid from a farm. I don't understand half of what you're telling me, and I'm terrified that I'll mess this up, that I'll fail when people are counting on me."

The guardians exchanged glances, and Sean saw something pass between them—a recognition, a memory, perhaps even a trace of affection.

"Because," Mary said gently, "that's exactly what each of us said when we first stood where you're standing now. The fear, the doubt, the overwhelming sense of responsibility—these things don't disqualify you, Sean. They make you worthy. A person who isn't afraid of power is someone who shouldn't have it."

"And because," Lyralei added, "you have something that many of us lacked in our time: you're not alone. The bonds you've formed with your friends and family—both blood and chosen—are a source of strength that many guardians never had. Cherish them. Protect them. And remember that sometimes the greatest magic is simply refusing to let the people you love face the darkness alone."

The guardians began to fade, but their voices remained clear and strong:

"We will be here when you need us," Mary promised.

"Call upon us in your darkest hour," Lyralei added.

"Remember the patterns," Khalil whispered.

"Choose your path wisely," Temporis warned.

"Trust in the magic of growing things," Seraphina said with a warm smile.

"And never forget," Thaddeus said as his star-robed form became translucent, "that you are not alone. The sanctuary remembers all, and we remember you. You carry our knowledge, our experience, our hope for the future. Make us proud."

As the last guardian faded from view, Sean found himself alone again, but the sanctuary felt different now. It no longer seemed like just a magical room—it was a living repository of wisdom. In this place, the greatest magical minds in history had chosen to remain as guardians and guides. The weight of that responsibility was immense yet strangely comforting.

Sean reached out and touched the wall, feeling the pulse of life within the ancient stone. "Thank you," he whispered. "All of you."

As Sean prepares to leave, Temporis pulls him aside privately.

"I must show you something," she said, her form flickering between youth and old age more rapidly than before—a sign of agitation. "A possibility I've glimpsed. Not a certainty, but a shadow of what might come."

She waved her hand, and the air shimmered. Sean saw himself, older, standing in the sanctuary. But it was wrong—the sacred space was cracked, damaged, dark energies seeping through wounds in reality. This older Sean was alone, desperately trying to hold together failing wards.

"This is the danger of the path you walk," Temporis whispered. "The sanctuary itself can become a target. If the enemy cannot break the guardian, sometimes they try to break the sanctuary itself. Guard not just against external threats but against the corruption of this sacred space."

The vision faded, leaving Sean shaken.

"How do I prevent this?" he asked.

"By understanding that the sanctuary's greatest strength isn't its magic or its knowledge," Temporis replied. "It's the connections between those who protect it. A guardian alone, no matter how powerful, can fall. But a true coven, bound by love and purpose... that is infinitely harder to break."

The sanctuary glowed brighter for a moment as if acknowledging his gratitude, and Sean knew that whenever he returned, the guardians would be watching over him. The weight of his magical heritage was heavy, but knowing he had such powerful allies made the burden more bearable.

As he left the sanctuary and made his way back through the cave, Sean's mind buzzed with everything he'd learned. The battle ahead would be difficult, more challenging than anything he'd faced before. But he was no longer just a boy discovering his powers—he was a guardian in training, backed by the wisdom of ages and the love of those who had walked this path before him.

The real adventure was just beginning, and for the first time since discovering his magical abilities, Sean felt truly ready to face whatever darkness lay ahead.

Chapter 8: The Thresholder's Toll

The discovery was made not with a shout but with a sudden, profound silence. They had delved deeper into the sanctuary than ever before, following a faint, almost imperceptible current of air that hinted at chambers beyond the main library. It led them to an archway that wasn't on any of the sanctuary's hand-drawn maps, a gaping maw of darkness that seemed to swallow the light from their enchanted lanterns.

The air that bled from it was cold—not the simple chill of subterranean stone, but an ancient, breathless cold that carried no scent of earth or water. It was the absolute zero of a place that had been sealed for millennia.

"I don't like this," Kim murmured, her arms wrapped tightly around her chest. Her innate connection to the earth, usually a comforting, steady hum beneath her feet, was gone. Here, the ground was just a dead stone, a foundation of silence.

Sean held his lantern higher, stepping forward cautiously. The archway was framed not by carved rock but by something that looked, impossibly, like a thicket of petrified thorns. The vines were as thick as his arm, twisted into a gnarled, impenetrable lattice, their surface the color and texture of old, rusted iron. There was no visible door, no seam, only this thorny, unwelcoming barrier. Sprouting from the iron-hard vines were blossoms, dozens of them pale and colorless. They shed a ghostly, internal luminescence—a ghostlight that cast no shadows but painted their faces in the pallid, shifting glow of a dying moon.

"Thornwall magic," Sam whispered her voice tight with a mixture of academic awe and primal fear. She ran a gloved hand near the surface, not daring to touch it. "This is pre-Celtic. Maybe older. It's not a wall, Sean. It's a spell woven and hardened into a physical form. It's a lock."

As she spoke, Todd, who had been hanging back, his face a pale mask of unease, took an involuntary step closer. "Is it just me, or are those flowers... watching us?"

He was right. The pale blossoms seemed to track their movements, their faint light intensifying as the coven's own magical auras brushed against the barrier. The sight was deeply unsettling, a beautiful, silent warning.

"It's a Thresholder Room," Sean said, the knowledge surfacing not from a book, but from a deep, instinctual part of his warlock heritage that the sanctuary seemed to amplify. "A test for initiates. It's designed to filter out anyone unworthy of seeing what lies beyond."

"Is it going to try to kill us, or just give us a pop quiz?" Matthew muttered, trying to break the tension with a joke that fell flat in the unnerving silence.

"Stay close," Sean commanded, ignoring him. "And don't try to force it. It's not about power." He took a deep breath, centering himself, and stepped toward the gate.

The moment his foot crossed the threshold, the ghostlight from the blossoms flared, and a low hum vibrated through the chamber, a sound that felt like it was coming from the back of Sean's own skull. The Thornwall didn't open. Instead, a narrow, shimmering gap appeared in its center, a distortion in the air like a heat haze. It was an invitation.

One by one, their hearts pounding, they passed through the shimmering tear in reality.

The world on the other side was a vast, silent chamber of impossible scale. The ceiling was lost in an oppressive darkness, and the floor was a perfectly flat, polished obsidian that reflected the blackness above, making it feel as though they were floating in a starless void. Suspended in the surrounding air, motionless as sleeping birds, were hundreds, perhaps thousands, of razor-sharp obsidian shards. They ranged in size from tiny splinters to blades as long as Sean's forearm, each one a perfect, non-reflective black. The silence was absolute, the air unnervingly still.

For a long moment, nothing happened. They stood clustered together, a small, terrified island in a sea of suspended knives.

"Okay," Katie whispered, her strategic mind already trying to dissect the threat. "It's a construct. A magical trap. Let's form a defensive triangle, just like we practiced. We put up a shield, and we—"

She was cut off as the shards... woke up.

They didn't move, not physically. But a low, discordant hum began to emanate from them, and with it came a wave of pure psychic venom. It wasn't a vague feeling of dread; it was a targeted, surgical strike on their deepest insecurities.

Sean was suddenly gripped by a cold, suffocating certainty that he had failed his grandfather, that his leadership was a sham that would get them all killed. Beside him, he felt Katie flinch, her mind suddenly flooded with a vivid, horrifying image of Sean, pale and lifeless, his body consumed by the cost of his own magic. Matthew saw his friends looking at him with contempt, his humor revealed as nothing but foolish bravado. And Todd was frozen, reliving the moment he'd abandoned his family, the old guilt a fresh, gaping wound.

"It's feeding on our fear!" Sam cried out, her own face a mask of anguish as she fought off the phantom echoes of her first coven's destruction. "It's turning our own minds against us! Form the shield! Now!"

With a collective gasp, they snapped back to the present. Katie, her face pale but set with fierce determination, began the incantation. *"Clypeus unitatis, nos defendat!"*

A translucent dome of shimmering turquoise energy flickered into life around them. The instant it formed, the shards reacted. They began to move, not randomly, but with a cold, terrifying intent. They swarmed like angry hornets, their sharp edges clattering against the shield like a hailstorm of black glass, each impact sending a jarring vibration through the coven.

The shield held, but the psychic assault intensified, now amplified by the dome. The whispers grew louder, the visions more vivid.

"It's not working!" Matthew yelled, his hands pressed to his temples. "The shield is trapping the feeling in here with us!"

"We're broadcasting too much power," Sam analyzed, her voice strained. "Five auras, all lit up and screaming with fear. We're fueling it. Kim, can you ground it? Pull the psychic filth out of the air and into the earth!"

Kim, her face ashen, nodded grimly. This was her specialty. She was the anchor, the root. She dropped to her knees and slammed her palms flat against the polished obsidian floor. She closed her eyes, shutting out the horrifying whispers, and reached down with her magic, seeking the familiar, steady heartbeat of the living earth.

But there was nothing there. The floor beneath her palms was not connected to the world they knew. It was a cold, sterile, alien foundation. And as her magic searched for purchase, the room responded. It didn't reject her power; it welcomed it. It drank it.

"Kim?" Sean asked, sensing the shift.

She didn't answer. A horrifying transformation had begun. Her fingers, pressed against the floor, began to lose their color, turning a pale, stony gray. The change moved with an unnatural speed, creeping up her hands, her skin taking on the texture of rough granite. Stone veins erupted along her arms.

"No," she choked out, her voice a strangled gasp. Her eyes flew open wide with a terror beyond anything the psychic assault had conjured. "It's... turning me. It's making me part of the room."

The petrification was crawling up her neck. A choked scream died in her throat as her jaw stiffened.

"Break the connection!" Sean roared, pure panic seizing him.

Katie reacted instantly, hurling a blast of cleansing, white-hot fire not at Kim but at the floor beneath her hands. The obsidian sizzled and cracked. The flow of energy was severed. Kim collapsed onto her side, sobbing, her arms still a terrifying, mottled gray, her fingers locked into stony claws.

The floating shards, their power source interrupted, stilled. The psychic whispers faded. The room relaxed, its test complete. Their horrifying, near-fatal lesson had been learned.

They scrambled to Kim's side. She was shivering violently, her eyes darting around the chamber in terror. Sean reached for her arm, and it felt like touching a cold statue.

"She's still locked in the backlash," Sam said, her voice trembling. "The petrification... it's not receding."

They were faced with a new, more immediate horror. They had survived the room, but they were about to lose one of their own to its after-effects.

Thinking fast, Sean ignored the complex spells from the sanctuary. He reached for a different kind of magic, the kind his uncle had talked about on the porch. The power of what you fight *for*. He knelt beside Kim, took her stony, unmoving hand in his, and focused not on breaking the curse but on reminding her of what she was.

He didn't use an incantation. He pushed a feeling into her. Not raw power, but a memory: the feeling of soft, warm earth after a spring rain. The scent of her herb garden. The sensation of a new sprout pushing its way toward the sun. He poured every ounce of his own connection to the living world, to the farm, into her, a desperate transfusion of pure, chaotic, beautiful life.

For a moment, nothing happened. Then, the gray on Kim's arm began to recede, not quickly, but like frost melting in the morning sun. Color returned to her cheeks. Her fingers twitched, then curled into a fist. She took a deep, shuddering breath, the sound impossibly loud in the silent chamber.

When they finally helped her to her feet and half-carried her back through the Thornwall gate, the sanctuary felt like a haven of impossible warmth and safety. Kim collapsed onto one of the ancient sofas, still trembling, her connection to the earth feeling bruised and raw.

They looked at each other, their faces pale and streaked with sweat. The bravado was gone. The easy confidence was shattered. They had passed the test, but the price of failure was now terrifyingly clear. The old Gatekeepers who had built this place wielded a magic that was cold, dominant, and utterly unforgiving. It was a power that did not collaborate with life but sought to command it.

"That's the lesson," Katie said, her voice a quiet, shaken whisper as she looked at her friends. "We can't use their magic. We can't become what they were. We have to find our own way. Or this place... it will consume us, too."

They had survived the Thresholder's Toll, but the true test—the battle for their own souls against the seductive, destructive power of their own heritage—had only just begun.

Chapter 9: Echoes in the Grooves

The afternoon sun hung heavy and still over the Murphy farm, casting everything in an amber haze that made the air shimmer like water. It was the kind of oppressive heat that made even the cicadas fall silent, their usual drone replaced by an expectant, almost waiting quietly. Matthew wiped the sweat from his brow as he walked between the rows of ancient pear trees, his weathered canvas satchel bouncing against his hip with each step. The list Sam had given him was crumpled in his back pocket—willow bark for cleansing rituals, mandrake root for protection wards, elderflower for truth-seeking—but his mind kept drifting from the mundane task at hand.

Something was calling him.

It wasn't a voice, exactly, more like a persistent itch at the back of his consciousness, a magnetic pull that seemed to emanate from somewhere deeper in the orchard. He'd felt it for days now, growing stronger each time he passed this way. At first, he'd dismissed it as residual anxiety from their recent battles with the ancient texts in the sanctuary. The Thresholder's Room had left all of them more sensitive to magical currents, their psychic defenses still raw and in the process of healing.

But this was different. This felt... old. Expectant. Patient in the way that only stone and earth could be patient.

Matthew paused beneath the gnarled canopy of the centermost tree, an ancient pear whose trunk was so thick three grown men couldn't wrap their arms around it. Local folklore claimed it was over three hundred years old, having been planted by the first European settlers who had cleared this land. Its bark was a patchwork of deep furrows and moss-covered scars, and its roots had long ago buckled and cracked the neat rows the orchard had once maintained.

The pull was strongest here.

He knelt, brushing away the carpet of fallen leaves and rich, black soil that had accumulated around the massive root system. His fingers, already stained green from gathering herbs, worked methodically, following an instinct he couldn't name. The earth was surprisingly loose as if it had been disturbed recently, though he knew no one had been working this section of the orchard.

Three inches down, his fingertips struck stone.

Matthew's breath caught. He dug faster now, his hands working with the focused intensity that came over him when he was carving when his kinetic magic flowed through wood and stone with perfect precision. The object he uncovered was a circular slab of weathered granite, roughly three feet in diameter and worn smooth by centuries of weather and time.

But it wasn't the stone itself that made his heart race; it was what was carved into its surface.

Spirals. Not the flowing, organic curves of Celtic knotwork he'd expected to find on something this old, but precise geometric patterns that hurt to look at directly. Concentric circles that seemed to fold in on themselves, creating an optical illusion that made his eyes water and his head spin. The lines weren't carved, he realized with growing unease. They were burned into the stone as if someone had drawn them with lines of pure, white-hot fire.

As he stared at the spirals, they seemed to pulse with a faint, rhythmic light that matched his own heartbeat. The temperature around the stone was noticeably cooler, creating a pocket of almost winter-cold air that raised goosebumps on his arms despite the sweltering afternoon heat.

And then he heard the sound that had been drawing him here all along.

Children's laughter, high and sweet and wrong. It seemed to bubble up from somewhere deep beneath the stone, muffled by layers of earth and time, but unmistakably present. As Matthew leaned closer, the laughter grew clearer, and with it came other sounds: the splash of water, delighted squeals, the kind of joyful chaos that came from a summer day at a swimming hole.

Except there was no water here. There never had been.

Matthew scrambled backward, his hands leaving muddy prints on the stone's surface. The sounds faded as he put distance between himself and the spiral-carved slab. Still, the memory of them lingered, along with a growing certainty that what he'd uncovered was far older and more significant than a simple grave marker or property boundary.

His hands shaking slightly, he pulled out his battered notebook and quickly sketched the spiral pattern, trying to capture the dizzying, impossible geometry. Even as a rough drawing, it made his stomach lurch. There was something fundamentally wrong about those angles, something that suggested dimensions his mind wasn't equipped to process.

When he'd finished the sketch, Matthew carefully covered the stone with leaves and soil, though he suspected it wouldn't stay hidden for long. Things like this had a way of making themselves known when they were ready. He gathered his scattered herbs and hurried back toward the farmhouse, his mind racing with possibilities and fears.

The others needed to see this. Sean would know what it meant, or at least where to start looking for answers. But as Matthew walked away from the ancient pear tree, he couldn't shake the feeling that uncovering the stone had been more than an accident. It felt like a test, or worse—like an invitation.

***

An hour later, the entire coven was gathered around the kitchen table, Matthew's crude sketch lying in the center like an accusation. The late afternoon sun slanted through the windows, but somehow the drawing seemed to absorb the light, creating a small zone of shadow that made everyone unconsciously lean away from it.

"I've never seen anything like this," Sam said, her voice tight with concentration as she compared Matthew's sketch to several open books spread around her. "The closest analog I can find is in some pre-Columbian texts, but even those are different. These spirals... they're not meant to be decorative. They're functional."

Sean leaned back in his chair, his hazel eyes dark with worry. The silver streak at his temple—a permanent reminder of his sacrifice with the Wayfinder—caught the light as he shook his head. "Functional, how?"

"Think of them as a circuit board," Sam explained, tracing one of the spirals with her finger without actually touching the paper. "Each line channels energy in a specific pattern. But the power source..." She looked up at Matthew. "You said you heard children playing? In water?"

Matthew nodded, suppressing a shiver at the memory. "It was so clear I looked around, thinking there might be a stream I'd missed. But there's nothing. Just dry earth and those ancient roots."

Katie, who had been unusually quiet, suddenly straightened in her chair. Her blue eyes had taken on a distant, unfocused look, indicating that she was accessing deeper layers of magical knowledge. "Not children playing," she said slowly. "Children drowning."

The temperature in the kitchen seemed to drop ten degrees.

"What?" Sean's voice was sharp with alarm.

Katie blinked, and when she looked at them again, her expression was haunted. "I touched the sketch—just for a second—and I saw... fragments. Images. There was water here once, Sean. A lot of water. And something went wrong." She wrapped her arms around herself, as if trying to ward off a chill only she could feel. "The laughter you heard, Matthew... it wasn't joy. It was the sound children make when they're trying to be brave. When they're scared, but don't want the adults to know."

Uncle Todd, who had been listening from the doorway with his characteristic quiet intensity, stepped into the kitchen. "How old did that stone look to you, son?"

Matthew considered the question carefully. "Old. Really old. The weathering patterns suggest it has been exposed to the elements for centuries, but the carvings themselves... they look almost fresh. Like they were made to last."

Todd nodded grimly and disappeared down the hallway. They could hear him rummaging in the study that had once been Tom's office, moving boxes and shuffling through papers. When he returned, he carried a thick manila folder with yellowed documents and faded photographs.

"Your grandfather kept every survey and historical document he could find about this property," Todd explained, spreading the papers across the table. "He was obsessed with the land's history, always said you couldn't protect something if you didn't understand where it came from."

The oldest document in the collection was a hand-drawn map from 1847, created by the county surveyor who had originally platted the Murphy family's homestead. The faded ink showed the familiar boundaries of their property. Still, with one crucial difference: where the orchard now stood, the map clearly showed a significant, natural depression labeled "Drowned Meadow—seasonal lake, dangerous currents."

"Jesus," Matthew breathed, staring at the map. "There really was water."

But it was the photograph that made Katie gasp aloud. Taken sometime in the 1920s, it showed a group of local children posed beside what was clearly a swimming hole, their old-fashioned bathing costumes dark with water, their faces bright with the kind of unguarded joy that only came from a perfect summer day. Behind them, clearly visible in the background, was the massive pear trees smaller than, but unmistakably the same ancient giant that now stood guard over Matthew's discovery.

And there, barely visible at the edge of the frame, was a corner of the spiral-carved stone.

"Granddad mentioned this place once," Todd said quietly, his finger tracing the faces of the long-dead children. "Said there had been an accident back in the twenties. A group of local kids were swimming when a flash flood came down from the hills. The natural dam that formed the swimming hole was unable to handle the sudden volume. It burst."

"How many?" Sean's voice was barely a whisper.

Todd's expression was grim. "Seven children. Ages six to twelve. They never found all the bodies."

The kitchen fell silent except for the steady tick of the old wall clock. Seven children, lost to a sudden, violent flood in what should have been their safe, familiar swimming hole. Seven young lives were cut short by the kind of random, natural disaster that left communities scarred for generations.

But as Matthew stared at his sketch of the impossible spirals, he knew with a growing certainty that what had happened here hadn't been natural at all.

"Sam," he said slowly, "those spirals you mentioned—the ones that channel energy. What kind of energy, exactly?"

Sam's face had gone pale as the implications became clear. "Emotional resonance. Fear, joy, pain... but especially traumatic memories. They act like a psychic battery, storing and amplifying the emotional energy from significant events." She looked around the table, her sea-green eyes wide with horror. "If those children died in terror if their last moments were filled with panic and desperation..."

"Then their deaths would have charged that stone like a lightning rod," Katie finished, her voice hollow.

Sean stood abruptly, his chair scraping against the floor. "We have to go back. Now. If that thing has been sitting under our orchard for almost a century, feeding on the psychic imprint of those children's deaths..." He didn't finish the sentence. He didn't need to.

They all understood. The spiral stone wasn't just a historical curiosity or a tragic memorial. It was a weapon. A psychic bomb that had been slowly building power for decades, fed by the echo of seven young lives lost in terror and confusion.

And somehow, Matthew's gift with earth magic had resonated with it, called to it across the years and through layers of concealing soil. The question now was whether his discovery had been a coincidence—or if something else had guided his hand, something that wanted the stone to be found.

As they prepared to return to the orchard, armed with salt circles and protective wards, none of them noticed the way the shadows in the kitchen had begun to move independently of their light sources. None of them saw the faint, translucent figures of seven children who had begun to gather at the edges of their vision, their old-fashioned clothes dripping with spectral water, their young faces etched with an eternal, patient sorrow.

The spiral stone had been waiting for almost a century to be uncovered. And now that it had been found, the dead children who powered it were finally ready to tell their story—whether the living were prepared to hear it or not.

***

The walk back to the orchard felt like a funeral procession. The sun was beginning to set, painting the sky in shades of orange and red that reminded Matthew uncomfortably of fire. Each step toward the ancient pear tree felt heavier than the last, as if the very air was growing thicker, more resistant to their passage.

Sean led the way, his hand resting on the rowan wood staff he now carried everywhere—a replacement for the destroyed Wayfinder, though nothing could truly replace that ancient artifact's power. Behind him, Katie walked with her fingers trailing through the protective salt she carried in a leather pouch, leaving a faint white trail in their wake. Sam had her emergency kit of herbs and crystals. At the same time, Matthew carried a small digital camera to document whatever they might find.

Uncle Todd brought up the rear, and though he carried no magical implements, his presence felt solid and reassuring. There was something about having a normal, non-magical person as witness that made their supernatural encounters feel more real, more grounded in the everyday world they were fighting to protect.

The ancient pear tree loomed before them, its gnarled branches reaching toward the deepening sky like arthritic fingers. In the dying light, the massive trunk looked less like a plant and more like a sleeping giant, its bark-covered surface seeming to rise and fall with slow, patient breaths.

Matthew approached the spot where he'd made his discovery but stopped short with a sharp intake of breath.

The stone was uncovered.

Not partially exposed, as he'd left it, but completely revealed, its entire surface clear of the leaves and soil he'd carefully arranged to hide it. The spiral carvings seemed to glow with their own faint, phosphorescent light, pulsing in a rhythm that matched the distant sound of water moving over stone.

"I buried it," Matthew said, his voice tight with anxiety. "I know I buried it."

"The earth remembers," Katie whispered, kneeling at the edge of the stone circle. Her fingers hovered inches above the carved surface, not quite touching but close enough to feel the cold energy that radiated from it. "It wants to be seen. It's been waiting so long to tell its story."

Sean began laying out the salt circle, his movements precise and practiced. "Everyone inside the boundary," he commanded. "We don't know what kind of defenses this thing might have, or what it might do if it feels threatened."

As they arranged themselves in a protective circle around the stone, the sounds began again. At first, it was just the phantom splash of water and distant laughter that Matthew had described. But as the last light faded from the sky and the first stars appeared overhead, the audio landscape became richer, more detailed.

They could hear the children's voices now, not just their laughter but their words, their conversations, spoken in the flat, nasal accents of rural South Carolina from decades past:

"Come on, Billy, don't be such a baby!"

"I can hold my breath longer than anyone!"

"Mama said we shouldn't swim after eating, but I'm fine..."

"Look how deep it is in the middle! I bet it goes all the way to China!"

The voices were so clear, so immediate, that all of them found themselves looking around for the speakers. But there was nothing to see except the empty orchard and the spiral stone, which now pulsed with a steady heartbeat rhythm of cold, blue light.

Sam pulled out a small recorder and set it on the ground outside their salt circle. "If we're going to document this, we need evidence," she said quietly. "Something to study later, when we're not in the middle of whatever this is."

As if responding to her words, the children's voices grew louder, more urgent. The playful chatter gave way to something else confusion, then concern, then rising panic:

"Where did all this water come from?"

"I can't touch bottom anymore!"

"Something's pulling me down!"

"Help! Help me!"

"Mama! MAMA!"

The final scream was so full of terror and desperation that Katie instinctively reached out toward the stone, her protective instincts overwhelming her caution. Sean caught her wrist just before her fingers made contact with the carved surface.

"Don't," he said firmly. "We don't know what it will do if you touch it directly."

But it was too late. The moment Katie's hand had moved toward the stone, something fundamental had changed. The phantom sounds of the drowning children cut off abruptly, replaced by a silence so completely it felt like being underwater. The air grew thick and humid, carrying the scent of river mud and summer rain.

And then, in the space between one heartbeat and the next, they were no longer alone in the orchard.

Seven translucent figures stood around the spiral stone, their forms wavering like heat mirages but clearly visible in the starlight. They were children, just as the photograph had shown, but their old-fashioned bathing costumes were now torn and muddy, their hair streaming with spectral water that never quite seemed to drip to the ground.

The oldest couldn't have been more than twelve, a serious-faced boy with his arm protectively around a smaller girl who might have been his sister. The youngest was perhaps six, a tiny thing whose wide eyes held a confusion that was heartbreaking to witness.

They were all looking at Katie with expressions of desperate hope as if she might be the answer to a question they'd been asking for almost a century.

"You can see us," the oldest boy said, his voice carrying the hollow, distant quality of an echo in a deep well. "You can finally see us."

Katie nodded, tears streaming down her face. "Yes. I can see you. What... what do you need? How can we help?"

The little girl stepped forward, her small hand reaching toward Katie but stopping just short of touching her. "We've been trying to warn people," she said in a voice like wind through dry leaves. "The bad thing... it's still down there. In the deep water. It's what made the dam break. It's what pulled us under."

"What bad thing?" Sean asked gently, his hand still on Katie's wrist, ready to pull her back if necessary.

The children turned toward him as one, their translucent faces etched with remembered terror. "The spiral thing," the oldest boy said. "It was already in the water when we came to swim. We thought it was just a pretty rock covered in carved pictures. But when Billy touched it..."

"It woke up," a red-haired girl finished. "And it was hungry. So very, very hungry."

Matthew felt his stomach lurch as the implications became clear. "The stone... it didn't just record your deaths. It caused them."

The little girl nodded solemnly. "It needed our fear, our pain. It consumed them and grew stronger. And now it's big enough to do it again."

"Do what again?" Katie whispered.

The children's forms began to flicker and fade as if the effort of maintaining their manifestation was becoming too great. But before they disappeared entirely, the oldest boy managed one final, desperate warning:

"It's going to make more water. Lots and lots of water. And when people come to see what happened... it will feed again."

The ghostly figures vanished, leaving only the spiral stone and the sound of distant thunder rolling across the night sky. Above them, clouds were gathering at an unnatural speed, building into the towering formations that often preceded flash floods.

Sean looked at the stone, then at the approaching storm, and felt the pieces of a terrifying puzzle clicking into place. The seven children had died almost a century ago, their terror and desperation absorbed by the carved spirals and converted into power. For decades, that power had been building, growing, and waiting for the right moment to repeat the cycle on a larger scale.

And somehow, Matthew's discovery had triggered the next phase of its plan.

"We have to get everyone away from here," Sean said urgently, already breaking the salt circle. "Not just us—everyone. If this thing is planning to flood the area again..."

"The whole town could be at risk," Katie finished, scrambling to her feet.

As they ran toward the farmhouse, the first fat raindrops began to fall, warm and heavy and far too early for the season. Behind them, the spiral stone pulsed with increasing intensity, drawing power from the approaching storm and the terror of its long-dead victims.

The ancient pear tree groaned in the rising wind, its massive branches swaying like the arms of a conductor leading a symphony of destruction. And deep beneath the stone, in a place that existed between memory and reality, something vast and patient and utterly without mercy began to stir from its century-long slumber.

The children's warning echoed in the wind: *It's going to make more water. Lots and lots of water.*

And this time, seven small voices wouldn't be nearly enough to satisfy its hunger.

Chapter 10: The First Echo

The hallways of Goose Creek High School were a river of familiar, chaotic life. Lockers slammed, sneakers squeaked on polished linoleum, and the air buzzed with the mundane, urgent dramas of teenage existence. For Sean, this daily immersion in normalcy had become a lifeline, a necessary fiction he clung to with a desperate grip. Here, surrounded by gossip about pop quizzes and weekend plans, he could almost forget the glowing ley line map spread across the table in his secret cave, a silent, terrifying blueprint of the coming apocalypse.

He and Katie stood at her locker, their shoulders pressed together, a small, quiet island in the churning river of students. A few days had passed since his uncle's arrival, and the farmhouse had settled into a new, strange rhythm. Todd was a quiet, almost ghostly presence, a man navigating the landscape of his own past regrets. He and Sean spoke in short, practical sentences about farm chores and groceries, the immense, magical truth of their situation a silent, acknowledged chasm between them.

"He tried to make toast this morning and almost set off the fire alarm," Sean murmured to Katie, a small smile touching his lips. "I think he's trying his best to be a guardian, but he might burn the house down before the Spirit gets a chance to."

Katie chuckled, the sound a welcome warmth in the cold knot of anxiety that lived permanently in Sean's chest now. "Be nice. He's trying. It can't be easy for him, coming back to all this." She stuffed a history book into her locker. "Speaking of things that aren't easy, did you do the reading for Abernathy? I swear he enjoys torturing us."

"Yeah, it's on my tablet," Sean said. "I can barely focus on it. My mind keeps..."

"I know," she cut him off softly, her eyes meeting his with a look of profound understanding. "Me too. But we have to. We have to be normal. We can't let this break us before the real fight even starts."

Her strength was his strength. He nodded, taking a deep breath. She was right. Normal. Just for a few hours.

It was as they turned towards the cafeteria that the first discordant note was struck. A sharp, ugly shout erupted from just down the hall, slicing through the ambient chatter.

"I saw you looking at him! Don't you lie to me!"

They turned to see a couple, a senior football player and a junior cheerleader who were famously inseparable, locked in a sudden, vicious confrontation. The boy's face was flushed a deep, mottled red, his neck muscles corded with a rage that was terrifying in its intensity.

"I was just talking to him about the game, you psycho!" the girl shrieked back, her own face pale with shock and fury. "You're so paranoid!"

"Paranoid? You were laughing! Flirting! In front of everyone!"

The fight escalated with a speed that was breathtakingly unnatural, their words turning from accusations to cruel, personal insults in a matter of seconds. It ended when the boy, with a snarl of disgust, slammed his fist into a locker inches from the girl's head, the bang echoing through the now-silent hallway. He stormed off, leaving her to collapse against the lockers in a storm of humiliated, heartbroken sobs.

Students stared, then quickly looked away, whispering amongst themselves.

"Wow," Katie murmured, her eyes wide. "I thought they were going to get voted prom king and queen."

Sean didn't answer. He felt a cold prickle of unease on the back of his neck. The sheer, unrestrained venom of the argument had felt wrong, disproportionate. He had felt a flicker of something else in the air, a faint, sour tang, like the smell of burnt static. He pushed the feeling down. He was just on edge. That's all it was.

The feeling returned, stronger this time, as they entered the cafeteria. The vast, noisy room was its usual lunchtime circus, but today, something was off. The usual joyful, chaotic energy was absent, replaced by a low-grade, irritable hum. The air felt heavy, thick with a psychic humidity that made the hairs on Sean's arms stand on end. He saw small arguments breaking out at tables and friends snapping at each other over trivial things. He saw a girl at a nearby table suddenly burst into tears for no discernible reason, her friends staring at her with annoyance rather than concern.

The coven had claimed their usual table in the back corner, a strategic spot that offered a clear view of the entire room. Sam was already there, slowly stirring a cup of yogurt, her brow furrowed in concentration.

"Do you feel that?" she asked in a low voice as Sean and Katie sat down.

"It's like the whole room is having a bad day," Katie said, unwrapping her sandwich.

"It's more than that," Sam replied, her gaze sweeping across the room. "The emotional atmosphere in here is... toxic. It's not just random anger or sadness. It feels... orchestrated."

As she spoke, the chaos began to coalesce. A heated argument over a video game at a table of freshmen suddenly erupted into a full-blown shoving match. Across the room, a food fight started, but there was no laughter, only the angry splat of milk cartons and hurled pieces of pizza. It was a riot in miniature, fueled not by youthful exuberance but by a strange, free-floating malice.

Teachers blew whistles and shouted, trying to restore order, but their voices were shrill with a frantic, uncharacteristic panic. They began snapping at the students, their own tempers flaring.

It's a spell. The thought came sharp and clear from Matthew, who was sitting with some of his friends near the lunch line. *A wave of psychic interference. I can feel it trying to get in.*

Sean felt it too, an insidious whisper at the edge of his own consciousness, telling him that his friends were annoyed with him, that Katie was pitying him, that his uncle secretly blamed him for his grandfather's death. Vicious, irrational thoughts designed to prey on his most profound insecurities. He slammed his mental shields into place, the effort requiring a sudden, sharp focus.

Everyone shields up! Now! Sean commanded telepathically, his voice a calm, authoritative center in their minds. *This is a magical attack. It's an area-of-effect spell, designed to sow chaos and feed on the negativity. Don't fight it head-on. Just protect yourselves and stay calm.*

He could feel the immediate response, the mental presence of his coven members solidifying, their own shields flaring to life like small, steady flames in a psychic storm.

Katie, you're the most sensitive, Sean sent. *Can you trace the energy? Find the source.*

He saw her close her eyes, her uneaten sandwich forgotten. Her fork hovered over her tray for a moment, then she set it down. Her brow was creased with intense concentration. The noise in the cafeteria was reaching a crescendo, a cacophony of shouts, accusations, and hysterical crying.

It's not coming from a person, she thought, finally came back, strained and tight with effort. *It's like a broadcast tower, blanketing the whole room. It's everywhere. But the signal... it's strongest over there. By the trash cans.*

Sam, Kim, and Sean directed. *Work together. Create a calming aura. Don't try to erase the anger, just soothe it. Push out waves of peace and clarity. Muffle the broadcast.*

Matthew ground the energy. Visualize all this psychic filth as dirty water and create a drain. Pull it down into the earth beneath the school. Give it somewhere to go so it doesn't just keep swirling around.

He could feel them working, their combined magic a subtle but powerful counter-current to the chaos. The ambient rage in the room was lessened by a few crucial degrees. It was enough. Now he had to get the source.

He looked over at the cluster of tables near the trash receptacles. His eyes scanned the area. There was nothing out of the ordinary. The source had to be hidden.

"I'm gonna get rid of my tray," he said aloud to Sam, who gave him a tiny, almost imperceptible nod. He stood up, his heart beginning to pound a heavy, anxious rhythm against his ribs. He had to walk through the heart of the madness, appearing completely normal, while a psychic storm raged around him.

He took his first step, and it was like wading into a current. A jock, his face contorted with rage, shoved past him, snarling, "Watch it, hero." Sean ignored him. He passed a table where a girl was accusing her friend of stealing her boyfriend, her voice thick with a paranoia that was terrifyingly absolute. He felt the waves of their misery washing over his shields, and he had to constantly reinforce them, his focus absolute.

He needed a diversion.

Matthew, he sent. *On my count. Create a distraction. Opposite side of the room. Make it loud.*

On it, came the confident reply.

Sean continued his slow, deliberate walk toward the trash cans. *Three... two... one...*

CRASH!

On the far side of the cafeteria, Matthew, feigning a clumsy misstep, went down hard, his entire lunch tray flying through the air and hitting the floor with a spectacular, attention-grabbing clatter of plastic and silverware. Every head in the room, including the teachers', snapped toward the sound.

It was the opening Sean needed.

He reached the designated area. He bent down as if to tie his shoe, his eyes scanning the grimy undersides of the tables. And there it was. Taped to the bottom of a table leg, almost perfectly concealed in shadow, was a small, cold, ugly object. It was a coin-sized idol carved from a greasy-feeling, non-reflective black stone. Its features were a distorted, leering mockery of a human face, its mouth open in a silent, hateful scream.

The moment his fingers brushed against it, a jolt of vile, cold, *familiar* energy shot up his arm. It was the Malevolent Spirit's signature—unmistakable, arrogant, and hungry. He felt a psychic whisper of its presence, a faint, mocking echo of its ancient consciousness. *I see you, little warlock.*

Sean suppressed a gasp, his fingers recoiling before he forced them to close around the object. The cold was intense, a soul-deep chill. He quickly wrapped it in the napkin from his pocket, insulating it, containing its poisonous broadcast.

The effect was instantaneous and breathtaking. The oppressive psychic pressure in the room vanished as if a switch had been thrown.

The food fight sputtered to a halt. Students stood frozen, looking down at the splattered milk on their clothes, at the trays in their hands, their faces filled with a dawning, bewildered confusion. The vicious arguments died, replaced by a sudden, awkward, embarrassed silence. The teachers stopped shouting, blinking, and looking around the room as if waking from a collective, inexplicable nightmare. The fever had broken.

Sean stood up, his heart hammering, and calmly walked to the trash can. He dropped his tray, with the napkin-wrapped idol hidden beneath his leftover food, into the bin. He turned and walked back to his table, his legs feeling weak and shaky, the gazes of his coven members filled with a mixture of awe and shared terror.

That evening, they stood in the clean, quiet air of the sanctuary. Sean, using a pair of iron tongs, had retrieved the idol from the school dumpster after the final bell. Now, it sat on a flat stone slab in the center of the room. Its power was spent, but the foul, lingering residue of the Spirit's magic still clung to it like a shroud of grave dirt.

"It was feeding," Katie said finally, her arms wrapped tightly around her chest as she stared at the ugly object. "The whole school... it was a psychic feeding trough.

It was siphoning off all that negative emotion, all that fear and anger, and using it to charge itself."

"It was more than that," Sam said, her voice grim. "It was a probe. A way to test our response time, to see if we were sensitive enough to even detect this kind of subtle, widespread attack. It was gathering intelligence on us."

Sean nodded, the chilling truth of their words settling deep in his bones. He looked from Katie's pale, determined face to Sam's worried one, and then to the idol itself. "It was both," he said, his voice quiet but hard as steel. "And it was a message." He met their eyes. "It was a message to me. It was telling me that it can touch us anywhere. That nowhere is safe. That it controls the board, and we are just pieces on it."

He raised his hand, and a sphere of clean, white, wiccan fire bloomed in his palm. He hurled it at the idol. The object didn't just burn; it screamed, a high-pitched, psychic shriek of pain and rage, before dissolving into a puff of greasy, black smoke that was instantly purified by the sanctuary's magic.

They had stopped the attack. They had won the skirmish. But the victory was deeply unsettling. The first echo of their enemy's return had faded, but it had taught them a terrifying lesson. They were no longer just preparing for a future war. The Cold War had already begun, and its battlefields were the hallways of their school, the hearts of their friends, and the quiet, vulnerable spaces of their own minds.

Chapter 11: The Other Guardians

T he letter arrived on a Thursday morning, three days after the psychic assault at the school. It wasn't delivered by any postal service—it simply appeared on the kitchen table while the family ate breakfast, materializing between Todd's coffee mug and Katie's plate with a soft whisper of displaced air.

The envelope was ancient, made of parchment that felt more like skin than paper, sealed with black wax that bore a symbol none of them recognized—a tree whose roots and branches formed an endless knot. Sean's name was written across it in ink that seemed to shift between deep purple and midnight blue.

"Magical correspondence," Sam said, her voice tight with caution. "Could be trapped."

Sean held his hand over the letter, sensing for hostile magic. Instead, he felt something else—a resonance that echoed his own power but in a different key, like hearing a familiar song played on an unfamiliar instrument.

"It's safe," he said, breaking the seal.

The letter inside was written in a flowing script that was almost archaic:

To the Guardian of the Murphy Line,

Your recent activities have not gone unnoticed. The echo of your battle with the Spirit's manifestation has rippled across the ley lines, and we of the Council of Trees have taken note.

You are not alone in your vigil, young Guardian. Others keep watch at other Gates, face other threats, guard other seals. The time has come for you to know of us as we know of you.

If you would meet your fellow Guardians, come to the Crossroads Oak at midnight on the new moon. Come alone or with your bonded if you have one. Speak the words: "By root and branch, I answer the call."

We have much to discuss regarding the stirring darkness.

In service to the Light, Guardian Ashworth of the Eastern Seal

Katie looked up from reading over his shoulder. "Other Guardians? Other Gates?"

"Grandfather's letter mentioned them," Sean said slowly. "But I thought... I guess I thought we were the only ones left actively fighting."

"It could be a trap," Matthew pointed out. "The timing is suspicious. Right after we fought off an attack?"

But Todd shook his head. "Tom spoke of the Council once, years ago. Said they were real but scattered. Said they only gathered when the threat was bigger than any one family line could handle."

The debate continued throughout the day, but Sean had already made his decision. If there were others like them—other families standing against the darkness—he needed to meet them. They needed allies, knowledge, and perspective beyond their own limited experience.

Three nights later, under a dark sky with no moon, Sean and Katie made their way to the Crossroads Oak. It was an ancient tree that stood where three old roads met, five miles from the farm. Local legend said it had been there since before the first settlers when Native American tribes considered it a sacred meeting place.

As they approached, Sean could feel the power radiating from the massive oak. Its trunk was so vast that six people holding hands couldn't encircle it, and its branches spread like a canopy of frozen lightning against the stars.

"By root and branch, I answer the call," Sean said clearly.

The air around the tree shimmered, and suddenly, they weren't alone.

Five figures materialized from what had seemed like empty air. They were diverse in age and appearance, but all carried the same unmistakable aura of power carefully controlled.

The first to step forward was a woman in her fifties with steel-gray hair woven into an intricate braid. She wore simple clothes, but power radiated from her like heat from a forge. "Guardian Murphy," she said with a slight British accent. "I'm Eleanor Ashworth. I keep watch over Glastonbury Tor."

A young man, perhaps twenty-five, with intricate tattoos covering his arms, nodded in greeting. "Marcus Chen. I guard the Pacific Gate, out of San Francisco."

An elderly Black woman with eyes that seemed to hold starlight smiled warmly. "Rosalie Thibodaux, child. New Orleans. Been keeping the Southern Crossroads locked for longer than you've been alive."

A severe-looking man with Nordic features simply stated, "Erik Nordahl. Iceland. The Fire and Ice Seal."

The last was a girl who looked no older than fourteen, though her eyes suggested otherwise. "Yuki Tanaka," she said softly. "Kyoto. The Cherry Blossom Gate."

Eleanor gestured to a circle of stones that hadn't been there moments before. "Sit. We have much to discuss and little time to discuss it."

As they settled into the circle, Sean felt the weight of history, of shared purpose. These people—these Guardians—understood the burden he carried in a way even his coven couldn't fully grasp.

"The spirit you fought," Eleanor began without preamble, "was indeed what you call a Keystone. But it wasn't working alone. We've all felt stirrings at our own Gates. Whatever ritual it attempted was meant to weaken not just your seal but create a sympathetic weakening in all of them."

Marcus leaned forward. "Three weeks ago, something tried to breach the Pacific Gate. It came from beneath the ocean, speaking in languages that predate human civilization. I barely held it back."

"The Crossroads have been... restless," Rosalie added. "Spirits that have slept for a hundred years are beginning to wake. They whisper about a Convergence."

Sean and Katie exchanged worried glances. "Convergence?" Katie asked.

"A theoretical event," Erik explained, his voice like a grinding stone. "If enough Gates weaken simultaneously, they could create a cascade failure. One break, they all break. The barriers between worlds collapse entirely."

"Which is why," Eleanor said firmly, "we need to coordinate. The old ways—each family guarding their territory in isolation—won't work against a coordinated assault."

Yuki spoke for the first time since introductions. "There are prophecies in the East. They speak of a time when the Guardians must become as one, or all will fall as many."

"How many of us are there?" Sean asked.

"Active family lines?" Eleanor considered. "Perhaps thirty worldwide. But many are weakened, their bloodlines thinned, and their knowledge fragmented. You're lucky—your grandfather maintained the old ways better than most."

"What about the ones who aren't lucky?" Katie asked.

A shadow passed over Rosalie's face. "The Brennan line in Ireland—their last Guardian died without passing on the knowledge. Their Gate stands are protected only by automated wards two centuries old. The Petrova family in Russia lost three generations to Stalin's purges. They're down to one thirteen-year-old girl who doesn't even know what she is yet."

The weight of it settled on Sean's shoulders. They weren't just fighting for their own Gate—the entire network was vulnerable.

"What do you need from us?" he asked.

Eleanor smiled, the expression transforming her stern face. "For now? Keep doing what you're doing. You've already proven yourselves remarkably capable for one so young. But stay in contact. Share what you learn. And be ready."

She produced a small silver compass from her pocket. "This will always point toward the nearest active Guardian. If you need help, if your situation becomes desperate, follow it. We'll come."

Marcus handed Katie a smooth stone covered in Chinese characters. "This is linked to mine. Speak to it during the full moon, and I'll hear you. The Pacific Gate has some of the oldest archives on spirit binding—if you need research, I'm your man."

Each Guardian offered something—a token, a connection, knowledge freely shared. Sean felt a warmth spreading through his chest. They weren't alone. They'd never been alone.

As the meeting concluded and the other Guardians began to fade back into the ley lines that had brought them, Eleanor lingered.

"Your grandfather would be proud," she said softly. "I met him once, years ago. He spoke of you even then—the grandson who would carry on when he couldn't."

"You knew him?"

"All of us older Guardians knew of Tom Murphy. He was... remarkable. He once held the Carolina Gate alone for three days against a full assault while his coven was recovering from a plague. Lesser men would have broken." She placed a hand on Sean's shoulder. "You have his strength. I can see it. But remember—strength alone won't win this war. The connections you forge, the allies you gather, the love you protect—that's what will make the difference."

With that, she, too, faded, leaving Sean and Katie alone beneath the ancient oak.

They walked back to the farm in contemplative silence, the silver compass warm in Sean's pocket. The world had suddenly become both larger and smaller—larger in scope, smaller in the sense that they were no longer isolated defenders but part of an ancient network.

"We need to tell the others," Katie said finally.

"We do," Sean agreed. "And we need to start thinking bigger. If this Convergence is real..."

"Then we're not just protecting our town anymore," Katie finished. "We're protecting everything."

Above them, the stars wheeled in their courses, and Sean couldn't shake the feeling that they were being watched—not just by the Witness that would later plague them, but by forces even older and more patient, waiting to see if this generation of Guardians would prove worthy of their inheritance.

The war for reality had more players than they'd imagined. And for the first time since his grandfather's death, Sean felt the stirring of something that might have been hope.

Chapter 12: The Uncle's Guidance

The ancient, preserved air of the sanctuary had grown stale with frustration. For three nights straight since the incident at the school, the coven had sequestered themselves in the hidden library, driven by a frantic urgency. They had subsisted on protein bars and water bottles, their sleep measured in stolen hours on the enchanted sofas, their dreams filled with shadowy creatures and the faces of frightened classmates. The initial surge of adrenaline from their victory in the cafeteria had long since evaporated, leaving behind the gritty residue of fatigue and a growing, gnawing sense of hopelessness.

They were drowning in information. They had stacks of translated scrolls detailing the history of the *Vatra Sângelui*, also known as the Blood Weavers. They had stone tablets describing the tactics of the *Yawar-Machaq*, the Shadow drinkers. They knew more about the different clans of Malevolent Spirits than any living soul had a right to, but it was all history, all lore. It told them what the monsters *were* but not where their own local monster *is*.

"This is useless," Matthew said, throwing his hands up in exasperation. He gestured to the chaotic piles of books and parchments surrounding them. "We know there's a Keystone spirit out there, preparing a nexus for some kind of magical apocalypse, but we have no idea where it is or what it's doing. For all we know, its host is the mayor, or the mailman, or that creepy guy who runs the bait and tackle shop. We're blind."

"We just need to look deeper," Katie insisted, though her voice was strained, her usual fiery optimism worn thin. She was rubbing her temples, a clear sign of the headache that came from hours of magically assisted reading. "There has to be a scrying spell, a ritual of seeking..."

"We've tried three different scrying rituals, Katie!" Sam countered, her voice sharper than usual. "All we get is static. Its magic is too strong, or it's warded itself against observation. It knows we're looking. It's toying with us."

The frustration in the room was palpable, a bitter fog that clung to them all. Sean felt the weight of their despair pressing down on him, the burden of leadership a physical ache between his shoulder blades. He was their leader, the most powerful among them, and he was failing. He was leading them in circles while a world-ending threat gathered its strength somewhere out in the darkness. He pushed himself up from the sofa, the ancient leather groaning in protest.

"I need some air," he mumbled, turning his back on the sympathetic, worried faces of his friends.

He walked through the silent outer chambers of the cave, the oppressive sense of failure following him. He didn't head back to the empty farmhouse. Instead, on instinct, he found himself walking towards the barn. The huge, weathered structure stood as a dark silhouette against a sky littered with a billion indifferent stars. It was a place of work, of tangible reality, a place that had always belonged to his grandfather.

A single, dim light bulb glowed from within, casting a weak, golden rectangle out of the open side door. Sean stepped inside, the familiar scent of hay, old wood, and dry earth washing over him. His uncle was there, sitting on an overturned milking stool in the center of the vast, quiet space. He wasn't working. He was just sitting, a long-forgotten whetstone in his hands, staring at nothing. He was surrounded by the ghosts of a life he had run away from.

Todd looked up as Sean entered, his expression unreadable. "Couldn't sleep either?"

Sean shook his head, leaning against the rough-hewn wood of a horse stall. The silence stretched between them, not the comfortable quiet he had shared with his grandfather, but one filled with unspoken history and awkward regret.

"We're lost," Sean said finally, the admission feeling like a betrayal of his role as a leader. "We know a hurricane is coming, but we have no idea where it's going to make landfall. We're just sitting here, reading old books, waiting to get hit."

Todd set the whetstone down carefully, his gaze dropping to the dusty floor. "Maybe you should stop looking for it," he suggested, his voice low. "Maybe the best you can do is prepare for the impact. Strengthen your wards, keep your head down."

It was the advice of a man who had chosen flight over fight his entire life. A flare of anger, hot and unfair, shot through Sean. "Keep our heads down? While it plants cursed idols in schools? While it walks around in some person's body, planning to rip a hole in the world?" He took a step forward, his fists clenching at his sides. "Grandpa wouldn't have hidden. He would have fought."

"And he would have been smart about it!" Todd shot back, rising to his feet, the sudden fire in his voice startling Sean. "He wouldn't have charged into the darkness without a lantern! He knew the price of recklessness!"

"Then what's the answer?" Sean demanded, his voice cracking with desperation. "He's gone. He left me in charge, and I'm failing. I don't know what to do." He looked at his uncle, his pride stripped away, leaving only the raw fear of a boy in over his head. "He must have known something. In his last days... he was trying to tell me something, warn me about something more specific. I can feel it."

He reached into his pocket and pulled out the small, carved wooden bird. He held it out on his palm. "He gave me this. The night before he died. He called it a 'Wayfinder.'"

Todd froze. All the color drained from his face, and his eyes fixed on the small object as if it were a venomous snake. He looked, for the first time since he'd returned, truly and utterly terrified. He took an involuntary step back, shaking his head.

"Put it away, Sean."

"What is it?" Sean pressed, stepping closer. "You know what it is. You have to tell me."

"He should never have given that to you," Todd whispered, his voice hoarse. "He should have thrown it in a fire." He looked up, his eyes filled with a pained, frantic energy. "Don't you understand? Some doors are meant to stay closed. Some secrets are meant to stay buried. That thing... it's a shortcut through a dark wood, and the path always demands a toll."

"I don't care about a toll!" Sean's voice rose, echoing in the cavernous barn. "I need a path! What does it do?"

His uncle stared at him for a long, agonizing moment, a silent battle waging behind his eyes. Finally, with a sigh that sounded like the surrender of his soul, he gestured for Sean to sit on a nearby hay bale. He took the bird from Sean's hand, his own fingers trembling as he held it.

"It's older than this farm," Todd began, his voice barely a whisper. "Older than the Murphys who came to this country. The story... the story my father told me was that it was carved by the first of our line to be cursed with the Sight. Carved from the heart of a lightning-struck yew tree." He turned it over and over, his thumb tracing the impossibly small runes. "It doesn't point north. It points to where magic is being broken. To where the fabric of the world is being torn. It points to trouble."

Sean's heart hammered in his chest. This was it. The lantern in the dark. "So it can find the Spirit. It can lead us to the nexus."

"Yes," Todd said, his voice flat and dead. "It can. But you didn't listen to me, Sean. I said it demands a toll."

He finally looked Sean in the eye, and the fear and regret there were so profound they were almost tangible. "My grandfather—the man who gave this to my father—he was a powerful man, in his way. The stories say he used it to track a creature that was preying on the children of his village back in the old country. A thing that stole their breath while they slept. He took the bird and followed it. He was gone for three days. When he came back, the creature was gone, and the children were safe."

"So, he won," Sean said, a surge of hope rising in him.

"Yes," Todd said, his voice breaking. "He won. But he was a man of forty when he left. When he came back... his hair was snow white. He had a tremor in his hands that never left him. And he died of old age before he was forty-five. My father said the bird doesn't just use your magic to find its way, Sean. It uses *you*. It burns your time as fuel. Minutes, hours, maybe even years off your life, depending on how hard you ask it to look and how far away the trouble is. It feasts on your future to show you the present."

The hope in Sean's chest turned to ice. He stared at the beautiful, terrible object in his uncle's hand. A compass that ran on the years of his life.

"Tom was afraid of it," Todd continued, his voice heavy. "He never touched it after my grandfather died. He locked it away. The fact that he gave it to you... that tells you how desperate he believed the situation was about to become. He was leaving you a choice he never dared to make himself."

A terrible, agonizing choice. He could protect himself, protect his future, and let the world burn. Or he could use this horrifying gift, pay the ultimate price, and give them a fighting chance. He thought of Katie's face, of the fear in Kim's eyes, of his grandfather's belief in him. He thought of the snarling paranoia in the cafeteria, a small taste of the world the Spirits wanted to create. There was no choice at all, not really.

"I have to use it," Sean said, his voice quiet but unshakable.

Todd's shoulders slumped in defeat. He looked at Sean, and the fear in his eyes was replaced by a deep, sorrowful respect. "I ran from this kind of choice my whole life," he said softly. "You're a better man than I am, Sean. A better man than I ever was." He pressed the Wayfinder back into Sean's palm. Its wooden surface was no longer neutral. It felt hungry. "Just... be careful. Please. Don't ask more of it than you can afford to give."

Sean nodded, unable to speak. He stood up and walked out of the barn, leaving his uncle alone with the ghosts of his past. The Wayfinder felt impossibly heavy in his pocket now, a lead weight pulling him toward a future he might not live long enough to see. The path back to the cave was dark, each step a conscious decision, a move toward his own sacrifice.

He entered the sanctuary to find the coven still hunched over their texts, their faces drawn with exhaustion. They all looked up as he entered, their expressions questioning, hopeful. He didn't say a word. He just walked to the center of the room, to the table with the glowing map, and held up the small, unassuming wooden bird.

"I think I found a way," he said, his voice heavy with the knowledge of the price.

Seven pairs of eyes fixed on the small artifact. And in the flickering candlelight of the ancient library, they saw not just a piece of carved wood but a sliver of hope, a terrifying chance, and the dawning, awful understanding of what their leader was willing to pay to give them one.

Chapter 13: A Call for Allies

The heavy silence of the Murphy farmhouse was a poor cloak for the frantic energy buzzing beneath it. Two days had passed since the psychic assault at the school, and the coven's sanctuary had become a claustrophobic prison of dead ends. The ancient texts offered a thousand terrifying descriptions of the enemy but not a single, actionable strategy for finding it. They were a tiny, isolated island of knowledge in a vast, dark ocean, and the tide was rising.

Sean paced the worn floorboards of the living room, the frustration a bitter, metallic taste in his mouth. He ran a hand through his hair, a gesture of anxiety he'd inherited from his grandfather. On the sofa, Katie was cross-referencing a 17th-century demonology text with a modern geological survey map, her brow furrowed in concentration. Sam, who had spent the better part of the last forty-eight hours with them, was quietly meditating in the corner, trying to sense any new disturbances in the town's emotional atmosphere.

"It's no good," Sean burst out, the words erupting from him. "We're just reacting. We neutralized that idol at the school, but that was just one symptom of a larger issue. We're trying to cure a plague by swatting at a single fly. It knows we're here; it knows we're a threat, but we're completely blind to it."

Katie looked up, her eyes shadowed with fatigue. "So what do we do, Sean? We can't just walk down Main Street casting 'find evil' spells. We need more information, a new approach."

"We need more than that," Sean said, stopping his pacing to look at her. The idea had been taking root in his mind for hours, a desperate, risky gambit. "We need more power. Not just my power, or yours. We need more allies."

Katie's expression immediately hardened, her protective instincts rising like a physical shield. "Allies? Who? We can't just put an ad in the paper: 'Local coven seeking witches to fight ancient evil. Must be okay with potential dismemberment.' We don't know who we can trust."

"I know," Sean said, walking over to the small table where he'd left his schoolbooks. He shuffled through a stack of papers and pulled out a small, folded slip. It was the note Sam had given him after the football game, the one with her phone number. He hadn't thought he'd ever use it. "There's her. The witch from the game."

Katie's eyes narrowed. "Sam? The one who was actively using magic to make your team lose? That's your brilliant idea for an ally?"

"She wasn't trying to hurt anyone, Katie, she was just helping her cousin. And her magic was... clean. I could feel it. There was no malice in it," Sean argued, though he understood her hesitation. "Think about it. She's powerful enough to affect a whole football field, and knowledgeable enough to find us. She's alone. Maybe she's looking for a coven as much as we're looking for members."

"Or maybe she's a spy for another faction we don't even know about," Katie countered, her voice sharp. The auras of jealousy and protectiveness coming off her were so strong Sean could practically see them shimmering in the air. "I don't like it. It's too risky. We have no idea who she is."

"Which is why we don't just invite her in for tea," Sean said, his voice softening as he sat on the edge of the coffee table, facing her. "We test her. We take her measure. We find out if she's a friend or a foe. Katie... we can't do this alone. Matthew was right. We're just kids on a farm. The world is a lot bigger than we thought, and it's a lot darker. We need help."

He saw the conflict in her eyes, the war between her fierce, protective caution and her pragmatic intelligence. She knew he was right. He could feel her resolve beginning to waver.

"Fine," she conceded finally, with a heavy sigh. "Fine. We test her. But we do it our way. On our terms. And if I feel even a whisper of dark magic from her, Sean, I swear, we end it immediately. Agreed?"

"Agreed," he said, relief washing over him. He picked up his phone, his thumb hovering over the numbers on the slip of paper. He dialed, and the phone rang twice before she answered.

"Hello?" Her voice was calm, confident, and held a hint of amusement, as if she'd been expecting his call.

"Sam, it's Sean Murphy."

"I know," she said. "I've been wondering when you'd call. Your coven's wards are impressive, but they hum like a power station. A bit obvious if you know what to listen for."

Sean's grip on the phone tightened. She wasn't just powerful; she was perceptive. "We need to talk. We have a proposition for you. A test, really."

There was a pause, and Sean could almost hear her smiling. "I love tests. Where and when?"

"The old barn at the edge of my property. Sundown."

"I'll be there," she said, and the line went dead.

***

As dusk settled over the farm, painting the sky in bruised shades of purple and orange, the interior of the barn felt like a sacred, ancient space. The air smelled of generations of hay, old leather, and the clean, mineral scent of the earth. Sean and Katie had spent the last hour preparing. This wouldn't be a simple conversation; it would be a ritual.

Katie, using her deep knowledge of the sanctuary's texts, had insisted on tradition. With painstaking care, she poured a thin, unbroken line of purified rock salt across the threshold of the main door, whispering an ancient ward of truth-seeing with each grain that fell. "No creature with a duplicitous heart or malicious intent can cross this line without revealing itself," she explained, her face serious in the dimming light.

Sean, meanwhile, had set up a testing ground in the center of the barn's wide, swept floor. On a rough-hewn worktable, he placed a single, perfect green apple, its skin so taut and shiny it looked like polished jade. Beside it sat a small, empty iron cauldron and a collection of herbs and crystals he'd brought from the cave: lavender for purity, obsidian for protection, quartz for clarity.

Their preparations were done in a tense, purposeful silence. The weight of their decision hung between them. This was a turning point. They were either about to gain a powerful new ally or invite a viper into their home.

"She's here," Katie whispered, her eyes fixed on the open barn door.

Sean extended his senses and felt it too—a steady, confident magical signature approaching. It was strong, like Sam's, but there was something else with it... a faint, almost undetectable trace of something ancient and wild. His hand instinctively went to the Wayfinder in his pocket. It remained cool and dormant.

A moment later, Sam appeared in the doorway, a dark figure silhouetted against the fading light. She was dressed practically in jeans and a dark jacket, her striking sea-green eyes taking in the entire scene at a glance. Her gaze fell upon the line of salt, and a slow smile spread across her face. It was a smile of respect.

"Wise," she said, her voice echoing slightly in the vast space. "A classic for a reason. You honor the old ways."

She took a deliberate step, her boot crossing the shimmering line of salt without any hesitation or ill effect. The first, most basic test was passed. The tension in Sean's shoulders eased by a fraction.

She walked toward them, her steps confident, her eyes missing nothing. "So," she said, her gaze falling upon the items on the table. "This is a test of some kind. I'm intrigued."

"It is," Sean said, his voice level. "We need to know who you are. And what you're capable of."

Katie stepped forward, her arms crossed, her expression a mask of cool assessment. "We'll start with a contest of wills. Change the apple. Turn it red. Then, protect your spell. Sean will try to change it back."

Sam's smile widened into a grin. "An interesting challenge. I accept."

She stood five feet from the table, her posture relaxed but focused. She raised a hand, her fingers tracing a slow, deliberate pattern in the air. "DER OT EG-NAHC TCETORP," she murmured, her voice a low hum of power. A shimmer of emerald light enveloped the apple, and when it faded, the fruit was a deep, luscious crimson. A faint, invisible shield of energy now pulsed around it.

Sean stepped up to the table. He didn't use an incantation. He simply reached out with his mind, with the deep, elemental power that was his birthright. He didn't try to break her shield; he went under it, touching the very essence of the apple, the memory of its greenness. He felt her power pushing back, a well-constructed but ultimately yielding force. *NEERG OT EGNAHC,* he thought, and the apple flickered, then reverted to its original, vibrant green.

Sam's eyes widened slightly, a flicker of surprise crossing her features. She refocused her own concentration doubling. The air crackled. The apple began to strobe, flashing rapidly between red and green like a faulty traffic light. Sam was straining now, a bead of sweat tracing a path down her temple. She was powerful, more powerful than Sean had even guessed, but his own connection to the earth, to the life force of the apple itself, was deeper, more fundamental.

He gave one final, decisive mental push. *TCETORP NEERG OT EGNAHC.*

The struggle ceased. The apple remained a defiant, solid green. Sam, seeing she was beaten on this front, did not surrender. Instead, she poured one last, frustrated burst of energy at her own failed spell.

SMUSH.

The apple didn't just explode; it detonated. A fine mist of apple juice and a shower of pulp rained down on the three of them. For a moment, they just stood there, stunned and sticky. Then Sam burst out laughing, a genuine, hearty laugh that echoed through the barn. Sean, surprised, found himself grinning. Even Katie couldn't suppress a smile.

"Okay," Sam said, wiping a piece of apple off her cheek. "I concede. You are far more powerful than I am, which is exactly why I'm here." The laughter faded, and her expression grew serious once more. "I would like to join your coven. If you'll have me."

As they cleaned apple pulp from their faces and clothes, Sean caught Katie watching him with an unreadable expression. The afternoon sun slanted through the barn's high windows, turning her hair to spun gold and making her eyes impossibly blue.

"What?" he asked, suddenly self-conscious.

"Nothing," she said, but a small smile played at her lips. "Just... do you remember the first time we did magic together?"

Sam made an interesting sound as she continued to wipe the apple from her jacket. "I don't think I've heard this story."

Katie's smile widened. "We were thirteen. Sean had just started manifesting, couldn't control anything. Every time he got emotional, things would randomly catch fire or freeze solid."

"You're exaggerating," Sean protested, his ears turning red.

"Am I? What about Mrs. Henderson's rosebush?"

"That was an accident!"

"You turned it into an ice sculpture because she gave us a pop quiz!"

Sam laughed. "Please tell me there are pictures."

"Better," Katie said, her eyes dancing. "I have the security footage from the school library."

"We agreed never to speak of the library incident," Sean groaned.

"What happened?" Sam asked, delighted.

Katie settled onto a hay bale, clearly enjoying herself. "Picture this: young Sean, gangly and awkward, massive crush on the new girl who'd just moved to town—"

"Katie," Sean warned, but he was fighting a smile.

"—decides the best way to impress her is to show off his newfound magical abilities. In the middle of the school library. During finals week."

"Oh no," Sam breathed.

"Oh yes. He was trying to levitate my books for me. Sweet, right? Except he got nervous when I smiled at him. Instead of a controlled levitation, every book in a twenty-foot radius went flying. Three hundred years of accumulated knowledge, just..." She made an explosive gesture. "Whoosh."

"The librarian cried," Sean admitted. "Actual tears."

"But here's the part Sean doesn't like to tell," Katie continued, her voice softening. "When the books started falling, he threw himself over me. Took the full weight of an encyclopedia set to the back to keep me from getting hurt. That's when I knew."

"Knew what?" Sam asked.

Katie looked at Sean, her expression tender. "That he was the kind of person who'd always put others first. That his first instinct would always be to protect." She reached out and took his hand. "That I was completely doomed to fall in love with him."

The barn fell quiet except for the distant sound of wind in the rafters. Sam cleared her throat. "That's... actually really romantic. In a chaotic, destructive sort of way."

"Story of our lives," Sean said, squeezing Katie's hand. "Beautiful chaos."

"Anyway," Katie continued, "after we cleaned up the library—took six hours and a lot of magical help from Tom—Sean was so mortified he avoided me for a week. Until I cornered him after school and suggested we practice together."

"And that's when you discovered your magical compatibility?" Sam guessed.

"That's when we discovered everything," Katie said simply. "The first time we joined our power, it was like... like finding a piece of yourself you didn't know was missing. Everything just clicked."

Sean remembered that moment perfectly. They'd been in this very barn, trying a simple light spell. The moment their magic touched, it had erupted into a brilliant display of golden and turquoise light that painted impossible patterns on the walls. They'd stood there, two thirteen-year-olds holding hands, watching their combined power dance through the air like living aurora.

"From that moment on," Sean said, "we were partners. In everything."

Sam looked between them with a knowing smile. "No wonder your magic harmonizes so well. You've been practicing together since the beginning."

"Six years of magical partnership," Katie confirmed. "Six years of him setting things on fire and me putting them out."

"Hey! You've caused your share of magical accidents."

"True. Remember the incident with the frogs?"

"We swore never to speak of the frogs."

"What happened with the frogs?" Sam asked eagerly.

"No," Sean and Katie said in unison, then burst out laughing.

As their laughter died down, Katie's expression grew more serious. "Sam, I need you to understand something. What Sean and I have... it's more than just romantic. Our magic is intertwined at a fundamental level. When we cast together, it's not just addition—it's multiplication. That's why I trust your magic. I can feel it's clean nature, yes, but also... you understand partnership. Your power has that same quality of connection."

Sam nodded slowly. "In my old coven, we called it resonance. Some people's magic just... sings together."

"Exactly," Katie said. "And your magic doesn't clash with ours. It harmonizes. That's rare."

"And valuable," Sean added. "Especially given what we're facing."

The conversation had turned serious again, but the warmth of shared memories lingered. As they prepared to continue Sam's tests, Sean caught Katie's eye and mouthed 'thank you.' She winked in response.

Some stories were worth telling, even the embarrassing ones if they reminded you why you were fighting in the first place.

Sean looked at Katie. He saw the grudging respect in her eyes. "Power is one thing," Katie said, her voice still cautious. "Loyalty is another. There are two more tests."

She gestured to the cauldron. "Brew a portion of protection. Strong enough to withstand a direct counter-spell."

Without a word, Sam approached the table. She moved with the quiet confidence of a seasoned practitioner. She chose her herbs with a discerning eye, crushed crystals into a fine powder. She whispered incantations that were different from the ones Sean knew, her voice rising and falling in a rhythmic, unfamiliar cadence. The potion, when she was finished, glowed with a soft, steady blue light. She drank a small amount without hesitation.

Sean raised his hand and muttered a sharp, guttural word of unraveling. A bolt of dark, disruptive energy shot from his fingertips and slammed into Sam. It hit the invisible shield created by her potion and dissipated with a harmless sizzle, like water on a hot skillet.

She had passed.

"One last thing," Katie said, her voice now softer. She stepped forward and produced a small, ornate dagger with a silver blade and a handle of dark, polished wood—an athame from the sanctuary. She also held a small, empty stone chalice. "An oath. To bind you to us in trust."

The mood in the barn shifted, becoming solemn, ancient. This was no longer a game or a simple test. This was a rite.

Sam looked at the athame, then at Katie, then at Sean. She nodded once, a gesture of profound understanding. She took the blade and, without flinching, drew a thin, clean line across her palm. A line of crimson welled up. She held her hand over the chalice, letting three drops fall.

Katie did the same, her movements precise and ritualistic. Then she handed the athame to Sean. He met Sam's gaze as he made his own cut, the sting of the blade a small price for the promise of a true ally. He let his own blood fall, mingling with theirs. He felt the magic of the oath seal itself, a new thread weaving itself into the tapestry of their coven, strengthening it, changing it forever.

"I accept you as my coven master," Sam said to Sean, her voice steady and clear, her sea-green eyes unwavering.

"And we accept you as our sister," Sean replied, a genuine smile finally reaching his eyes. "Welcome to the coven."

He looked at Katie, who was now smiling too, her earlier suspicions replaced by a look of relief and burgeoning friendship. They were no longer just two. They were three. Their small circle of light in a world growing darker had just expanded. It was a start. And for the first time in days, the crushing weight on Sean's shoulders felt just a little bit lighter.

Chapter 14: The Spirit's Gambit

A fragile, tentative peace had settled over the Murphy farm. The days following the addition of Sam to their coven were marked by a focused and determined energy. The raw, gaping wound of Tom's death had begun to scar over, leaving a persistent, tender ache that Sean knew would be with him always, but it no longer threatened to swallow him whole. Now, it was fuel.

The new normal was a carefully constructed balancing act. Mornings were for chores and the clamor of high school, afternoons for homework and magic practice in the barn, and late nights for poring over ancient texts in the sanctuary. Uncle Todd had settled into a quiet, awkward rhythm of his own. He would spend his days working remotely from the small office he'd set up in the guest room, and his evenings attempting to cook large, often slightly burnt, dinners for the entire coven. He never asked about their practice, never ventured near the cave, but they would find tools sharpened, fences mended, and the pantry inexplicably full. He was a silent, practical guardian, holding the mundane world together so they could fight the battles in the shadows. It was in these small, unspoken acts that they were slowly and cautiously building a family.

One evening, the whole group was gathered in the living room, the scent of Todd's overcooked pot roast still lingering in the air. A comfortable camaraderie filled the space. Matthew was showing Kim a small, intricate puzzle box he'd carved, its wooden gears clicking softly. Katie was quizzing Sam on American history for an upcoming test, their laughter mingling with the low murmur of the television. It was a moment of such profound and simple normalcy that Sean felt his heart ache with the fierce desire to protect it.

"Oh, quiet down, everyone," Todd said from his armchair, turning up the volume on the TV. "This is supposed to be big news for the whole region."

On the screen, a local news anchor stood in front of a backdrop of lush, undeveloped marshland, her expression beaming. "We're live at what will soon be the site of the most ambitious private research initiative this state has ever seen," she announced.

The camera panned to a man standing at a podium. He was handsome in a way that seemed algorithmically generated for maximum appeal—wearing a sharp suit, boasting perfect teeth, and sporting a charismatic smile that radiated trustworthiness. A banner behind him read: "The Aethelgard Institute: Powering a Greener Future."

"For those of you just joining us," the anchor continued, "that is visionary tech billionaire Alistair Finch, who is about to make a landmark announcement."

Finch stepped up to the microphone, and the crowd of reporters and local politicians erupted in applause. He held up a hand, and the crowd fell silent, captivated.

"Thank you," Finch said, his voice a smooth, confident baritone that was impossible to dislike. "For too long, this beautiful region has been overlooked. For too long, we have relied on old, outdated forms of energy. But the earth itself provides answers." He gestured to the wilderness behind him. "Here, on this land, we will build the Aethelgard Institute. Not just a campus, but a state-of-the-art geothermal and atmospheric research facility, a place where the brightest minds will come together to unlock the planet's own power, creating clean, sustainable energy for generations to come."

"He seems impressive," Todd commented, leaning forward. "Bringing a lot of jobs to the area."

But Sean wasn't listening. He was staring at the screen, a cold, sickening dread beginning to pool in his stomach. It wasn't just the man's unnerving charisma; it was something else, a predatory wrongness he could feel even through the electronic filter of the television. His gaze flicked to the map displayed on the screen behind Finch, a graphic showing the proposed 5,000-acre site. A jagged finger of ice traced its way down his spine.

Katie gasped beside him. "No," she whispered, her face draining of color. "It can't be."

She scrambled up from the floor, ran to the hallway closet where they'd stashed their research materials, and returned with their own ancient ley line map. She spread it out on the floor, her hands shaking. The coven gathered around, their lighthearted mood shattered.

The location of the proposed Aethelgard Institute, a project being hailed as the region's savior, was a perfect, yet horrifying, match for the brightest and most powerful ley line nexus in the entire southeastern United States.

The Malevolent Spirit hadn't just found a new host. It had executed a strategic masterstroke. It had cloaked itself in progress, in philanthropy, in the handsome, unimpeachable guise of a beloved public figure with the power, money, and influence to build its apocalyptic ritual machine with the full blessing and funding of the state.

Sean looked from the ley line map on the floor to the smiling face of Alistair Finch on the television. He couldn't sense the magic, not through the screen, but he could feel the truth of it in his bones, in the sudden, icy coldness of the Wayfinder in his pocket. They were no longer fighting a simple monster. They were fighting an idea, a public works project, a celebrated hero. How could they possibly win?

***

The sanctuary, their refuge, now felt like a war room. The glowing map of the world was their enemy's battle plan, and they had just witnessed a major offensive.

"He's building it," Sam said, pacing back and forth in front of the stone shelves. "Right under everyone's noses. The 'geothermal research'... he's going to tap the ley lines directly. The 'atmospheric facility'... he'll use it to focus the energy of the eclipse. It's brilliant. It's horrifyingly brilliant."

"We can't expose him," Matthew said, running a hand through his hair. "Who would believe us? 'Excuse me, Mr. Governor, your state's biggest benefactor is actually an ancient soul-eating demon building a doomsday device.' They'd lock us up."

"So we can't fight him in the open," Sean said, his mind racing, piecing together a desperate plan. The initial shock was giving way to a cold, hard resolve. "So we fight him in the shadows. His world and ours. We have to know what he's doing. We need intelligence." He looked around at the faces of his coven, their expressions a mixture of terror and determination. "We have to go there. Tonight."

A heavy silence fell over the room.

"To the site?" Kim asked, her voice a small, trembling whisper.

"Yes," Sean confirmed. "We need to see what's really there. We need to scry the land itself, feel the energy on the ground, and find out what kind of magical preparations he's made. We can't fight what we can't see." He paused, letting the weight of his words sink in. "It's dangerous. He'll have wards up. If he detects us, he'll know we're onto him. This has to be a stealth mission. Small team. Just me, Katie, and Sam."

No one argued. The decision was made. The first real adventure of their new, terrifying war was about to begin.

The swamp at night was a different world. Oppressively humid, thick with the smell of decay and damp earth, and alive with a symphony of unseen things. Frogs bellowed their guttural calls, insects buzzed in a relentless cloud, and every splash in the dark water nearby sent a fresh jolt of adrenaline through Sean. They moved in silence, following the faint glow of surveyor's stakes that marked the edge of Finch's property.

Sean took the lead, his senses pushed out to their absolute limit, tasting the air for any hint of magical traps. Katie was behind him, her eyes scanning the darkness, her own magic a low, protective hum around them. Sam brought up the rear, her steps preternaturally silent, her gaze constantly moving.

"Headlights," Sam whispered suddenly.

Instantly, they dove for cover behind a massive, moss-covered cypress tree, their hearts pounding. A heavy-duty security truck rumbled past on a nearby access road, its searchlight cutting a stark white swath through the primordial darkness. They held their breath until the sound of its engine faded into the chorus of the swamp.

"He's not just relying on magic," Katie breathed once they were sure it was gone. "He has mundane security, too."

"Makes sense," Sean whispered back. "It makes him look thorough, professional."

They continued on, deeper into the property until Sean felt it. A change in the air. A palpable pressure, a vibration in the soles of his feet. The air grew thin, charged with a clean, electric power that had nothing to do with the swamp's humidity.

"We're here," he said. "This is the center. The nexus."

They had reached a small, natural clearing, a raised hummock of dry land in the middle of the marsh. The energy was so thick here it was almost visible, making the air shimmer.

"Quickly," Katie said, already pulling purified salt from a pouch at her belt. "Let's get the circle up."

She and Sam worked in a seamless, practiced unison, creating a shimmering circle of protection around them. Sean stepped to the center of it, the ground beneath his feet buzzing like a live wire. He closed his eyes and reached down with his senses, not with a spell, but with his innate connection to the earth, trying to read the secrets held in the soil.

The vision, when it came, was dizzying. He saw the land not as it was but as it would be. A horrifying palimpsest of steel and stone overlaid with shimmering, sinister lines of power. He saw the gleaming, benign architecture of the Aethelgard Institute, and beneath it, its true purpose. He saw massive subterranean conduits, not for geothermal steam, but designed to channel raw magical energy from the ley lines. He saw a central, circular chamber deep underground that was undeniably a ritual altar. And woven through it all, he saw the wards. Finch's wards. They were powerful, layered with a cold, cruel, alien intelligence that felt thousands of years old.

It was a machine. A soul-engine. And it was aimed at the heart of the world.

As he pushed his senses deeper, trying to understand the final function of the central chamber, he felt a sudden, violent shove against his mind.

WHO ARE YOU?

The mental voice was not a voice at all. It was a spear of ice and malice, the raw, undiluted essence of the Malevolent Spirit. It had felt him. An alarm, not a sound but a wave of hostile, searching magic, pulsed out from the nexus.

"He knows we're here!" Sean gasped, stumbling back, the vision shattering.

"The wards are lighting up!" Sam yelled, pointing to the edge of their protective circle, where sparks of dark energy were beginning to sizzle against their shield.

"We have to go. Now!" Katie commanded.

They broke the circle and ran, crashing through the underbrush, the feeling of a vast, unseen eye now fixed upon them. They didn't stop running until they had burst out of the swamp and were back on the familiar dirt road leading to the farm, their lungs burning, their clothes soaked with sweat and swamp water.

They collapsed by the side of the road, breathless and shaken. The reconnaissance had been a terrifying success. They knew the horrifying truth of Finch's plan. But now, the Spirit knew them. It knew they were not just a minor nuisance, but an active threat investigating its most sacred project.

Sean looked at his friends, their faces streaked with mud and fear in the moonlight. The game had just changed catastrophically. Their enemy was brilliant; he was publicly adored, and now, he was hunting them.

Chapter 15: The Scrying

A palpable sense of dread had taken root in the sanctuary. It was a cold, creeping thing that leeched the warmth from the magical air and made the ancient silence feel less like peace and more like the stillness of a tomb. For two days since their harrowing reconnaissance mission, the coven had been trapped in a state of agitated paralysis. They knew the enemy's location and the horrifying scope of its plan, but this knowledge was a curse, not a weapon. It had only illuminated the sheer, terrifying scale of their own insignificance.

They were gathered in the hidden library, the ley line map spread across the central table like a patient on an operating table, its glowing lines a diagram of the world's sickness. Alistair Finch's handsome, charismatic face stared up at them from the screen of Katie's tablet, the article praising his "visionary project" a bitter, mocking joke.

"We're missing a piece," Sam said, breaking the heavy silence. She was tracing the nexus point on the map with her finger. "We know the *where,* and we know the *what*. But we don't know *when*. A ritual of this magnitude would require a specific celestial alignment. An equinox, a solstice, a planetary conjunction... something. Without the timing, we're still just waiting in the dark."

"Then we have to find it," Sean said, his voice flat with exhaustion. He pushed away from the table, the weight of their collective fear a physical pressure on his shoulders. He walked over to a small, velvet-lined box on one of the shelves. He opened it and stared down at the small, carved wooden bird nestled within. The Wayfinder.

When he turned back to the group, holding the artifact, the shift in the room was instantaneous. The air grew thick with a new kind of tension, sharp and electric.

Katie shot to her feet, her chair scraping harshly against the stone floor. "No," she said, her voice low and trembling with a fierce, protective anger. "Absolutely not, Sean. Put it back."

"It's the only way, Katie," he said, his gaze not leaving the terrible, beautiful object in his hand. "It can show us. I know it can."

"And I know what it will cost you!" she cried, her control finally snapping. She rushed to him, her hands grabbing the front of his shirt. Her blue eyes were wide with a desperate, terrified plea. "Your uncle told you. It burns your life away to fuel its magic. Did you not hear him? Years, Sean! It could take years from you! We'll find another way. We can research more, we can try another scrying spell, we can—"

"We're out of time!" he cut her off, his own voice rising to match hers. He gently but firmly pried her hands from his shirt, holding them in his own. Her fingers were ice-cold. "Don't you understand? Finch knows we were there. He felt me. He knows he has an active, magical opposition now. He's not going to wait. He's going to accelerate his plans. Every day we waste searching for another way is a day he gets closer to ripping a hole in the world. This is our only chance to get ahead of him."

"I don't care!" she sobbed, tears finally spilling over and tracing paths down her cheeks. The sight of her tears was like a physical blow, harder than any magical attack he had ever faced. "What good is saving the world if I lose you to do it? What good is a future if you've burned yours away to get there? Don't do this to me, Sean. Please."

The raw, desperate love in her voice was an agony. He looked past her to the faces of his coven. He saw their fear, their indecision. They were looking to him, their leader, but for the first time, he wasn't leading them into a fight. He was asking them to watch him sacrifice a piece of himself.

He pulled her closer, his forehead resting against hers, his voice dropping to a raw whisper. "What good is my future if you're not safe in it? If none of them are?" He glanced at Sam, Kim, and Matthew. "My grandfather gave me a choice, Katie. He trusted me to make it. And my choice is you. It's always been you. This... this is how I protect you. This is the only way I know how."

He could feel her surrender, not an agreement, but a heartbreaking acceptance of his will. Her sobs quieted into shudders that wracked her body. She pulled back, wiping her eyes with the back of her hand, her expression one of profound, loving despair. "Then we do it together," she said, her voice thick but steady. "I won't let you go into that darkness alone. I'll be your anchor. I'll pull you back."

A grim understanding settled over the coven. The debate was over. The decision was made.

They prepared the library for the ritual. It was a somber, focused affair. Sam, using her knowledge of older, more complex traditions, helped Katie draw a containment circle around a clear space on the floor, not to keep things out but to focus the energy inward and, she hoped, mitigate the cost to Sean. Kim crushed herbs into a silver bowl—mugwort to enhance the vision, rosemary for protection, and valerian to calm the heart—setting them to smolder, their fragrant smoke filling the chamber. Matthew, silent and grim-faced, carved temporary runes of strength and endurance into the flagstones where Sean would kneel. It was a coven working as one, each member contributing their unique strength to protect their leader.

Sean watched them, his heart a painful knot of love and gratitude. He walked to the edge of the sanctuary and saw his uncle standing in the shadows of the outer cave, his face a mask of pained resignation. Their eyes met, and in that silent glance, a universe of regret and understanding passed between them. Todd gave him a single, almost imperceptible nod before melting back into the darkness.

It was time.

Sean took off his shoes and knelt in the center of the circle. Katie knelt just outside it, directly in front of him, her hands resting on the chalk line. She would be his lifeline. He took a deep, steadying breath and placed the Wayfinder on the floor before him. In the flickering candlelight, it seemed to throb with a faint, eager light, a sleeping predator sensing a meal.

"Ready?" Katie whispered, her eyes locked on his.

He nodded. He placed his hands over the wooden bird, not quite touching it, and closed his eyes. He didn't focus on the question he needed to ask. Instead, he focused on Katie. On the memory of her laughter, the exact shade of her eyes in the sunlight, the feeling of her hand in his. He wrapped the feeling of his love for her around his mind like a shield. Then, he poured his will, his energy, his very essence into the artifact.

The connection was instant and violent. The Wayfinder didn't just take his power; it drank it greedily, a siphon plunged directly into his soul. The world behind his eyelids exploded.

The vision was not a picture. It was a chaotic, multi-sensory assault.

He heard it first. A cacophony of whispers in a thousand dead and forgotten languages, the dry, sibilant hissing of the Spirits. Underneath it, a low, triumphant hum—the sound of the ley lines being twisted, corrupted, forced to sing a song of wrongness. And through it all, the high, thin shriek of reality tearing like old cloth.

Then came the images, not in sequence, but all at once, a nightmarish flood. He saw Alistair Finch standing at the heart of the nexus, his arms outstretched. But he wasn't just a man anymore. A shimmering, indescribable shape of pure, featureless shadow was superimposed over him, the Malevolent Spirit wearing the billionaire's body like a cheap suit. He saw the faces of the other twelve Spirits, not as people, but as living symbols of horror—one was a vortex of blood and teeth, another a skeletal figure of rot and decay that withered everything it looked upon, a third a gibbering embodiment of pure madness that seemed to claw at the edges of Sean's own sanity.

He saw the sky, and the sun was a black, lightless hole, its corona a ring of ethereal, sickly green fire. The solar eclipse.

He saw the ground at the nexus split open, and it did not reveal rock and earth, but a glimpse into a sanity-shattering abyss—a sky filled with wrong-colored stars and constellations that drew themselves into symbols of pain. He saw dark, writhing things begin to crawl and pull themselves through the tear, eager to enter a world that was no longer protected.

He felt the Spirit's mind. It was a vast, cold, and ancient thing, its arrogance as boundless as a galaxy. It held nothing but a clinical, contemptuous hatred for the messy, chaotic vibrancy of life. He felt the agony of the earth itself, its veins of magic being poisoned and turned to a dark, unholy purpose. He felt himself being pulled apart, his consciousness dissolving into the horrifying vision, his own identity threatening to be extinguished by the sheer scale of the evil he was witnessing.

Sean!

Katie's voice. Not in his ears but in his soul. A single, pure, desperate note of love in the damned chorus. He clung to it, to the memory of her face, to the feeling of her hand in his. It was his anchor. His lifeline. He pulled, fighting his way back from the abyss, back from the edge of dissolution.

With a final, ragged gasp, he tore his mind away from the vision and collapsed forward, the connection broken. The sanctuary slammed back into his senses—the smell of the herbs, the flickering candlelight, the feel of the cold stone floor against his cheek. The Wayfinder lay an inch from his nose, inert and cold, its hunger sated.

"Sean!" Katie was scrambling into the circle, ignoring the broken ritual. Sam was right behind her. They gently rolled him over. He was shivering violently, his skin pale and clammy.

"I'm okay," he managed to choke out, his voice a weak, unfamiliar croak.

Katie was cradling his head, her tears dripping onto his face. "Sean, your hair..." she whispered in horror.

He lifted a trembling hand to his head. At his right temple, where there had been only dark hair, there was now a stark, thick streak of pure, silvery white. The toll. The price had been paid, and it was visible to all.

They helped him sit up, and Kim rushed forward with the restorative potion she had prepared. He drank it, the warm, earthy liquid chasing away some of the deathly chills but doing nothing to erase the terrible images seared into his mind.

He looked at the frightened faces of his friends, his family, his coven. He saw the horror in Katie's eyes as she stared at the silver in his hair. But he also saw their resolve.

He took another shaky breath, his own voice sounding distant to his ears. "The eclipse," he said, the words heavy and final. "It's the solar eclipse. Next month. On the 23rd." He met Katie's tear-filled gaze. "That's the day. That's when it's going to open the gates."

A terrible certainty settled over the small group in the heart of the ancient sanctuary. They had their answer. They had a date for the end of the world. The clock was now ticking, its sound a deafening roar in the sudden, terrified silence.

Chapter 16: A Coven Divided

The immediate aftermath of the vision was a thick, ringing silence, broken only by Sean's ragged breaths and Katie's frantic, whispered reassurances. He was back, but the abyss he had looked into had left its mark, not only in the shocking silver streak that now cut through his dark hair but in the deep, haunted knowledge that now lived behind his eyes. The coven gathered around him, their faces a mural of shock and awe. They had their answer. And it was worse than any of them could have possibly imagined.

The solar eclipse. Less than a month away.

The knowledge did not bring clarity; it brought a paralyzing terror. The threat was no longer a vague, shadowy concept. It now had a deadline. A countdown timer had begun on the end of their world, and the sound of it was a deafening roar in the quiet of the sanctuary.

It was Matthew who broke first. His youthful face, usually open and quick to laugh, was pale and taut with a fear that had curdled into anger. He slammed his fist down on the ancient wooden table, making the scrolls and crystals jump.

"So that's it!" he exclaimed, his voice tight and high. "We know when and we know where. We can't just sit here reading anymore! We have to hit him. Now!

We go to the nexus, all of us, and we throw everything we have at him. A full-on magical assault. We take him out before he can even begin the ritual."

His words, born of a desperate need for action, hung in the charged air. For a moment, several of the younger coven members nodded in agreement, their own fear seeking the simple, direct outlet of a fight.

"And we'd be incinerated before we got within a hundred yards of the site."

Sam's voice was quiet, cold, and sharp as a shard of ice, cutting through Matthew's bravado. She had been a part of a coven before, one that had been broken by loss, and her eyes held the weary caution of someone who knew the true cost of underestimating an enemy.

"We all saw what Sean went through just to *look* at that place from a distance," she continued, her gaze unwavering. "His wards are ancient and powerful. A direct assault isn't a battle, Matthew. It's a suicide mission. We'd be walking into a meat grinder."

"So what's your plan, Sam?" he shot back, whirling to face her. "We just wait? We let him finish building his doomsday machine and hope he invites us in for tea before he pushes the button?"

"Of course not," she retorted, her voice dangerously calm. "But we don't fight him on his terms. We don't fight his magic with our magic. Not yet. We're outmatched there, and you know it."

The battle lines were drawn. The coven, their unity so new and fragile, began to fracture under the immense pressure. Kim, whose magic was rooted in the slow, defensive strength of the earth, sided with Sam, her expression troubled. "She's right, Matthew. We need to be smarter than this. Charging in is what he'll expect."

But the others were swayed by Matthew's desperate urgency. The need to *do something*, to fight back against the overwhelming helplessness they all felt, was a powerful intoxicant. The argument grew louder, their voices echoing off the ancient stone walls, their fear manifesting as angry, jagged words.

It was Katie who finally silenced them. She stepped into the center of the fray, her presence so commanding that the argument died in their throats. Her face was pale, her eyes red-rimmed from the tears she'd shed for Sean, but her expression was one of fierce, unshakable intelligence.

"Both of you, stop," she said, her voice cutting through the tension like a blade. "Yelling at each other is a luxury we don't have. And Matthew, your plan is reckless. Sam is right, we'd be slaughtered." She held up a hand before he could protest. "But she's also right that we can't just wait. So we don't attack the Spirit. We attack the man."

She strode over to the table and tapped the glossy image of Alistair Finch on her tablet. "This is his weakness. The Spirit is ancient and powerful, but its vessel is human. Alistair Finch has weaknesses. He has a board of directors, investors, and a public image to maintain. I guarantee you that a man this rich and powerful didn't get there without breaking a thousand human laws. That's where we attack."

Her eyes burned with a cold, "tragic fire. "We can't beat him with a fireball right now. But we can use our magic to make his life a living hell. We can magically corrupt data files and send them to investigative reporters. We can create discord among his board members, whispering seeds of doubt and paranoia into their minds. We can plague his construction site with delays—floods, equipment malfunctions, and union disputes sparked by magically fueled bad tempers. We tie him up in so much mundane, human chaos that the Aethelgard Institute becomes a logistical and financial nightmare. We buy ourselves time. Time to get stronger. Time to find a real weapon in these books, a real way to counter the ritual itself."

It was a brilliant plan, a masterful blend of magical thinking and real-world strategy. But to Matthew, it sounded like a coward's gambit.

"Time?" he scoffed, his voice dripping with disbelief. "We have less than a month! While we're playing games with his stock portfolio, he'll be finishing his real work in secret. This is just poking at the edges! We need to strike at the heart of the problem, not give him a series of inconvenient papercuts!" His gaze swung to Sean, who had been listening in silence, his face drawn and exhausted. "Sean, tell her. We have to fight!"

All eyes turned to Sean. He felt the immense weight of their expectations, the pull of two opposing, equally valid arguments. He looked at Katie, at her fierce, intelligent plan designed to protect them, to protect *him*. He saw the desperate love behind her strategy. Then he looked at Matthew and saw his own desperate need to act, to fight, not to let his grandfather's sacrifice be in vain. The silver streak at his temple seemed to throb with a dull, phantom ache, a constant reminder of the price of their only piece of intelligence.

His head was pounding. He closed his eyes, leaning back against a stone shelf, the coven's fractured, fearful energy a chaotic storm around him. Katie thought he was too weak, that he couldn't handle a direct confrontation. Matthew thought a strategic delay was the same as surrender. They were both right. And they were both wrong.

He opened his eyes, and the exhaustion and pain had been replaced by a quiet, unwavering authority. He pushed himself off the shelf and walked slowly to the head of the table, placing his hands flat on the glowing map. The room fell silent.

"You're right, Katie," he began, his voice quiet but ringing with a finality that commanded their full attention. "A direct assault on the nexus now would be a massacre. Finch is expecting it. He wants us to throw ourselves against his wards and burn out. Your plan is smart. It's our best chance of slowing him down in the real world, and we are absolutely going to do it."

A wave of relief washed over Katie's face. Matthew opened his mouth to protest, but Sean cut him off, his gaze shifting to him.

"And you're right too, Matthew," he said, his voice hardening slightly. "We can't just hope that a few stock market fluctuations and construction delays will be enough to stop the apocalypse. That's a fantasy. While we're creating chaos in his human life, he will still be working. We have to be preparing for the inevitable battle at the nexus. We have to be ready to fight him on his terms when the day comes."

He looked around the room" meeting each of their eyes, forging them back into a single weapon with the force of his will.

"So this is what we're going to do. We're splitting into two teams. Katie, you and Sam will lead the first. Your mission is subterfuge. I want you to be a plague on Alistair Finch's life. Use your magic to find his secrets, his crimes, his pressure points, and squeeze until he bleeds. I want him so buried in lawsuits, federal investigations, and shareholder revolts that he can barely remember his own name. Create a smokescreen so thick he won't see our real attack coming."

He then turned to the other side of the room. "Matthew, Kim, the rest of us... we have the other mission. While Katie's team buys us time, we will focus on one thing and one thing only: dismantling his magical defenses. We're not attacking the nexus. We're going to be invisible. We will find the weakest points in his words. We will study these texts until our eyes bleed, and we will craft specific, targeted counter-spells for every ward he has. We will unravel his fortress, one thread at a time. So that when the day of the eclipse finally comes, we won't be charging at a wall of impenetrable power. We'll be walking through an open door, ready to face the monster inside."

The plan settled over the room, audacious and terrifyingly complex, yet it was a cohesive whole. It gave purpose to both caution and aggression. It honored every member's strengths. The division in the coven healed, the tension bleeding out of the air, replaced by the cold, sharp focus of a shared, impossible goal.

They huddled around the map again, but this time, they were not arguing. They were a single unit. Katie was already pointing out the location of Finch's corporate headquarters. Sam was suggesting ways to influence key board members psychically. Matthew, his earlier bravado replaced by a grim focus, was sketching out the ward patterns Sean had described from his vision, looking for a place to begin their assault.

They had a plan. A desperate, terrifying, two-front war against an enemy of immense power and cunning. Sean looked at the faces of his friends, his family, all of them looking to him, and the burden felt heavier than ever. But for the first time since he'd woken the Wayfinder, it felt bearable. Because he wasn't carrying it alone. He looked at the stark white streak in his hair reflected in the dark screen of Katie's tablet. It was a reminder of the cost. A down payment on a victory they had to earn, one piece at a time.

You are a great novelist. Write a 3,500-word chapter 13 using the same style, making the character likable with enhanced fear, detail, tension, and mystery.

Chapter 17: The Shape of Failure

The air in the barn was thick with the smell of ozone and burned herbs, a testament to three nights of failed attempts. They were working from a fragment of a Gatekeeper scroll Sam had unearthed, its edges scorched, its text maddeningly incomplete. It described a complex defensive lattice, a ward of such power that the scroll claimed it could hold a tear in reality shut. To the desperate coven, it felt less like a lesson and more like their only hope.

"The resonance matrix is unstable," Sam stated, her voice flat with exhaustion. She pointed a slender finger at a diagram she'd chalked onto the dusty barn floor. "Every time we try to channel the final stabilizing flow, the structure fractures. The old Gatekeepers used a different kind of power—colder, more singular. Our magic is too... alive. It's like trying to build a clock with water."

"So we try again," Matthew said, his jaw tight. The easy jokes had long since evaporated, replaced by a grim, dogged determination. He felt the weight of their slow progress as a personal failure.

Tonight, they were adding a new, volatile element: Todd. He stood awkwardly at the northern point of the great chalk circle, a cold iron ingot in each hand. He couldn't channel magic, but Sam theorized that a mundane, non-magical human could act as a grounding rod, a psychic anchor to the real world that might prevent the lattice from spiraling into pure abstraction. To Todd, it felt like being asked to stop a lightning strike by holding up a fork. He had never felt more useless or more terrified.

Sean stood at the center, the designated conductor. "Everyone ready?" he asked, his gaze sweeping over his coven. He saw their fatigue, the dark circles under their eyes. He saw the tremor in Todd's hands. "Positions."

They began the chant. The air grew heavy, pressing in on them. Kim, kneeling, placed her palms flat on the floor, coaxing a soft, green energy from the earth. Sam wove intricate patterns with her hands, her voice a low, melodic hum that shaped the ambient magic. Matthew fed a steady, controlled stream of his own kinetic energy into the mix, a low, thrumming sound that made the teeth ache. At the center, Sean gathered the disparate threads, his own power the needle that would stitch them together.

The lattice began to form in the air above them. It was breathtakingly beautiful, a shimmering, three-dimensional web of interlocking sigils that glowed with pure, white light. It was a cathedral made of energy, intricate and impossibly fragile.

"It's holding," Katie breathed from her position opposite Todd. She was the weaver; her role to guide the final shape of the ward, to ensure its symmetry. "Stabilizing flow on my mark... Mark!"

This was the critical moment. Matthew was meant to feed one last, perfectly measured pulse of energy to lock the final rune into place. But as the lattice flared with near-blinding intensity, he saw a flicker in the structure, a momentary weakness near Kim's quadrant. Fearing a collapse, he pushed, just a fraction too hard. His intention was pure—to reinforce, to protect. But in the delicate architecture of the spell, his small surge of kinetic power acted not as a support but as a hammer blow.

A single thread in the lattice snapped. The sound was not loud, but it was horrifying—a high, crystalline *ping* that echoed in the sudden silence.

A spiderweb of glowing fault lines erupted from the break, spreading through the structure in a chain reaction. The beautiful cathedral of light began to implode.

"Hold the anchor!" Sean roared, but it was too late.

The lattice didn't just dissipate; it ruptured. As the central weaver, Katie took the full, explosive force of the collapse.

She didn't scream. The sound was ripped from her lungs as the feedback loop took hold. For the others, it was a blinding flash of white light and a concussive wave of energy that threw them back. For Katie, it was the universe turning inside out.

Her mind was ripped from her body and flung into a chaotic, shrieking void between realities. She saw the barn from a thousand different angles at once. She saw a version where the spell had worked, and they were cheering. She saw another where the barn was reduced to ash. She saw Matthew lying broken on the floor. She saw Sean with his hair turned entirely to silver. The conflicting sensory information was a physical agony, a feeling of being torn into a million pieces. Her body, lying on the barn floor, began to twitch violently, her eyes wide, pupils dilated, staring into the infinite horrors her mind was now forced to witness.

"Katie!" Sean scrambled to her side, his heart seizing with a terror that dwarfed anything he had felt at the nexus. Her skin was cold, her pulse a frantic, erratic flutter beneath his fingers. "She's locked in! The resonance feedback has her."

"We have to pull her out!" Todd yelled, his face bleached of all color.

"Her mind is trying to process too many energy fields at once," Sam cried, her analytical calm shattered. "If we try a counter-spell, we could just add another layer and shatter her consciousness completely!"

They stood frozen, helpless, watching their friend, their partner, their anchor, being consumed by a storm they had unleashed. Matthew was on his knees, his face a mask of utter self-loathing. "I did this," he whispered. "I pushed too hard."

Sean looked at Katie's vacant, terrified eyes, and his uncle's words from the porch echoed in his memory. *It's not about what you can break. It's about what you refuse to let be broken.*

Magic had failed them. Their power was the problem. They needed an anchor. A real one.

"Todd!" Sean yelled, his voice a sharp command that cut through the panic. "Get to her! Talk to her! Don't use magic, just... pull her back!"

For a second, Todd stared, uncomprehending. Then, seeing the desperate certainty in Sean's eyes, he acted. He scrambled past the smoldering chalk lines of the broken circle and dropped to his knees beside Katie. He ignored the faint, dangerous sizzle of residual energy still arcing from her skin. He grabbed her physical hand, his large, calloused grip a startling intrusion of the mundane into the magical chaos.

"Katie!" he yelled, his voice rough with fear. "Katie, listen to me! It's Todd! You're in the barn. You feel that? That's my hand. It's real. The floor is real. It's dusty and it smells like hay. Can you smell the hay, kid?"

He didn't know if it was working, but he kept talking, his voice a desperate, grounding litany. He described the splinter in the floorboards beside her, the smell of the coming rain, the sound of his own frantic breathing. He gave her senses something solid to cling to, a single reality in the storm of possibilities.

Slowly, agonizingly, it began to work. The violent twitching of Katie's limbs subsided to a fine tremor. A flicker of recognition returned to her eyes. She gasped, a deep, shuddering intake of breath, and her gaze focused on Todd's face. She was back.

The aftermath was a landscape of quiet, shaken horror. They helped Katie to a hay bale, wrapping her in old horse blankets. She was no longer convulsing, but she was deeply traumatized. When she looked at Sean, he could see faint, ghostly after-images flickering at the edge of her form. Her magical senses were scrambled, the world a discordant symphony of sights and sounds she couldn't quite parse.

Matthew sat apart from the group, his head in his hands, refusing to meet anyone's eyes, the weight of his guilt a tangible shroud around him. The rest of the coven was silent, the near-loss of Katie a wound in their collective soul. They had sought a weapon and had nearly executed one of their own.

Long after the others had retreated to the house, Sean remained in the silent, chilly barn. He couldn't shake the feeling that they were missing something vital. He walked back to the great chalk circle, his lantern casting long, dancing shadows. The energy of the failed spell had left scorch marks on the wooden floor, a permanent record of their failure.

He knelt, tracing the jagged, blackened lines with his finger. They weren't random. There was a pattern, a horrifying, deliberate geometry to the chaos. The cracks radiated from a central point and branched out, not in a starburst, but in a precise, six-pointed spiral.

His blood ran cold.

He scrambled to his feet, his mind racing, pulling together the disparate threads. The glyphs in the orchard. The diagram in the Book of Umbrae. And now this.

A horrifying realization dawned, so simple and so monstrous it stole the breath from his lungs. The incomplete scroll they had found hadn't described a defensive ward. It had described a trigger. The spell wasn't meant to hold. It was designed to fail. It was designed to collapse into this exact, specific, recurring symbol.

The Fracture Drill wasn't a drill at all. It was a key. And in their desperate attempt to build a shield, they had just turned it in a lock they didn't know existed.

Chapter 18: The Drowned Library

The story, like most local ghost stories, started as a whisper. A dare between teenagers, a broken fence, and a trip into the skeletal remains of the old Goose Creek High School abandoned for two years since the ground beneath its west wing had decided to swallow itself. But this time, the story came back wrong. Three teens went in; only one came out. He was found by a sheriff's deputy at dawn, curled on the fifty-yard line of the football field, shivering and soaked to the bone on a dry night, muttering the same chilling, nonsensical phrase: "The substitute knows your name. The substitute knows your name."

"He's catatonic," Sam said, scrolling through a grainy photo of the boy on her tablet. The coven was gathered in the farmhouse kitchen, the comforting aroma of Todd's coffee doing little to dispel the chill of the story. "The other two are still missing. The official theory is a bad drug trip, but the boy's system was clean."

"What does it mean, 'the substitute knows your name'?" Matthew asked, leaning forward, his fascination warring with his unease.

"It means something there is intelligent," Sean answered grimly. "And it means we have to go."

A heavy silence fell over the kitchen. This wasn't a Malevolent Spirit or a world-ending ritual. This was smaller, more intimate, and somehow more terrifying.

"A scouting mission," Katie said, her strategic mind clicking into place. "Small team. Non-combat at first. We need to assess the threat." She looked at Sean, her eyes silently pleading with him to stay. The silver in his hair was a constant, stark reminder of the cost of their last battle, and the thought of him walking into another unknown was unbearable.

He understood. "Not me, and not you," he agreed, the decision costing him. "Sam, you know more about hauntings and residual energies than any of us. Kim, we need your senses. You can feel a place, read its history in the soil."

"I'll go," Todd said suddenly. Every head turned to him. He stood awkwardly by the counter, holding a dishrag. "You need a baseline, right? A canary in a coal mine? I'm the most normal person here. If I feel something, you'll know it's not just magical static."

Sean hesitated, but Sam nodded slowly. "He's right. A mundane witness can sometimes ground a psychic event or, at the very least, provide us with a clearer perspective. It's a risk but a calculated one."

And so the team was chosen: the scholar, the sensor, and the anchor.

They arrived at dusk. The abandoned high school sat slumped against the bruised, purple sky like a forgotten carcass. A high chain-link fence, topped with rust-pocked barbed wire, did little to hide the graffiti that scarred its brick walls or the darkness that pooled in its shattered windows. The silence was the first indication of something amiss. The familiar chorus of cicadas and tree frogs that filled a Carolina evening was completely absent here. Nature itself seemed to be giving the place a wide berth.

"The wards are inside out," Kim whispered, her hand hovering over a fence post. She crouched, her fingers tracing a faint, almost invisible symbol etched into the concrete base. "I've never felt anything like it. It's a repellent sigil, designed to ward off something. But the polarity... it's reversed. They weren't trying to keep something out. They cast this to trap something *in*."

That chilling revelation hung in the air as they found a gap in the fence and slipped through. The moment they stepped onto the school grounds, the air changed. It grew heavy, damp, and cold, carrying a faint, briny smell like low tide on a winter beach.

"Feel that?" Todd asked, his voice tight as he rubbed his arms. "It's like the temperature just dropped twenty degrees."

"Psychic cold spot," Sam murmured, her eyes scanning the building. "It's a classic sign of a residual emotional imprint. Something terrible happened here."

They entered through a set of double doors that had been pried open, the warped metal groaning in protest. The air inside was thick with the smell of mildew, wet paper, and a deeper, more profound scent of decay and forgotten sorrow. Their footsteps echoed unnaturally in the long, silent corridor, the sound swallowed by the oppressive quiet.

They were drawn, as if by an invisible current, toward the library. The large oak doors were closed. As they approached, a low, scraping sound came from within, the unmistakable noise of a single wooden chair being dragged across a linoleum floor. They froze, their hearts hammering in their chests.

Sam held up a hand, signaling for silence. She slowly, carefully pushed the door open.

The library was a disaster zone. Books were strewn across the floor, their pages swollen and warped as if they'd been soaked in water. A thick layer of dust and grime covered everything, but the air was freezing, and the salty, marine smell was overpowering. At the far end of the room, behind the main reference desk, a single chalkboard was clean, a stark black rectangle in the gray sea of decay.

As they stepped inside, the doors swung shut behind them with a deep, final boom, plunging them into near-darkness.

"It knows we're here," Kim breathed, her voice trembling.

A new sound began a soft, rhythmic dripping. Drip. Drip. Drip. But there were no leaks in the ceiling. The sound seemed to be coming from everywhere at once. Then, on the clean chalkboard, a single, wet word began to appear as if written by an invisible, dripping finger.

Listen.

The dripping coalesced into whispers, faint and sibilant, the voices of children. They weren't speaking words, but conveying feelings—panic, cold, the desperate, burning need for air.

"This isn't a ghost," Sam whispered her academic calm fraying at the edges. "This is a psychic recording. An echo trapped in a loop."

Then, they felt it. A crushing pressure, as if the weight of an entire ocean were pressing down on them. The air grew thick, making it hard to breathe. The floor beneath their feet seemed to shimmer and turn dark, like looking down into deep, murky water.

"It's a projection," Sam gasped, struggling against the psychic pressure. "A memory bleed. It's trying to pull us into the loop!"

Todd cried out, stumbling back. "My clothes... they're wet!" He looked down. His jeans were soaked from the knees down, though the floor was bone dry.

The illusion intensified. The library dissolved around them, replaced by a horrifying vision. They were standing in the school's hallway, but it was submerged in murky, green-black water. Rusted lockers lined the walls, their doors hanging open like gaping mouths. And floating in the water, their forms pale and indistinct, were the children, their eyes wide and dark, their mouths open in silent screams.

"Break the illusion!" Kim cried out. This was not the living earth, but she was a child of it, and she would not let this place of death claim them. She closed her eyes, ignored the terrifying vision, and focused on a single, powerful memory of her own: the feeling of the sun on her face in her garden, the solid, unyielding strength of the world beneath her feet. She channeled that feeling, not as an attack, but as an anchor, a statement of pure, living reality against the tide of remembered death. "*Terra firma!*" she shouted, slamming her foot down.

The vision shattered. The water vanished. They were back in the dusty, freezing library.

And they were no longer alone.

A man was standing behind the reference desk. He was in his mid-forties, with salt-and-pepper hair and wearing a neat, if slightly dated, suit. He was translucent, a figure made of memory and regret. His face was kind, but his eyes held a sorrow so profound it was a physical ache in the room. This was the substitute.

"You don't belong," he said, his voice not a sound but a thought that appeared directly in their minds. It was a voice weary of repeating the same lesson for eternity. "The door is closed. The Gate failed. The children drowned."

"What Gate?" Sam asked, her voice trembling. "Who are you?"

The substitute's expression didn't change. He raised a hand, and the whispers returned, but clearer this time, forming a single, heartbreaking phrase, repeated over and over. *He tried to save us. He told us to hold the line. The water came too fast. He tried to save us...*

"My God," Todd breathed, the pieces clicking into place. "He wasn't a substitute teacher. He was a guardian. A witch. Like you. And this... this was his failure."

The entity—the psychic echo of the guardian—nodded slowly. *The lesson is learned. Failure is the only outcome. You should not have come.*

It fixed its sorrowful gaze on them, and they felt a new wave of psychic energy, not an attack, but a dismissal. It was trying to erase them from its memory, to eject them from its eternal, looping tragedy.

"Run," Sam commanded. They turned and fled, throwing themselves against the heavy oak doors, which now swung open easily. They didn't stop running until they had burst out of the school's oppressive atmosphere and were back on the other side of the fence, gasping in the clean, living air of the evening, the sound of crickets a welcome, deafening roar.

They stood there for a long moment, shaken to their core.

"It wasn't a haunting," Kim said finally, her voice still shaky. "It was a warning. Left behind by a coven that tried and failed."

"But it reacted to us," Sam added, her eyes wide with a new, dawning fear. "Our presence... it changed the loop. It became aware." She looked back at the dark, silent school. "What if we didn't just witness its memory? What if we woke it up?"

Back in the cold, silent library, the echo of the guardian stood alone. For the first time in decades, the loop of his failure had been broken. A new thought, a new directive, entered his fragmented consciousness. They had come. Others. Guardians. The Gate he had failed to protect was not the only one.

He turned to the clean chalkboard. The dripping finger of a ghost began to write again. But it was not the single, looping word from before. It was a new set of symbols, a fresh set of instructions. Coordinates. A location deep in the swamplands, near an old farmhouse.

The substitute lesson was over. A new one was about to begin.

Chapter 19: The Oldest Pact

<hr>

The storm arrived just after midnight, but it was not a storm of wind and rain. It was a storm of silence so profound it seemed to have weight, pressing down on the Murphy farm like an invisible hand. The air itself grew thick and oppressive, causing Todd's ears to pop and his lungs to work harder with each breath. Outside, the world had gone unnaturally still—no cricket songs, no distant lowing of cattle, no whisper of wind through the corn. Even the old barn cat, who usually prowled the grounds with feline confidence, had vanished, seeking shelter from something that existed beyond the reach of ordinary senses.

Todd sat alone on an overturned milking stool in the cavernous barn, the solitary lantern at his feet casting a small, defiant circle of golden light in the encroaching darkness. He'd volunteered for the watch—insisted on it, really—though the gesture felt almost laughably inadequate. What could a middle-aged man with no magical abilities do against the kinds of threats that haunted his nephew's world? He was armed with nothing more than a thermos of bitter coffee, a cell phone with spotty reception, and a profound sense of his own uselessness.

But it was his family now. His watch. His responsibility.

The horses in the stable had been restless for hours, their nervous whinnying and the sharp crack of hooves against wooden stalls providing a counterpoint to the unnatural quiet. Animals always knew when something was wrong when the very fabric of the world was being stretched thin. Their fear was honest, uncomplicated by human attempts to rationalize the impossible.

Todd took another sip of coffee, grimacing at its burnt taste. He'd made it too strong again, but the bitter caffeine helped keep him alert. Sleep felt like a luxury he couldn't afford, not when every instinct he possessed was screaming that danger was approaching. He might not have inherited the Murphy family's magical gifts. Still, he had their stubborn streak, their bone-deep refusal to abandon their post when others were counting on them.

The charm bracelet Sam had woven for him—a delicate thing of silver thread and midnight-black raven feathers—began to vibrate against his wrist. The sensation was subtle at first, barely more than a tickle, but it quickly intensified until the feathers seemed to flutter with their own inner wind. Todd's heart began to hammer against his ribs as he understood what the warning meant.

Something's coming.

He stood slowly, his joints protesting after hours of sitting, and moved toward the open side door of the barn. The night beyond was awash in a sickly, green-tinged gloom cast by a moon that seemed too large, too bright, too close to the earth. The familiar landscape of the farm looked alien under that otherworldly light, shadows falling at impossible angles, the very air shimmering with an oily iridescence that made his eyes water.

And there, at the far edge of the western field where the tall grass met the tree line, stood a figure.

Todd's breath caught in his throat. The thing was tall and impossibly slender like a scarecrow stretched beyond all proportion. It was draped in what looked like a cloak woven from white reeds and river cane, the material rustling despite the complete absence of wind. Its face was hidden deep within a hood of twisted vines and Spanish moss, creating a hollow of absolute blackness that seemed to drink the moonlight.

But it was the ground around the figure that made Todd's blood run cold. In a perfect circle extending ten feet in every direction, the lush summer grass had withered and died. The earth itself looked poisoned, cracked, and blackened as if struck by lightning or doused with acid. Whatever this thing was, its very presence was toxic to life itself.

A wave of primal terror washed over Todd, the kind of fear that existed in the deepest parts of the human brain, the ancient warnings encoded in DNA by millions of years of evolution. This was not just another supernatural threat—this was something older, something that predated human civilization, human language, human understanding. It was entropy given form, death walking on two legs, the cold silence that waited at the end of all things.

His hands shaking, Todd fumbled for the two-way radio clipped to his belt. He had to warn Sean, had to alert the others before—

The radio erupted in a shriek of static so loud and violent it felt like an ice pick driven through his eardrums. The sound was more than noise—it was wrongness made audible, a frequency that attacked the very concept of communication. Todd cried out and dropped the device, watching it clatter to the concrete floor, where it continued to emit a screeching sound until something vital inside it burned out, leaving behind only the acrid smell of fried electronics.

Then, impossibly, a voice spoke directly inside his skull. It was not a voice in any human sense—it was the rustle of a billion dry leaves, the whisper of wind through a graveyard, the sound of time itself grinding forward toward an inevitable end.

The oldest pact was not with fire, nor with blood. The oldest pact was with the living earth. You have forgotten the words.

The figure took a step forward, and the circle of death expanded with its movement. Another step, and the blight spread further, consuming healthy grass and leaving behind only sterile, poisoned soil. It was walking toward the farmhouse with the unhurried gait of something that had all the time in the world, secure in its ancient power and terrible purpose.

Walking toward Sean. Toward Katie. Toward all the young people sleeping peacefully in their beds, unaware that something had come to collect a debt they didn't even know they owed.

In that moment, Todd's paralyzing fear was incinerated by something far more powerful—the fierce, protective instinct that had been dormant in him for fifteen years but never truly gone. These weren't just Sean's friends or fellow witches. They were his family now, the children he'd never had, the second chance he'd never thought he deserved. And something was threatening them.

He didn't think about strategy or magical theory. He didn't consider the odds or calculate his chances of survival. He simply acted on an instinct older than magic itself—the need to stand between danger and the people he loved.

Todd sprinted from the barn, not toward the house to wake the others, but toward the small pantry off the kitchen. His movements were quick and sure despite his fear, guided by half-remembered childhood lessons and the desperate improvisation of a man with everything to lose. He grabbed a box of coarse sea salt from the shelf, its weight familiar and comforting in his hands. From the breadbox, he took the hard, stale heel of a sourdough loaf—bread made with his own hands from grain grown in this very soil. Then he ran to the toolshed, his boots pounding on the hard-packed earth, and ripped a heavy, rust-pitted iron horseshoe from the nail where it had hung for fifty years.

Salt, bread, and iron. The peasant's trinity. The working man's magic. It wasn't the elaborate ritual work of trained witches and warlocks. Still, it was older, deeper, rooted in the same primal forces that had guided humanity's first fumbling steps toward understanding the unseen world.

By the time he returned to the front yard, the entity had reached the halfway point between the tree line and the house. Its approach was relentless but unhurried, like a tide that knew it would eventually claim everything in its path. The circle of blight around it had expanded to encompass fifteen feet in every direction, and the very air seemed to wither in its presence. Behind it, a trail of dead earth marked its passage like a scar across the face of the world.

Todd planted himself squarely in the entity's path, between the approaching darkness and the warm, sleeping farmhouse. With movements that were steadier than he had any right to expect, he poured the salt in a thick, unbroken line across the creature's route. The white crystals caught the moonlight, forming a barrier that looked laughably small against the approaching horror but felt significant in ways Todd couldn't articulate.

He held the bread in his left hand and the iron horseshoe in his right, simple tools that carried the weight of ten thousand years of human faith and tradition. His heart was hammering so hard he could feel his pulse in his temples, but his voice, when he found it, was surprisingly steady.

"I don't know what you are," he said aloud, the words carrying clearly in the supernatural stillness. "And I don't care. This is a protected place. You don't get past me."

The entity paused in its advance, its hooded void of a face tilting as if considering his words with the detached interest of a scientist examining an unusual specimen. When it spoke again, the voice of rustling leaves filled Todd's mind with images of cosmic emptiness, of stars dying in the cold dark between galaxies.

The pact is broken. The new magic is loud. It screams. It tears at the weave. It has woken that which should have slept. It must be silenced.

Todd felt a chill of understanding. The entity wasn't talking about magic in general—it was talking about Sean's magic, about the coven's magic. In its ancient, alien perspective, their power wasn't a defense against darkness but a source of chaos, a discordant noise in what should be a quiet, ordered universe. It had come to silence them, to restore what it saw as the natural balance.

But Todd had spent fifteen years running from his family's legacy, fifteen years denying the magic that flowed in his blood, and he understood something the entity didn't. Power wasn't just about force or ancient pacts or cosmic hierarchies. Sometimes, the most profound magic came from the simplest sources—love, loyalty, the willingness to stand between danger and the people who mattered.

His mind raced back through half-forgotten childhood memories, searching for the words his grandmother had sung to him during thunderstorms and dark nights. She'd been Irish to her bones, carrying the old songs and older wisdom across an ocean to a new world where such things were easily forgotten. But Todd remembered. In the deepest part of his soul, where love lived and fear couldn't reach, he remembered.

He took a shaking breath and began to sing. The words came slowly at first, the Gaelic thick and clumsy on his tongue, but as he continued, the melody grew stronger, more sure. It was a lullaby, ancient and simple, about protection, peace, and the kind of love that endures beyond death itself.

"Sé do bheatha, a leanbh liom, a chodlaíonn faoi sholas na ré..."

Welcome, my child, who sleeps beneath the moonlight...

His voice was raw and untrained, cracking with emotion and fear, but it carried across the poisoned ground with surprising strength. It wasn't a spell in any formal sense. There were no complex gestures, no precisely pronounced incantations, no carefully measured ingredients. It was simply a man singing to keep the darkness at bay, offering the only magic he possessed: memory, love, and the stubborn human refusal to let evil win without a fight.

The effect on the entity was immediate and profound. It stopped dead in its tracks, its hooded head tilting at an impossible angle as if hearing something it hadn't expected. The pressure in the air lessened, and the advance of the dead circle halted. For the first time since its appearance, the creature seemed uncertain.

The whispers in Todd's mind changed, losing their cold, judgmental edge and taking on something that might almost have been recognition or even regret.

A song of the cradle. You still remember. There are so few who still remember the quiet ways.

The entity stood motionless for a long, silent moment, and Todd could feel something like a vast, ancient sadness radiating from it. This wasn't a monster, he realized. It was a guardian, like Sean, like all the Murphys who had come before. But it was a guardian of silence, of endings, of the spaces between heartbeats where peace could be found. It had seen the universe grow noisy and chaotic, and it was trying to restore the quiet it remembered from eons past.

But it had forgotten that some sounds were worth preserving—laughter, conversation, lullabies sung to frightened children. It had become so focused on ending the noise that it had lost track of why silence was valuable in the first place.

The wild is walking again, the voice whispered, and now it carried a warning rather than a threat. *The old paths are overgrown, but they are not gone. Remind the loud ones of the quiet. The balance is failing.*

And then, as suddenly as it had appeared, the entity began to fade. Not vanishing in a flash of light or dramatic display, but simply becoming less solid, less present, until it was nothing more than a memory of darkness against the night sky. The circle of blighted earth began to green again, life returning in slow, tentative waves as the presence that had poisoned it withdrew.

The supernatural pressure lifted, and with it came the return of normal night sounds—the distant hoot of an owl, the rustle of small creatures in the underbrush, the whisper of wind through the corn. The world remembered how to breathe again.

Todd stood alone in the front yard, the salt line at his feet, the bread and iron still clutched in his shaking hands. His legs gave out, and he sank to his knees, the adrenaline finally deserting him and leaving behind a bone-deep exhaustion that threatened to pull him into unconsciousness.

He'd done it. Somehow, impossibly, he'd faced down an ancient cosmic entity with nothing but folk magic and a grandmother's lullaby. Not because he was powerful or specially trained but because he'd remembered something the entity had forgotten—that the point of protecting the quiet wasn't to eliminate all sound but to preserve the space where beautiful sounds could exist.

Sean found him twenty minutes later, drawn by the psychic shockwave of the entity's departure. Todd was still on his knees by the salt line, staring up at stars that seemed brighter and more numerous than they had any right to be. His nephew's face was pale with concern and something that might have been awe.

"What happened?" Sean asked, kneeling beside him. "I felt... something. A presence, and then it was gone."

Todd looked up at him, at this young man who carried so much responsibility on his shoulders, who fought battles that would have broken older, more experienced warriors. For the first time since returning to the farm, Todd felt like he belonged here like he had something valuable to contribute to the family legacy.

"Something came to call," he said quietly, his voice still hoarse from singing. "And I think... I think I sang it a song it needed to hear."

Sean helped him to his feet, and together, they looked out over the farm—at the fields and buildings that had been protected by love and stubbornness and an old man's half-remembered lullaby. In the distance, the ancient pear tree swayed gently in the returning breeze, its branches reaching toward stars that had witnessed the dance between noise and silence, chaos and order, since the beginning of time.

Todd had finally found his place in the story. Not as a warlock or a guardian of ancient knowledge but as something equally important—a keeper of the small magics, the human magics, the simple truths that even cosmic entities could not ignore. He was the bridge between the world of ordinary people and the realm of wonders his nephew inhabited, proof that love and memory were powers in their own right.

The next morning, he would teach Kim how to weave iron nails into a wreath of blackberry thorns, showing her the protective charms his grandmother had hung over every door and window. He would share the old songs and older stories, the folk wisdom that had kept families safe for generations before the first formal spell was ever cast.

But for now, in the quiet after chaos, he simply stood with Sean in the starlight and remembered what it felt like to be exactly where he belonged. The guardian was gone, but the garden remained, tended by love and protected by the simple, unshakeable truth that some things were worth fighting for.

In the house behind them, the rest of the coven slept peacefully, unaware of how close they had come to losing everything. But Todd knew, would always know, that he had stood between them and the dark. Not with magic or ancient power, but with the greatest force in any universe—a love so deep and stubborn that it could make even the oldest entities remember what they had once chosen to protect.

The lullaby still echoed in his mind as he and Sean walked back to the house, a melody that would stay with him for the rest of his days: a reminder that sometimes the most powerful magic was simply refusing to let the people you loved face the darkness alone.

Chapter 20: Preparations for War

T he sanctuary had transformed. Where once there had been the quiet, dusty reverence of a library, there was now the frantic, focused energy of a battle command center. The air, which had so recently been thick with the miasma of grief and despair, now crackled with a different kind of intensity—the grim, electric hum of preparation for an impossible war.

The two-pronged strategy had cleaved the coven's activities in two. One-half of the sprawling hidden library was now Katie's domain. Ancient scrolls had been carefully rolled and set aside, replaced by magically acquired corporate charts, satellite images of Finch's construction site, and complex diagrams of financial networks that looked like a madman's string theory. The other half of the room belonged to Sean. Here, the tables were littered with arcane diagrams of magical wards, runic alphabets copied from crumbling texts, and shallow bowls filled with arcane ingredients—powdered silver, crushed obsidian, sprigs of nightshade, and jars of murky, phosphorescent liquids.

It was a war room for a war being fought on two entirely different planes of existence.

Katie and Sam were huddled over a tablet, its screen reflecting in their focused eyes. They had been at it for hours, their fingers occasionally tracing glowing blue patterns on the screen—a modern form of witchcraft that was Katie's unique and formidable specialty. It wasn't hacking in a conventional sense; it was a dance of digital illusion and psychic infiltration. Katie wove spells of obfuscation that could make their magical intrusion look like a meaningless server glitch while Sam whispered quiet, binding words to bypass password protections that were less like locks and more like sentient guard dogs.

"I'm in," Katie breathed, her eyes widening. "Past the primary firewalls of Finch's personal server." A cascade of encrypted files filled the screen. "He's good. The layers of protection here are... unnatural."

"He's had centuries of practice hiding in human systems," Sam murmured, her hand resting on Katie's shoulder, feeding a small trickle of her own energy into the effort. "What are we looking for?"

"Anything that doesn't make sense. Large-scale purchases of materials that have nothing to do with a geothermal plant. Unexplained payroll, strange shipping manifests." Katie's fingers flew across the screen, her mind sifting through terabytes of data with a magically enhanced speed. She was in her element, her intelligence a sharp, precise instrument.

After nearly an hour of navigating the digital labyrinth, she found something. A series of heavily encrypted, massive wire transfers, all originating from offshore accounts and funneling into a handful of oddly named shell corporations.

"Got it," she said, her voice tight with excitement. "Look at these names. 'Nyarlatho Tech Solutions.' 'Azathoth Aggregate.' 'Shub-Niggurath Holdings."

Sam leaned closer, her brow furrowed. "Those names... they sound familiar, but I can't place them. They feel... wrong."

"They're more than wrong," Katie said, a chill running down her spine. "They're a thread. Let's pull on it."

***

Across the room, Sean's team was engaged in a more visceral and far more frustrating struggle. He, Matthew, and Kim stood around a miniature, replicated version of one of Alistair Finch's outer wards. It shimmered over a large, flat stone, a dome of sickly, purple-black energy about three feet in diameter. It was the simplest of the wards Sean had glimpsed in his vision, and it was proving to be almost unbreakable.

"Again," Sean said, his voice strained with effort.

Matthew, his face beaded with sweat, thrust his hands forward. A bolt of raw, kinetic force, the color of a thunderhead, slammed into the ward. The dark energy dome buckled, groaning under the assault, but it held firm; the impact sent a ripple of hostile energy back at Matthew, making him stagger.

"It's no good," he grunted, shaking his hands as if to rid them of the ward's foul energy. "It's like punching a wall of solid rubber. It just absorbs the force and throws it right back."

"Let me try," Kim said, her voice calm and steady. She knelt, placing her palms flat on the stone floor. Closing her eyes, she drew on her deep, innate connection to the earth. A low hum filled the air as she attempted to ground out the ward's power to pull its unnatural energy down into the planet's embrace.

For a moment, it seemed to work. The purple-black shimmer flickered and dimmed. But then, with a sharp, ugly pulse, the ward adapted. It severed its own connection to the stone, hovering an inch above the surface, fed by its own internal, alien power source. Kim gasped, her connection broken, the backlash leaving her pale and breathless.

"It thinks," Sean said, the realization dawning on him with a cold dread. "It's not just a wall. It's a living defense. It analyzes the attack and changes its nature to counter it." He remembered the feel of it from his vision—the cold, cruel, analytical intelligence. This was a magic far older and more complex than their own earth-based traditions.

He stepped forward, his mind racing. Brute force wouldn't work. Grounding it wouldn't work. They had to think differently. He closed his eyes, recalling the *feeling* of the ward—its coldness, its alien structure. It was a magic of pure, unfeeling intellect. What was its opposite?

Life. Warmth. Chaos.

"Okay," he said, opening his eyes. "New plan. We don't try to break it. We try to... poison it. With us." He looked at Kim. "Give me a feeling of new growth. Spring mud, a sprouting seed." He looked at Matthew. "Give me pure, unrestrained emotion. A victory cry, a shout of joy." He took a deep breath. "I'll provide the life force."

It was a strange, abstract strategy, and he saw the doubt in their eyes, but they trusted him. They focused, their expressions intense. Sean felt the trickle of their magic—Kim's green, earthy energy and Matthew's wild, chaotic power—flowing towards him. He took those energies and wove them together with a thread of his own vital essence, the same life force the Wayfinder so greedily consumed. He didn't shape it into a weapon. He shaped it into a single, warm, vibrant pulse of pure, messy, chaotic *life*.

He gently pushed the pulse of energy against the ward.

It didn't strike or buckle. For a moment, nothing happened. Then, the ward began to shudder violently, its smooth, dark surface breaking out in dissonant ripples. It was as if he'd introduced a beautiful, living note into a symphony of perfect, sterile silence, and the symphony couldn't handle the impurity. A high-pitched whine filled the air, and with a sound like shattering glass, a tiny, hairline crack appeared in the surface of the ward.

It was a small victory, almost infinitesimal, but it was a victory nonetheless. They had found a way. A slow, challenging, and profoundly draining way, but a way.

***

Hours later, the two teams took a much-needed break, gathering in the main chamber of the sanctuary. They were all bone-weary, but the air of hopelessness was gone, replaced by the electric buzz of progress. Uncle Todd, as had become his custom, had silently left a large cooler near the entrance. It was filled with sandwiches, fruit, and cold drinks. His quiet, practical support was a constant, comforting presence in their strange new lives.

"He almost gets the bread-to-meat ratio right," Matthew said, taking a large bite of a turkey sandwich, and they all laughed; the sound was a welcome release in the ancient chamber. The tension of the last few days broke. For a few wonderful minutes, they were just teenagers, joking, sharing food, and complaining about their respective tasks.

"You should have seen the firewalls on Finch's server," Katie said, leaning her head on Sean's shoulder. "It was like trying to break into a dragon's hoard. But we found his encrypted ledgers."

"Anything useful?" Sean asked, putting his arm around her.

"Just a lot of weirdness," Sam chimed in, pulling out her own phone to show them her notes. "Massive, untraceable payments to a series of shell corporations. The names are what's bothering me. Shub-Niggurath Holdings, Azathoth Aggregate, Nyarlatho Tech..."

Sam had a passion for ancient history and mythology, a skill that had already proven invaluable. She scrolled through her research. "I couldn't find them in any corporate directory. But the names... they're not just random. I found a reference. Not in a history book. In a crumbling, pre-Christian codex from a monastery in Northern Europe. A book my old coven leader called 'dangerous nonsense.'"

She looked up, her sea-green eyes dark with a new and profound fear. "They aren't corporate names, Sean. They're the names of... things. Ancient, pre-human entities of chaos. Cosmic horrors from the time before time. The book refers to them as the "Outer Gods.""

A deep, ringing silence fell over the group. The half-eaten sandwiches were forgotten.

"What are you saying?" Sean asked, his voice barely a whisper.

"I'm saying," Sam said, her voice trembling, "that the Malevolent Spirit we're fighting... it might not be the master of this plan. It might just be a servant. A high priest. And Alistair Finch... a man with that much power and influence doesn't just get randomly possessed. He was likely a human acolyte. A cultist who willingly opened the door and invited the monster in."

The world tilted on its axis. Their understanding of the conflict shifted from horrifying to apocalyptic. They weren't just fighting a clan of ancient, soul-eating spirits. They were fighting the foot soldiers of a Lovecraftian nightmare, a pantheon of chaos gods from beyond the stars. The ritual at the nexus wasn't just to free more spirits. It was to weaken the fabric of reality enough to allow these... Outer Gods... to gain a foothold in their world.

As this new, terrifying reality settled over them, a slow, rhythmic pulse began to throb through the sanctuary.

Thump-thump. Thump-thump.

It was a soundless beat, a feeling more than a noise. Sean's head snapped toward the velvet-lined box on the far table. The Wayfinder.

He scrambled over to it and threw open the lid. The small wooden bird was glowing with a faint, sickly, yellowish warmth. It wasn't the intense, demanding heat of the scrying. This was different. This was the slow, steady pulse of something observing them.

Thump-thump. Thump-thump.

Ice flooded Sean's veins. "He's watching," he breathed, the words barely escaping his lips. "He's close. He's watching us right now."

Instantly, the coven was on their feet, their brief respite shattered. Terror, sharp and immediate, seized them. Their sanctuary, their only safe place, had been compromised.

"Wards up! Now! Seal the entrance!" Sean commanded his voice to bark harshly with pure instinct.

They flew into action, their fear channeled into a frantic burst of defensive magic. They poured their combined will into the ancient wards of the cave, reinforcing them, layering them with every protective spell they knew. But even as the magic settled, creating a powerful, shimmering barrier between them and the outside world, the feeling persisted. The slow, rhythmic, observational pulse of the Wayfinder continued.

Thump-thump. Thump-thump.

It was a message. From the monster to them. *I see you. I know what you are planning. Your fortress is a fishbowl, and I am watching your every move.*

The adventure had become a siege. And they were the ones trapped inside.

Chapter 21: The First Strike

The two weeks leading up to the eclipse were the longest of Sean's life. The farm, once a place of sanctuary and peace, had become a fortress. A constant, low-grade tension hummed in the air, an invisible current running parallel to the familiar rhythms of their daily lives. They were living under siege, not from a visible enemy, but from the crushing weight of what was to come.

Every waking moment was dedicated to preparation. The hidden library in the sanctuary was in a state of organized chaos, its ancient quiet replaced by the murmur of strategy sessions and the frantic scratch of pens on paper. By day, they were high school students, dissecting frogs and debating the causes of the Civil War. By night, they were soldiers in a secret, desperate war, their homework assignments lying forgotten next to bowls of smoldering herbs and diagrams of arcane power.

Katie's subterfuge team had scored a minor but significant victory. A series of "unfortunate data corruptions" at one of Finch's subsidiary companies had triggered an internal audit. A magically nudged anonymous tip to a financial journalist had resulted in a scathing article about "accounting irregularities" at the Aethelgard Institute. Finch's stock had taken a small but noticeable dip. It wasn't a fatal blow, but it was a distraction, a tangle of mundane problems to occupy the man while the Spirit inside him plotted the end of the world.

Sean's team, meanwhile, had managed painstakingly to deconstruct and replicate three more of the nexus's outer wards. Their progress was slow, a grueling process of trial and error that left them magically and physically drained each night. Each small success felt monumental, a single brick removed from an insurmountable wall.

They had fallen into a new routine, this small, strange family of witches and guardians. Uncle Todd had taken over all the cooking, his culinary creations ranging from surprisingly delicious to heroically burnt. His quiet, steadfast presence was a comfort, a silent acknowledgment that he was in this with them, even if his role was to ensure they ate.

One evening, they were all gathered in the kitchen; the coven exhausted after a long night of practice, Todd serving up plates of spaghetti with a sauce that was just a little too smoky. For a moment, it felt normal. Matthew was telling a bad joke, Kim was laughing, and Katie was leaning against Sean, her head resting on his shoulder. In that instant, they were just kids. The illusion was so perfect, so deeply longed for, that when it shattered, the sound was deafening.

It began not with a bang, but with a sudden, unnatural silence. The chirping of the crickets outside ceased. The lowing of the cattle in the distant pasture cut off abruptly. All the ambient, living sounds of the farm simply stopped.

Uncle Todd was the first to react, his head snapping up from the pot he was stirring. "What was that?" he asked, his practical senses picking up on the wrongness before their magic did.

Then came the fog. It wasn't a natural mist rolling in from the creek; it was a thick, greasy, gray vapor that boiled up from the ground itself, swallowing the yard in seconds. It clung to the windows of the house, opaque and menacing.

The Wayfinder in Sean's pocket, which had been dormant for a week, suddenly flared with a sick, pulsing heat. At the exact moment, the protective wards they had painstakingly layered around the property began to scream. It wasn't a sound, but a psychic shriek of alarm that lanced through each of their minds.

"It's here," Sean breathed, the words turning to ice in the suddenly frigid air of the kitchen.

The moments of normalcy were over. The Spirit had come to call.

Chaos erupted, but it was an ordered chaos. They had drilled for this. "Positions!" Sean commanded, his voice cutting through the initial wave of fear. "Now!"

The coven scattered, each member racing to their designated post. Kim and Matthew charged out the back door to the western perimeter. Sam ran upstairs to the attic window, which overlooked the northern fields. Todd, his face grim and pale, grabbed the heavy, 12-gauge shotgun from the rack by the door. "I'll secure the house," he yelled, his voice tight with a fear he refused to let master him. "You kids do your thing."

Sean and Katie burst onto the front porch, the unnatural fog instantly clinging to them, cold and damp. The main ward around the farmhouse was visible now, a shimmering, transparent dome of pale blue light, already straining against the pressure of the assault.

The attack came first from the shadows within the fog. Vague, canine shapes, darker than the surrounding darkness, began to coalesce at the edge of the ward. They were the *Yawar-Machaq*, the shadow-hounds, just as the texts had described. They didn't bark or growl, but moved with a terrifying, silent purpose, throwing themselves against the glowing blue barrier. Their insubstantial forms sizzled and dissolved on impact, weakening the shield by a fraction with each one.

"They're testing the perimeter!" Katie yelled over the rising psychic hum. "Kim, Matthew, reinforce the outer ward! Don't let them break it down!"

As Kim slammed her hands onto the earth, drawing a wave of green, stabilizing energy up from the ground, and Matthew began hurling bolts of pure force at the bolder shadow-hounds, the second phase of the assault began.

It wasn't a physical attack but a mental one. A wave of pure, distilled despair washed over them. Sean suddenly felt the full, crushing weight of his grandfather's death, the grief so fresh and raw it threatened to bring him to his knees. Beside him, he felt Katie stumble, her mind suddenly flooded with an image of him, pale and lifeless, the silver streak in his hair having consumed him entirely.

"Illusion!" Sam's voice was a sharp, clear bell in their minds, cutting through the psychic filth. *It's the Desiccator's magic! It's feeding on your fear! Sphere of Truth, now! All of you!*

Together, they began the telepathic chant, their minds weaving a complex, protective sphere of clear, rational thought around the farmhouse. The horrifying illusions flickered and died, the wave of despair receding. But it had served its purpose. It had distracted them.

With a deafening CRACK, a bolt of raw, corrosive, purple-black energy—the Spirit's power—slammed into the central ward directly over the porch. The blue dome shuddered violently, and a network of spiderweb cracks appeared, sizzling with dark magic. The shield was failing.

The Spirit was no longer testing them. It was trying to break them.

"It's too strong," Katie gasped, her face pale with strain as she poured more of her own energy into the failing ward. "We can't hold it back!"

Sean's mind raced. They were in a battle of attrition against a being with a near-limitless supply of power, and they were losing. They couldn't just defend. They had to strike back. But at what? The Spirit was hidden, cloaked in the magical fog, its exact location unknown.

He looked at Katie, at the terror and determination warring in her eyes, and he knew what he had to do. The risk was immense, the potential cost unthinkable, but it was their only chance.

"Katie, I need you to anchor me," he said, his voice urgent. "Everyone else, forget the outer wards! Forget the hounds! All of you, pour every ounce of power you have into this main shield! Buy me thirty seconds!"

"Sean, what are you doing?" Katie cried, but there was no time to argue.

He closed his eyes, shutting out the chaos, the cracking shield, the swirling fog. He reached into his mind to the small, warm, vital spark of his life force, and he touched the Wayfinder in his pocket. He didn't ask it to perform a full scry—the cost would be too great, the time too long. He just gave it a single, desperate command. *Point.*

The wooden bird in his pocket flared with blistering heat, and the world behind his eyes went white with pain. It wasn't a vision, just a feeling. A single, pure, undeniable vector. A line of intention pointing from him to a spot seventy yards out, deep within the densest part of the fog. The source of the attack.

He opened his eyes, a sharp gasp of pain escaping his lips. He ignored the sudden, dizzying wave of weakness, the feeling of having run a marathon in a single heartbeat. His gaze was now locked on a spot in the swirling grayness.

"There!" he roared, his voice amplified by magic, a command that echoed across the besieged farm. "That's where it is! All of you are on my mark! Don't just reinforce the shield! Push!"

He felt the shift as the coven obeyed, their individual streams of power converging, no longer a defensive wall, but the tip of a spear.

"Now!" Sean bellowed.

As one, they unleashed their collective will. It wasn't a bolt of lightning or a fireball. It was a massive, concentrated wave of pure, untainted life force, a tidal wave of their combined hope and defiance. It erupted from them, pushing *through* their own cracking shield and lancing out into the fog, a brilliant, silent spear of pure white light aimed directly at the heart of the darkness.

For a moment, there was nothing. Then a shriek tore through the night.

It was a sound that did not belong in the world of living things, a sound of pure, unadulterated rage and pain, the sound of a god being wounded.

The assault stopped as if a switch had been thrown. The pressure on the main ward vanished. The shadow-hounds dissolved into harmless vapor. The unnatural fog receded with astonishing speed, boiling away into the clear night sky and revealing empty fields beneath a canopy of brilliant, silent stars.

It was over. The Spirit was gone.

A collective, shuddering sigh went through the coven. The main ward, its purpose served, shattered into a million glittering shards of light and vanished. On the porch, Sean's legs gave out, and he collapsed to his knees, Katie catching him before he could hit the floor. The coven was utterly, profoundly drained, their magical reserves scraped clean. But they were alive. They had held the line. They had won.

A few minutes later, after the initial wave of exhausted relief had passed, Uncle Todd came jogging back from the perimeter, the shotgun held loosely in his hands.

"Nothing," he said, his voice filled with a bewildered awe. "Not a single track. No broken twigs, no disturbed ground. It's like nothing was ever here."

Katie, helping Sean to his feet, looked out at the peaceful, empty field, then back at the exhausted faces of her friends. Her own face was a mask of dawning horror.

"It wasn't trying to win," she said, the words falling like stones into the quiet night. "If it had wanted to win, it would have kept attacking. Another minute and the shield would have failed completely. We were at our absolute limit."

Sean followed her gaze, his heart sinking with the cold, grim weight of her logic. She was right. This hadn't been an all-out assault. This was a test. A probe. It had thrown its minions at them, one type of magic after another, not to destroy them but to see how they would react. To measure their strength, to analyze their defenses, to learn their capabilities.

"It wasn't a battle," he said, his voice grim. The small spark of victory in his chest was extinguished, replaced by ice. "It was reconnaissance."

He looked at his coven, at his small band of teenage soldiers, and a new, more profound fear settled over him. They had survived. They had even struck back. But in doing so, they had shown their hand to an ancient, strategic enemy. And now it knew. It knew their strengths. It knew their weaknesses. It knew exactly how to break them.

Chapter 22: The Wayfinder's Memory

The night before the eclipse, Sean couldn't sleep. The Wayfinder lay on his nightstand, its carved surface catching the moonlight in ways that seemed impossible for simple wood. He'd been carrying it for weeks now, feeling its constant hunger, its pull on his life force even when dormant. Tomorrow, he knew, he would use it one final time.

Unable to resist, he picked it up. The moment his skin touched the ancient wood, the world... shifted.

He wasn't in his room anymore. He stood in a forest that predated human memory, where trees rose like cathedral pillars into a star-filled sky unmarred by any light pollution. The air smelled of moss and age, and something else—raw, primal magic that made his modern spells feel like children's toys.

"So, another Murphy comes to understand."

Sean spun around. An old man sat on a fallen log, but 'old' didn't begin to describe him. He looked like he'd been carved from the same ancient wood as the trees around them, his skin bark-rough, his hair white as birch bark. His eyes, though—his eyes were young, burning with a fierce intelligence that reminded Sean painfully of his grandfather.

"You're..."

"Cian Murphy. Though the concept of 'am' becomes complex when you exist primarily as a memory carved into heartwood." The ancient guardian smiled. "I made the Wayfinder, boy. Carved it from a branch of the World Tree itself, back when such things still grew in places mortals could reach."

Sean approached carefully, the Wayfinder warm in his hand. "The World Tree is a myth."

"Is it?" Cian gestured to the forest around them. "You're standing in a memory of the world as it was before the Gates, before the need for barriers between realities. When magic flowed like rivers and humans were just learning to cup it in their hands."

The scene shifted. Now, they stood on a hill overlooking a vast plain where darkness gathered like a living thing. Sean could see figures in the darkness—not the Malevolent Spirits he knew, but their progenitors. Older. Hungrier. Infinite.

"They came from the spaces between stars," Cian explained. "Drawn by the light of human consciousness. We were like flames to them—bright, warm, and eminently consumable. The first Gatekeepers weren't warriors. We were architects. We built the barriers not to fight them but to hide from them."

"But the Wayfinder—"

"Was never meant to find enemies." Cian's expression grew sad. "It was meant to find the lost. Children who wandered into the dark. Guardians separated from their circles. The innocent who needed guidance home." He looked at the artifact in Sean's hands. "I carved it with love, boy. Every line, every rune, was a prayer for the safety of those who would come after."

The forest returned, but now Sean could see other figures among the trees. Ghostly echoes of every Murphy who had carried the Wayfinder. His great-grandfather was young and fierce. His grandfather, Tom, was a middle-aged and grimly determined man. His father, David, laughing as he showed a toddler Sean how the bird's wings caught the light.

"Each guardian who uses it leaves an echo," Cian explained. "A memory of their purpose, their sacrifice. You're not just carrying wood, boy. You're carrying the accumulated will of twenty generations of protectors."

Sean felt the weight of it—not physical, but spiritual. "And the cost?"

Cian's expression darkened. "That came later. After the first corruption, when we realized the entities could use our own tools against us. The Wayfinder began demanding payment to ensure only the worthy could wield it. Better to burn years from a guardian's life than let it fall into the wrong hands."

"My grandfather never used it."

"Tom was wise. He understood that some prices are too high to pay unless the alternative is unthinkable." Cian studied Sean with those ancient eyes. "But you're facing the unthinkable, aren't you?"

Sean nodded, thinking of the forming portals and the cosmic horror that was preparing to unmake reality. "I need to See. Really See. The whole pattern, the full scope of what we're fighting. It's the only way to find a solution."

"And you're willing to pay the price."

It wasn't a question. Sean thought of Katie, of his coven, of every innocent soul who would suffer if the Spirits broke free. "Yes."

Cian stood, and suddenly he didn't look old at all. He looked eternal, a force of nature given human form. "Then let me show you what the Wayfinder truly is."

He reached out and touched the carved bird. Light exploded between them, and Sean saw—

The Wayfinder was more than just a tool. It was a key. A fragment of the original sight that had allowed the first humans to perceive magic. It was a piece of cosmic awareness that had allowed humanity to build the Gates in the first place. When activated fully, it didn't just reveal the location or expose the truth. It connected the user to the fundamental structure of reality itself.

"This is why it costs so much," Sean breathed, understanding flooding through him. "It's not taking life force as payment. It's burning through our limited human framework to access something infinite."

"Every moment of expanded awareness requires vast amounts of energy to maintain," Cian confirmed. "A human life contains only so much. Use it carelessly, and you'll burn through decades in minutes."

"But if I'm careful—"

"There is no careful with what you're planning." Cian's voice was gentle but implacable. "To See the full pattern of a cosmic threat, to understand beings that exist outside conventional reality... Sean, it will take everything you have."

Sean looked down at the Wayfinder. Such a small thing to carry such enormous potential. "Will it be enough? Will the knowledge be worth the cost?"

"That's not for me to say." Cian began to fade, the forest dissolving around them. "But I will tell you this—every guardian who has paid the ultimate price found that in their final moment, they understood something beyond knowledge. They touched the truth that makes all sacrifice worthwhile."

"What truth?"

But Cian was gone, the ancient forest was gone, and Sean was back in his room. Dawn was breaking outside his window. The Wayfinder lay in his palm, warm and waiting.

He understood now. Tomorrow, when he used it to See the Spirits' true form, he wouldn't just be burning his own years. He'd be adding his echo to the artifact's memory, joining the long line of Murphys who had given everything to protect what they loved.

The thought should have terrified him. Instead, he felt a strange peace. He was part of something larger than himself—a chain of sacrifice and love stretching back to humanity's first recognition of the darkness between the stars.

He kissed the wooden bird gently, feeling the pulse of all those accumulated memories. "Thank you," he whispered. To Cian, to his grandfather, to all who had carried this burden before him.

Tomorrow, he would use the Wayfinder one last time. He would pay the price in years and pain. But tonight, he understood that the true power wasn't in the artifact itself.

It was in the willingness to use it.

***

When Katie found him the next morning, he was sitting at his desk, writing in the Guardian Chronicle Lyralei had given him. The Wayfinder sat beside him, quiet and ready.

"What are you writing?" she asked softly.

"Instructions," Sean said. "For whoever comes after. About what the Wayfinder really is. What it really costs. Why it's worth it anyway."

She wrapped her arms around him from behind, resting her chin on his shoulder. "You're scaring me."

"I know." He turned to kiss her cheek. "But I need you to understand—when I use this today, I won't just be looking for answers. I'll be joining a tradition. Adding my voice to a chorus that's been singing the same song for a thousand years."

"What song?"

Sean smiled, thinking of Cian's eternal eyes, of his grandfather's last gift, of the chain of love that bound past to present to future.

"That the darkness is vast, but love is vaster. That every sacrifice creates light. That as long as someone remembers to stand watch, the dawn will always come."

He closed the Chronicle and stood, the Wayfinder secure in his pocket. Whatever happened in the coming battle, he was ready. He had touched the memory of his bloodline, understood the true weight of his inheritance.

And when the time came to pay the price, he would pay it gladly, knowing he was never truly alone. The Wayfinder would remember. The Chronicle would remember.

And somewhere in the space between heartbeats, every Murphy who had ever stood against the dark would stand with him one last time.

Chapter 23: The Longest Night

The last night fell not with a sense of peace but with the suffocating weight of a held breath. A swollen, rust-colored moon clawed its way into a sky that was already unnaturally dark, casting a sickly, bruised light over the farm. The world had gone silent. The familiar, living chorus of crickets and frogs had been erased, leaving an emptiness so profound it felt like a pressure against the ears. Every member of the coven felt it—the palpable sense that the world itself was bracing for impact.

Sleep was an impossibility, a distant country none of them could hope to visit. By unspoken agreement, they took turns on watch, each a lonely sentinel posted against the encroaching dread.

1:12 A.M.

Kim sat cross-legged at the edge of the orchard, her back to the reassuring warmth of the farmhouse, her gaze fixed on the black maw of the forest. She had come here seeking the comfort of the earth, the steady, grounding pulse that had been her lifelong companion. But tonight, the earth was sick. Beneath the surface, where there should have been the slow, peaceful dreaming of roots and stone, there was a low, dissonant *hum*. It was an ancient, sorrowful vibration, the sound of something vast and heavy stirring in a sleep it was never meant to wake from.

She pressed her palms flat against the cool grass, closing her eyes and pushing her senses deeper. The hum grew louder in her mind, and with it came a fragmented whisper, a thought that felt like it was made of cold, compressed soil.

...so long buried... the stone groans... the root remembers the rot...

A chill that had nothing to do with the night air traced its way up her spine. A memory bloomed unwanted in her mind: her mother, frail and fading in a hospital bed, her eyes glassy with fever and foresight. She'd gripped Kim's hand, her voice a dry rasp of Mandarin. *"Beware what sleeps beneath the sweet fruit,"* she'd whispered. *"The deepest roots feed on the oldest sorrows."* Kim had dismissed it then as delirium. Now, it felt like a prophecy. She felt a presence below her, something of immense patience and immense grief, and for the first time in her life, she was afraid of the ground beneath her feet.

2:06 A.M.

Todd walked the southern fence line, a heavy lantern in one hand, a solid iron pry bar in the other. He felt the foolishness of it—a mortal man with a lump of metal standing guard against cosmic horrors. But his profound sense of uselessness had curdled into a stubborn, grim resolve. This was his family now. This was his watch.

He felt the change in the air before he saw it. A pocket of unnatural cold, a sudden silence in the already-silent night. He stopped, peering into the gloom. A flicker of movement at the edge of his vision. It wasn't an animal. It was a shape, tall and impossibly thin, a thing of shadow that seemed to melt back into the darkness of the woods the moment he turned his head. He held his breath, straining his eyes, but it was gone.

He continued his patrol, his heart thudding, telling himself it was just a trick of the eerie lunar light. Then he saw the cairns.

They were small, neat stacks of three flat stones, balanced impossibly on top of five fence posts in a row. They hadn't been there an hour ago. He approached cautiously, the iron pry bar held tight in his grip. He nudged the nearest cairn with the tip of the bar. It tumbled apart silently. Tucked inside the stones was a small, tightly wound lock of hair, gray and coarse, bound with a single strand of red thread. It looked disturbingly like his father's hair.

A wave of nausea and rage washed over him. This wasn't a random threat; it was a message. A claim. He took a piece of chalk from his pocket, his hand shaking. On the post where the cairn had been, he drew a symbol of his grandmother had taught him to scratch onto door frames—a spiral folded inward on itself, a folk charm to ward off the "hungry dark." He didn't know if it had any real power, but it was an act of defiance. It was his voice shouting back into the darkness. *Not here. Not this family. Not tonight.*

2:58 A.M.

In the barn, the generators powering the string of work lights flickered twice, then died, plunging the vast space into near-total blackness. Sam didn't flinch. She clicked on a red-lensed headlamp and continued to stare at the horrifying mathematics scrawled across a whiteboard. She had been running simulations, cross-referencing their combined magical stamina against the projected energy output of the nexus ritual. The conclusion was always the same.

They were going to fail.

Under the strain of a full-scale assault, their most powerful combined warding spell would hold for approximately twelve minutes before collapsing. Twelve minutes stood between them and the end of the world. A cold sweat traced its way down her temples. Her hands trembled. For all their knowledge, for all their power, they were just a handful of children with a book of matches standing against a tidal wave.

Her phone, sitting on the table beside her, vibrated once. A text from an unknown number. There was no message, only an attached image.

Her blood ran cold.

The photo was old, sepia-toned, and grainy, dated 1971 in the corner. It showed five people—four of them young, their faces bright with a defiant hope that broke her heart, and one older man with the weary eyes of a seasoned guardian. They were standing in their orchard in front of their spiral tree. But in the photo, each of their faces had been violently scratched out with black ink. Taped to the bottom of the old photograph was a small, typed message:

We tried. The door doesn't stay shut. Don't make our mistake. Run.

Sam stared at the image, at the ghost coven that had stood where they now stood, that had faced what they now faced. The message wasn't a warning. It was an epitaph sent across fifty years of silence.

3:37 A.M.

Katie stood barefoot in the center of the yard, her head tilted back, her eyes fixed on the diseased-looking moon. The pressure was a physical thing now, a force that made the air shimmer at the edges of her vision. She felt the Gate, not as a concept, but as a presence, a vast, sleeping entity whose dreams were beginning to bleed into their world. The whispers were back, the faint, psychic echoes of the other Katies from the other failed spirals, their voices tempting her from the corners of her mind.

There is a version where we survive, one whispered. *We just have to let Sean take the full burden. His light is stronger.*

There is a version where we join him, another hissed. *His power is enough for two. We could be gods.*

She squeezed her eyes shut, fighting to hold onto the single, solid thread of her own identity. *I am Katie Rose Alden,* she thought, the words a desperate mantra. *I am the weaver. I am the anchor.* She whispered the names of the lost from the 1971 photograph, names she didn't know but felt in her soul. She whispered Matthew's name, and Kim's, and Sam's, and Todd's. She whispered Sean. A roll call of the souls she would not allow the darkness to claim. Her vigil was not against a monster outside, but against the ghosts within.

4:11 A.M.

Sean's patrol was a slow, deliberate circle. He could feel the strain on their wards, not as sharp impacts, but as a steady, grinding pressure, like the slow squeeze of a giant's fist. He moved through the familiar landscape of his home, but everything was rendered alien and menacing by the coppery twilight of the eve of the eclipse.

When he reached the southern tree line, he stopped. His heart felt like it had turned to ice in his chest. The old scarecrow, his grandfather's scarecrow, had moved again. It had been assembled from old fence posts and dressed in his father's forgotten work clothes. For weeks, it had been a silent, stoic sentinel. But tonight, its straw-stuffed head was no longer facing the fields. It was tilted up, its empty gaze fixed directly on the window of Sean's bedroom.

He walked toward it, his hand gripping the rowan wood staff he now carried. The air around the scarecrow was freezing. At the base of its post, arranged in a small, perfect circle, five candles burned. There was no smoke, and their flames did not flicker; each wick held a single, steady point of cold, blue light. He felt the magic coming off them—ancient, patient, and utterly tireless. These candles had not been lit tonight. They felt as if they had been burning for centuries.

And in their cold, magical light, he saw something he had never noticed before. Carved into the weathered wood of the central post, almost invisible with age, were five names. The last one was "Thomas Murphy." Above it was "Daniel Murphy." Above that, "Liam." The names of his father, his grandfather, his ancestors. There was a space at the bottom of the list, a blank stretch of wood waiting.

This wasn't just a scarecrow. It was a monument. A generational marker of the watch. And it was telling him that his time had come.

He didn't touch the candles. He simply whispered into the oppressive silence, "I understand."

A sudden, warm breeze, a stark contrast to the night's chill, rustled the straw of the scarecrow, a fleeting, gentle caress like a hand on his shoulder. *A final blessing from a long line of ghosts.*

As the first sickly light of the eclipse began to stain the eastern horizon, the coven was drawn from their lonely vigils by a new, impossible sight. In the orchard, the ancient spiral tree, which should have been dormant, had burst into bloom. Dozens of perfect, paper-white blossoms unfolded in the eerie twilight, their petals glowing with a faint, internal luminescence. And from them, a scent drifted on the still air—not of flowers, but of iron and roses. The smell of blood and magic.

They met at the edge of the orchard, their faces pale and drawn in the ghostly light. No words were needed. In the haunted eyes of his friends, Sean saw the reflection of his own sleepless night. They had each faced their own private horror and had each been given their own personal omen of the battle to come. They were terrified. They were exhausted. But they were together. And as the black disk of the moon began to kiss the edge of the sun, they stood as one, a small, fragile, and unbroken line against the coming dark.

Chapter 24: The Weeping Gate

The ritual began at the precise moment the sun vanished. They gathered in the cavernous upper loft of the barn, the air thick with the scent of beeswax and cold iron. A circle had been drawn on the floor in powdered silver and salt, intricate and shimmering in the eerie twilight of the eclipse. This was not a spell they understood; it was a desperate act of translation, pieced together from a scorched fragment of a Gatekeeper text that spoke of "walking the unseen path" and "mapping the world's sorrow."

Sean and Katie lay on woven mats at the center of the circle. The rest of the coven formed a living wall around them, their faces pale and grim in the half-light. This was their most dangerous gambit yet. They would send their consciousness out from their bodies, a tethered projection to scout the true nature of the ritual at the nexus. The text warned that the only anchor that could pull two souls back from such a journey was an unbroken, trusted link between them.

"Remember what I told you," Sam instructed, her voice low and tense as she anointed their foreheads with a pungent oil of crushed moonstone and mugwort. "No matter what you see, you are tethered to each other. Do not let go of that connection. It's your only way home."

Todd stepped forward, his face a mask of fear and resolve. He placed a heavy, cold iron chisel on Sean's forehead and another on Katie's. "The old tales say iron holds a soul to the earth," he whispered, his voice rough. "A mundane anchor. Just in case."

Sean reached out, his fingers finding Katie's. Her hand was cold, but her grip was firm. He squeezed once. *I'm here.*

She squeezed back. *Always.*

The coven began the chant, their voices weaving together into a low, resonant hum. Sean and Katie closed their eyes, and together, they leaped into the void.

The transition was not a gentle drift. It was a violent, tearing agony, a feeling of being ripped from the warm, familiar confines of flesh and bone and hurled into a screaming tempest. Their senses dissolved.

They were bombarded with a chaotic flood of color, sound, and feeling—the terror of a thousand forgotten battles, the joy of a million first kisses, the endless, patient silence of stone. It was the raw, untamed chaos of the Astral Plane, the psychic backstage of the world, and it threatened to shred their individual consciousnesses into meaningless confetti.

The only thing that kept Sean from dissolving was Katie. He clung to the feeling of her mind, a brilliant, turquoise star in the howling storm of everything. She, in turn, anchored herself to his steady, golden light. They were two swimmers in an infinite, raging ocean, holding fast to a single, shared lifeline.

Slowly, the chaos began to resolve. Their new, non-physical eyes opened, and they found themselves standing on a floor of shifting, crystalline fractals that seemed to be made of frozen thought. The sky above was not a sky, but a swirling, bruising vortex of deep violet and black, alive with the silent, crackling lightning of raw emotion. This was the Veilspace. And it felt profoundly, terrifyingly wrong. It was a realm that should have been neutral, but it felt claimed, tainted, like a holy place that had been desecrated.

"We have to find a stable point," Katie's thought echoed in his mind, clear and sharp despite the psychic din. "The scroll mentioned a 'scryer's perch.'"

They began to move, not by walking, but by an act of shared will, gliding over the crystalline ground. As they did, the map began to build itself around them. It was not a chart, but a living landscape of power. They saw the great ley lines not as lines, but as roaring, incandescent rivers of energy flowing across the globe.

And then they saw the Gate.

It was not a door or a portal. It was a wound. A vast, weeping scar of sickly, purple-black light that stretched from horizon to horizon, weeping a slow, steady torrent of dark energy into the Veilspace. Five other, smaller wounds—the other nexus points across the globe—pulsed in sympathetic agony, connected to the main scar by fraying threads of light.

"It's not a Gate to let things *in*," Sean realized, his astral form flickering with horror. "It's a wound to let reality *out*."

As they stared, they felt a new sensation: a terrifying, silent pull. It was a psychic vacuum, an absolute zero of cold and silence that tugged at the very edges of their souls. They looked down and saw it, near the center of the great scar: a second, smaller gate, but this one was inverted, a whirlpool of absolute blackness that was not weeping but *drinking*. It was a drain, siphoning the life and energy of their world into some unseen abyss.

Then they saw the guardians.

There were five of them, standing in a silent, solemn circle around the inverted gate. They were tall, robed figures, but their forms were static, like statues carved from sorrow. They were the dead Gatekeepers from a forgotten age. Spirals were carved into the vellum-like skin of their hands, glowing with a faint, resentful red light. They weren't looking at the Gate. They were facing *away* from it, their backs to the horror, their spectral hands outstretched as if in the midst of casting a final, desperate spell of containment. They were a dam made of souls, and they were failing.

"They tried to close it," Katie whispered in his mind, her thoughts trembling with awe and pity. "They failed... and they became its eternal jailers."

As if their presence had disturbed the ancient, static tableau, one of the robed figures began to turn. Its movement was stiff, unnatural, a thing of immense, grinding effort. It turned its head, revealing a face that was a smooth, featureless canvas of flesh, save for a single, empty eye socket that burned with a glyph of red light.

It fixed its gaze on them, and a voice entered their minds. It was not a voice, but a fractured, psychic echo, full of the static of ages and an unbearable, unending pain.

...walk the boundary... the hinge turns... the chain loosens...

The dead guardian raised a hand, and the Veilspace convulsed. The crystalline floor cracked, and from the fissures, tendrils of black vapor erupted—sentient memories of the guardian's own failure. Sean and Katie were assaulted with a vision: they saw the guardian alive, his face contorted in a scream of effort. They saw the Gate tear open completely, not to a place of monsters, but to a sky filled with wrong-angled stars and dead, black suns—the absolute nothingness of the void. They felt the guardian's final, soul-shattering despair as his magic failed and he was frozen into this eternal vigil.

The psychic echo of the guardian reached for them, not to harm them, but to pull them into its eternal, looping prison of failure. *...witness the sorrow... hold the line...*

"It's going to take us!" Sean screamed in their shared mind. "It thinks we're here to relieve the watch! We have to go back! Now!"

He focused on the single, most powerful anchor he had: the feeling of Katie's hand in his, not on this plane, but back in the barn. The mundane, physical reality of it. Together, they pulled. The Veilspace resisted, the pull of the inverted gate and the sorrow of the guardian trying to hold them fast. They fought against it, their combined will a desperate, clawing struggle back toward the land of the living.

With a final, violent wrench, the world snapped back into place.

They fell back into their bodies with a gasp, the transition an agony of reentry. They were shivering uncontrollably, the psychic cold of the Veilspace still clinging to them like a shroud. Sean sat up, his heart hammering, and looked at Katie. She was pale, a single tear tracing a path from her closed eye.

The rest of the coven rushed forward, their faces etched with worry. "What did you see?" Sam asked, her voice urgent.

Sean looked at Katie, and she looked at him. The truth of what they had witnessed settled between them, a shared burden of horrifying clarity. They now understood the true nature of the threat. The Malevolent Spirit wasn't trying to open a door for an army of monsters. That was a tragedy on a scale they could have understood. The truth was infinitely worse.

He looked at the frightened, hopeful faces of his friends.

"We were wrong," Sean said, his voice a hoarse, broken whisper. "All this time, we thought our job was to be Gatekeepers. To keep the door locked."

He took Katie's hand, his grip a lifeline. His eyes were dark with the reflection of the empty, starless sky he had just witnessed.

"But the Gate isn't a door to another place," he said, the terrible truth falling like a death sentence into the quiet of the barn. "It's a wound. And it's bleeding our world away into nothing. We're not here to keep it closed."

He met Katie's terrified gaze, and she finished his thought, her voice barely audible.

"We're here to figure out how to cauterize it before the entire world bleeds out."

Chapter 25: The Eve of Battle

The sun rose on the day of the eclipse, but it was a reluctant, anemic light. A strange, coppery haze clung to the horizon, filtering the dawn through a lens of deep unease. The air over the Murphy farm was unnaturally still, holding its breath. The usual morning chorus of birds was absent, the silence in the trees a profound and unsettling omen. The world itself seemed to know that this was a day when the rules would be broken and when the veil between worlds would be stretched to its breaking point.

Inside the farmhouse, a similar, solemn stillness reigned. The coven was gathered in the kitchen, but no one was eating. A plate of scrambled eggs grew cold on the table, a pot of coffee untouched. They sat in their familiar spots, a small band of teenage soldiers on the morning of a battle they couldn't possibly be prepared for, each lost in their own private universe of fear and resolve. The frantic energy of the past weeks had burned away, leaving behind this: the quiet, terrifying clarity of the final hours.

Sean looked at their faces, these friends who had become his family, and his heart ached with a love so fierce it was almost painful. He saw Kim, her hands clasped tightly in her lap, her knuckles white. He saw Matthew, for once not joking, his gaze fixed on some distant point beyond the kitchen window, his jaw tight. He saw Sam, her expression a mask of calm professionalism that didn't quite reach her haunted, sea-green eyes. And he saw Katie, who stared into her empty mug as if the fate of the universe could be read in the dregs; her face was pale, but her spirit was a defiant, unwavering flame that he could feel even across the room. He was their leader. He was responsible for every one of them. The thought was a crushing weight.

After the pretense of breakfast was abandoned, they moved to the barn. The vast, shadowy space had been transformed from a workplace into a makeshift armory. The scent of hay and old leather was now mingled with the sharp, clean smells of magical reagents: crushed silver, dried nightshade, and purifying salts.

They geared up in a ritualistic silence, each movement deliberate and imbued with a significance that transcended the physical. Katie carefully inspected a set of small, intricately woven silver charms, each one designed to emit a low-frequency psychic hum to disrupt illusions. Her fingers, normally so deft, trembled almost imperceptibly as she fastened the last one to her belt. Matthew sat on a hay bale, a whetstone in one hand and a flat, slate-gray throwing stone in the other. He sharpened the edges of the runic stone, then pricked his thumb with a small knife, smearing a single drop of his own blood over the central rune of force, binding it to his will. Kim, quiet and centered, was braiding living, supple vines into thick bracelets for each of them, whispering words of grounding and healing into the living wood.

Sean moved between them, his presence a quiet, steadying force. He offered a small nod to Matthew, placed a reassuring hand on Kim's shoulder. He was their leader, but in these final moments, he felt more like a brother, wanting only to ease their fear. He watched Sam as she stood by the far wall, her eyes closed, her lips moving in a silent, continuous chant. She wasn't reviewing a spell; she was wrapping her mind in a protective sheath of ancient words, a mental armor against the psychic horrors to come. They were as ready as they would ever be.

Sean stepped out of the barn's cool dimness and into the strange, coppery light of the morning, needing a moment alone. He found his uncle on the front porch, leaning against a post, a thermos in his hand, looking out at the sky. He had been waiting.

"Sky looks angry," Todd said, his voice low. He didn't look at Sean, just kept his gaze fixed on the hazy, unnaturally colored clouds. He unscrewed the cap of the thermos and poured a dark, steaming liquid into it. "Coffee. Your grandfather used to do this before a big storm was due. Just sit out here and watch the sky, as if he could face it down with a stubborn enough glare."

Sean took the offered cup, the warmth a small comfort against the chill that had settled deep in his bones. "He knew this was coming, didn't he? Not just a storm. This."

Todd finally turned to look at him, and Sean was struck again by the profound sadness in his uncle's eyes. It was the sorrow of a man looking at a path he himself had refused to walk. "I think he felt it," Todd said. "In his bones. In the land. That's something I never understood when I was younger. I thought his magic was all in the spells and the books in the cave. But I was wrong."

He gestured with his chin towards the sprawling fields. "Your grandfather's greatest power wasn't in the incantations he knew. It was on this farm. Every fence post he drove, every seed he planted, every drop of sweat he poured into this soil... it was a spell. A decades-long ritual of love and protection. He didn't just live on this land; he became a part of it. He drew his strength *from* it, Sean, not just from the ether. It was his anchor, his battery, his heart."

Sean looked out at the farm, and for the first time, he saw it as his uncle did not just as fields and buildings, but as a vast, living reservoir of his family's love and will, a legacy of power written into the very earth.

"The Spirit... this Finch creature... it's a parasite," Todd continued his voice barely a whisper. "It thinks power is about consumption, about control, about tearing things down to build its machine. That's its mistake. That kind of power is hollow. It has no roots. Real power, the kind that lasts, the kind your grandfather had... it isn't about what you can break. It's about what you refuse to let be broken. Inside yourself."

He met Sean's eyes, his gaze intense and full of desperate, urgent wisdom. "When you're out there, fighting... don't just fight the monster. That's what it wants. It wants a brawl. Don't give it to it. You fight *for* this." He swept his hand out again, indicating the house, the barn, the fields, and the quiet memory of a life well lived. "You fight for Katie. For your friends. For him." He nodded towards the small, private cemetery at the edge of the property where Tom now rested. "You fill your mind with that, and you let the magic flow. It will know the difference. Believe me."

It was the most he had ever heard his uncle say about magic, and it wasn't a spell or a secret weapon, but a perspective. A key. He was giving Sean the only guidance a man who had run from his own power could: a map of the heart.

Sean nodded, the lump in his throat too thick for words. He handed the empty cup back to his uncle, and they shared a final, silent look of understanding.

He found Katie in their clearing by the creek. The small, secluded spot where they had first formed their coven, where he had fallen in love with her a hundred times over. She was sitting on the grass, skipping small, smooth stones across the water's surface, each one leaving a trail of perfect, concentric rings that spread out until they vanished. She didn't look up when he approached, but he knew she'd felt him coming. After Sean's declaration about taking a day at the coast, they sat in silence for a moment, each lost in the bittersweet fantasy of a normal future.

"Tell me more," Katie whispered. "About that day. I need to see it."

Sean pulled her closer, resting his chin on top of her head. "We'll leave early, before sunrise. Drive with the windows down, singing along to whatever's on the radio—probably badly."

"Speak for yourself. I have a lovely singing voice."

"You really don't," he said affectionately. "But I love it anyway. We'll stop at that little diner in Georgetown, the one with the pancakes the size of plates."

"The one where the waitress calls everyone 'honey' and knows your order before you sit down?"

"That's the one. Then we'll drive all the way to Myrtle Beach, but not the touristy part. That little stretch of sand near Pawleys Island where it's just dunes and wild grass and ocean."

Katie closed her eyes, letting herself see it. "What will we do there?"

"Nothing," Sean said firmly. "Absolutely nothing productive. We'll swim until we're exhausted. Build the world's most pathetic sandcastle because neither of us actually knows how. Read books—real books, not spell books. Take a nap in the sun."

"I'll get sunburned," Katie murmured. "I always do."

"I'll put sunscreen on your back. Make sure to get all the spots you can't reach." His voice dropped lower. "Might take a while. Have to be thorough."

She laughed softly, sadly. "And dinner?"

"That little shack that sells the best shrimp and grits you've ever had. We'll eat outside, watch the sunset. Get ice cream from the place where it's made fresh. Walk on the beach in the dark, look for ghost crabs."

"Dance," Katie added. "On the beach, no music, just the sound of the waves."

"Yes," Sean agreed. "Dance until we're dizzy, then collapse in the sand and look at the stars. Talk about everything and nothing."

"Make plans," Katie said. "Real ones. About the future. About kids with your eyes and my stubbornness."

"God help us," Sean laughed, but it was wet with unshed tears. "They'll be terrible. Powerful and terrible."

"The best kind," Katie agreed.

They were both crying now, silent tears for a day that might never come. But somehow, speaking it aloud made it real and gave them something concrete to fight for beyond abstract concepts of duty and protection.

"Sean," Katie said suddenly, pulling back to look at him. "I need you to promise me something."

"Anything."

"If something happens to me—"

"Katie, no—"

"Listen." She pressed her fingers to his lips. "If something happens to me, promise you'll still go. Take that day. Live that life. Find someone—"

"Stop." He caught her hand, his eyes fierce. "There is no 'someone else.' There's you. There's only ever been you. If we don't both make it through this, then that day stays a dream. I won't live it without you."

"That's not fair," she whispered.

"None of this is fair." He cupped her face, thumbs brushing away her tears. "But it's true. You're not just my girlfriend, Katie. You're my other half. My magic doesn't work right without yours. My life doesn't work right without you in it."

"Then we both have to survive," she said fiercely. "No heroic sacrifices. No noble gestures. We fight smart, we fight together, and we both walk away."

"Deal," Sean said, though they both knew it was a promise they might not be able to keep.

They stayed by the creek until the last of the daylight faded, holding each other and memorizing the feeling of being young, in love, and alive. Tomorrow would bring battles, choices, and prices to be paid.

But tonight, they had this: the sound of water over stones, the feel of each other's heartbeats, and a dream of a perfect day that would give them strength for all the dark ones ahead.

When they finally walked back to the farmhouse, hand in hand, the first stars were appearing overhead. Katie stopped suddenly, tugging Sean to a halt.

"What?" he asked.

"I just... I want to remember this moment. Right here. The way the light from the house looks so warm. The way your hand feels in mine. The sound of the crickets. All of it." She looked up at him. "Whatever happens tomorrow, I want to remember that tonight, we were happy."

Sean pulled her close, pressing a kiss to her forehead. "We'll have a thousand more moments like this," he promised. "Tomorrow is just another battle. We've won before. We'll win again."

But as they resumed walking, both felt the weight of unspoken truth—that tomorrow's battle would be unlike any they'd faced before. That love, no matter how strong, might not be enough to save them both.

Still, they walked toward the warm light of home together, and for now, that was everything.

He sat beside her, the quiet of the clearing a fragile bubble against the looming dread of the day. The air was getting cooler, the light dimmer, as the moon began its inexorable transit.

"After this is over," Sean said, his voice soft, breaking the silence.

Katie kept her eyes on the water. "Don't."

"I have to," he insisted gently. "After this is over, we're going to take a day. A whole day. No magic, no chores, no coven business."

She finally turned to look at him, a single tear tracing a path through the light dust on her cheek. "And do what?" she whispered.

"Nothing," he said, a small, sad smile touching his lips. "We'll drive to the coast. We'll sit on the sand and feel the warmth of the sun. We'll eat fried shrimp from a paper basket. We'll just... be. Like normal people."

The simple, beautiful image of it was so painful, so impossibly distant, that it made her catch her breath in a sob. She launched herself into his arms, burying her face in his neck, holding onto him with desperate strength, as if she could physically keep him tethered to this world, to her.

"I love you, Sean Murphy," she murmured into his skin, her voice muffled and thick with tears. "Don't you forget that? No matter what happens out there."

He held her just as tightly, his eyes squeezed shut against the image of a future without her in it. He could feel the silver streak at his temple, a cold reminder of the price he had already paid and a chilling foreshadowing of the price still to be demanded. "There is no me without you," he whispered back, the words a sacred, unbreakable vow. "So you'd better be there when I get back."

She pulled away enough to look him in the eye, her expression one of fierce, heartbreaking love. "You come back," she ordered, her voice regaining a sliver of its usual fire. "That's not a request. It's a command from your partner in all things. You come back to me."

He leaned in and kissed her, a deep, lingering kiss that was filled with the terror of goodbye and the desperate promise of return. It was a kiss that sealed their past and gambled everything on their future.

When they returned to the farm, the rest of the coven was assembled in the yard. The sky had darkened to a deep, bruised twilight, though it was only mid-morning. The temperature had dropped, and the world was bathed in a strange, ethereal silver glow. The eclipse had begun.

They stood together, a small, determined unit armed with handmade charms and ancient knowledge. They exchanged final looks, quiet nods of encouragement and friendship. No more words were needed.

Uncle Todd stood on the porch, a solitary figure watching over them, his face a mask of grief and pride. He held up a single hand, a gesture of farewell and blessing.

Sean took Katie's hand, his fingers lacing through hers, offering a familiar and grounding comfort. He looked at the faces of his coven, his friends, his family. He felt the silent, heavy weight of the Wayfinder in his pocket. He gave a single, sharp nod.

Together, they turned away from the safety of the farmhouse and began their silent march across the fields, heading toward the swamp. Toward the nexus. Toward the battle that would decide everything. The light was failing; the air was cold, and the storm was finally upon them.

Chapter 26: The Ritual Begins

The world had gone silent. It was the first thing Sean noticed as they slipped through the tangled, overgrown perimeter of the Aethelgard Institute property. Not quiet, but silent—a complete absence of sound that felt like a physical weight pressing against his eardrums. The ceaseless thrum of the swamp's nightlife —the bellowing frogs, the chirping insects, the rustle of unseen things in the undergrowth —had been completely erased, smothered by an oppressive, magical pressure that made breathing feel like work.

Even the air itself seemed wrong. It was thick and viscous, clinging to their skin like invisible syrup, carrying the metallic taste of ozone and something else—something that reminded Sean of the smell of a house fire, acrid and choking. The very atmosphere felt hostile to life, as if the approaching ritual was poisoning the world at a molecular level.

They moved like ghosts through the gnarled cypress and black gum trees, their feet making no sound on the damp, peaty earth. The eclipse was well underway now, the sun reduced to a rapidly shrinking crescent that cast the world in an eerie, bruised twilight. The light that remained was wrong—not the warm gold of natural sunlight, but a cold, silver radiance that leached all natural color from the landscape, leaving only stark, skeletal shapes and deep, menacing shadows that seemed to move independently of their sources.

Every member of the coven had their shields up, shimmering barriers of personal magic that did little to ward off the profound sense of dread that permeated the air. It was like walking through the dreams of something vast and malevolent. In this place, the normal rules of reality had been suspended in favor of something older and more terrible.

Sean was in the lead, the broken Wayfinder in his pocket a cold, dead weight against his leg. He didn't need it now—every fiber of his being, every nerve ending, was screaming that he was getting closer to the source of the world's sickness. His senses were pushed out to their absolute limit, not in a powerful wave but in a delicate, spider-like web, feeling for the magical tripwires he knew would be laid in their path.

Behind him, he could feel Katie's presence, a steady, familiar warmth in the encroaching cold. Their minds were linked by more than just their magical bond now—the astral fusion had left them permanently connected, their thoughts flowing together like streams joining a river. Her fear was his fear, her determination his strength.

Anything? she sent, her thought a tight beam of focus that cut through the psychic static filling the air.

Not yet, he replied, pausing to examine a stand of dead trees that looked too perfectly arranged to be natural. *The wards feel... distant. Concentrated. He's pulled all his defensive energy back to the center. He's so focused on the ritual that he's left the perimeter almost undefended.*

It was a tactical mistake born of arrogance, the kind of oversight that came from believing yourself so far above your enemies that their existence barely registered. Sean had seen it before in the Malevolent Spirit's approach. This ancient, cosmic intelligence viewed human opposition as barely worth acknowledging.

Or it's a trap, Katie warned, her tactical mind immediately grasping the implications. *He could be drawing us in, making us think we have the advantage.*

Maybe, Sean acknowledged. *But we don't have a choice. This is our only window.*

They finally reached the edge of the tree line, crouching low behind the broad, moss-covered trunk of a fallen oak. Sean peered through a curtain of Spanish moss, and the breath caught in his throat. He motioned for the others, and one by one, they joined him, their faces paling as they took in the scene before them.

The nexus was a perfect, circular clearing, a hundred yards across, carved out of the ancient swampland with surgical precision. But this wasn't the work of bulldozers and chainsaws—the trees hadn't been cut down so much as convinced to leave, their absence leaving no stumps or debris, just smooth, dark earth that looked like it had never known the touch of growing things.

The natural beauty of the place had been utterly desecrated, replaced by a terrifying, alien geometry that hurt to look at directly. The ground itself was inscribed with a massive, complex glyph that seemed to exist in more dimensions than the human eye could process. The lines of the symbol pulsed with a sickening, purple-black light that cast no shadows but seemed to drain illumination from everything around it, creating pockets of absolute darkness that twisted and writhed like living things.

The design was simultaneously beautiful and horrifying, it's impossible angles and spiraling, nested patterns suggesting a mathematics that operated according to rules that had never applied to Earth. Looking at it directly caused a peculiar form of vertigo, as if the symbol was trying to convince the observer's brain that up was down, that straight lines could curve back on themselves, that three-dimensional space was just a comforting illusion.

At key intersection points along the glyph, a dozen metallic pillars had been driven deep into the earth. They towered twenty feet into the air, their surfaces made of a metal that seemed to absorb light rather than reflect it. The material was unlike anything Sean had ever seen—not quite black, not quite silver, but something that existed in the spaces between colors. Each pillar hummed with a low, resonant thrum that he could feel in his bones, in his teeth, in the hollow spaces of his skull. The sound was deeply unsettling, like the groaning of some vast machine struggling to contain forces beyond its design.

These were the conduits, the arcane machinery that was drawing raw power from the planet's ley lines and refining it for the ritual. As Sean watched, he could see streams of energy flowing between them—not visible light, but something his magical senses could perceive, like heat shimmers made of pure, concentrated malevolence.

And then there were the followers.

Perhaps two dozen men and women stood at precise intervals around the great glyph, their bodies positioned according to some arcane formula that turned them into components of a vast, living circuit. They were dressed in simple, drab gray robes that seemed to drink the available light, making them appear as vague, shadowy figures even in the eclipse's wan illumination.

But it was their faces that made Sean's blood run cold. They weren't the wild-eyed fanatics he had half-expected, driven mad by exposure to cosmic truths. Instead, they stood perfectly still, their heads bowed, their expressions utterly vacant. Their eyes were open but seeing nothing, their mouths slightly ajar, their breathing so shallow it was barely perceptible.

They were living batteries, their life forces being gently and inexorably siphoned to refine the raw energy of the ley lines into a form the Spirit could use. It was a quiet, passive horror that was far more chilling than any frantic ceremony could have been. These people—teachers, office workers, parents, grandparents—had been reduced to components in a machine, their individuality erased, their souls slowly consumed to fuel an apocalypse.

"My God," Matthew whispered, his voice barely audible even in the complete silence. "They're just... empty."

At the absolute center of it all, on a raised dais of black stone that seemed to have been carved from a single, massive piece of obsidian, stood Alistair Finch. Even at this distance, his presence was overwhelming, a gravity well of malevolent power that seemed to bend space around him. He stood with his arms raised to the eclipsing sun, his head tilted back, his eyes closed in an expression of rapturous concentration.

The man who had once been a charismatic billionaire was gone, replaced by something that wore his face like an ill-fitting mask. The Spirit's true nature was becoming visible now that the ritual was underway—Finch's skin had taken on a waxy, translucent quality, and dark veins were visible beneath the surface, pulsing with the same purple-black energy that powered the glyph. His perfectly styled hair had turned white as bone, and when he opened his mouth to continue his chanting, his teeth were sharp as razors.

The air around him shimmered with heat distortion, but Sean knew it wasn't temperature causing the effect. It was the sheer density of magical energy, reality itself straining under the weight of forces it was never meant to contain. Above Finch's head, the air was beginning to tear, hairline cracks appearing in the fabric of space itself.

"The portals," Katie breathed, pointing upward.

Sean followed her gaze and felt his heart sink. High above the clearing, barely visible against the dark sky, thirteen translucent, wavering shapes were beginning to form. They looked like wounds in the air, ragged tears that revealed glimpses of other places, other realities. Through one, Sean caught a flash of a landscape of rust-colored dust under a bloated, crimson sun. Another showed a writhing mass of organic matter that might have been vegetation if plants could scream. A third revealed only swirling chaos, a maelstrom of impossible colors that made his eyes water just to glimpse.

These were the prison realms of the other Malevolent Spirits, the cosmic horrors that had been banished eons ago by the first Gatekeepers. And now, powered by the energy being drawn from Earth's own life force, those prisons were beginning to weaken. Soon, the ancient locks would fail completely, and thirteen cosmic nightmares would be free to remake reality according to their own twisted desires.

The sight of the forming portals broke their paralysis. The existential terror was incinerated by a hot, desperate surge of adrenaline. They had found the ritual, confirmed their worst fears, and now they had to act. There was no more time for planning, no more room for doubt. The fate of every living thing on Earth hung in the balance, and a small group of teenage witches and warlocks were the only ones who could tip the scales.

Sean looked at Katie, memorizing her face in the eerie light of the eclipse. In her eyes, he saw his own love and fear reflected back at him, along with a fierce determination that had never wavered, not even in their darkest moments. It was a final, silent exchange of promises—to fight with everything they had, to protect each other as much as possible, and to make their sacrifice count if the worst came to pass.

"Everyone ready?" he whispered, though the words were barely necessary. They all knew what came next.

The coven spread out along the tree line, taking their assigned positions. This wasn't a frontal assault—that would be suicide against an enemy of this magnitude. Instead, they would strike simultaneously at multiple points, disrupting the delicate balance of the ritual before Finch could adapt to their presence.

Sean felt the familiar weight of leadership settle on his shoulders, but it no longer felt crushing. These weren't just his friends or his followers—they were his family, bound together by shared trials and unbreakable love. Whatever happened in the next few minutes, they would face it together.

The last sliver of the sun disappeared behind the moon's dark bulk, and the world was plunged into the otherworldly twilight of totality. The sun's corona blazed around the lunar disc like a crown of fire, casting everything in silver and shadow. The temperature dropped ten degrees in as many seconds, and the very air seemed to crystallize with potential energy.

Above the clearing, the thirteen portals flared to life, their ragged edges beginning to stabilize as the ritual reached its critical phase. Through the gaps in reality, Sean could see movement—vast, impossible shapes pressing against the weakening barriers, eager to break through into a universe that had been denied to them for millennia.

Alistair Finch's chanting reached a crescendo; his voice was no longer remotely human, but a harmony of frequencies that made the ground itself vibrate. The followers swayed in unison, their life force being drawn out of them in visible streams of light that flowed toward the central dais.

It was now or never.

Sean gave the signal—not a gesture or a word, but a pulse of pure intention that flowed through their mental link to every member of the coven. As one, they exploded from the cover of the trees, their magic blazing to life as they launched their desperate, coordinated assault.

The final battle for the soul of the world had begun.

The moment their feet crossed the boundary of the great glyph, reality convulsed around them. The alien geometry of the symbol responded to their presence like an immune system detecting infection, its lines flaring with blinding intensity as defensive subroutines activated. The air became thick as honey, each step forward requiring tremendous effort as the ritual's accumulated power pressed down on them like the weight of an ocean.

But they had trained for this. Sean's coven moved with practiced precision, their individual abilities combining into something greater than the sum of its parts. Matthew's kinetic blasts struck the nearest conduit pillar, sending ripples of disruption through the energy network. Kim's connection to the earth allowed her to sense the ley lines beneath their feet, guiding the others away from the most dangerous convergence points. Sam's encyclopedic knowledge of occult lore let her identify the ritual's weak points, the places where a precisely applied counterspell could cause maximum disruption.

And Katie—brilliant, tactical Katie—wove it all together, her mind processing the chaos of battle and finding the patterns, the opportunities, the split-second decisions that would mean the difference between victory and annihilation.

They had one chance to stop the end of the world. The eclipse was reaching its peak, the portals were stabilizing, and somewhere in the distance, ancient horrors were stirring from their eons-long slumber.

But Sean Murphy and his coven had not come this far to fail. They had lost too much, sacrificed too much, loved too much to let darkness win. As they charged across the cursed ground toward their impossible destiny, they carried with them the hopes of everyone they had sworn to protect—and the memory of a stubborn old farmer who had taught them that the greatest magic of all was refusing to give up, even when all hope seemed lost.

The war for reality itself had begun, and the guardians were ready to pay whatever price victory demanded.

Chapter 27: The Siege of Souls

The moment their feet crossed the threshold of the great, pulsing glyph, the world dissolved into a maelstrom of ordered chaos. The air, already thick with a pressure that felt like being at the bottom of a deep ocean, grew dense enough to taste—a bitter, metallic tang of ozone and raw, untamed magic. Above them, the sun was a black hole punched in the sky, its corona a wrathful, shimmering crown of pale green fire that cast no warmth, only an eerie, spectral light that made a mockery of shadows.

"Now!" Sean's command was not a shout but a sharp, telepathic crack of a whip in the minds of his coven.

They split, their practiced movements a stark contrast to the terrifying alienness of their surroundings. There was no time for fear, only for action. The plan was their only prayer, a desperate piece of sheet music in the face of a hurricane.

Sean watched as Matthew and Kim veered west, their faces set in grim, mask-like expressions of concentration. Matthew, a living engine of kinetic force, began hurling shimmering discs of pure power at the nearest humming, metallic pillar. The impacts didn't create explosions but deep, dissonant *thuds* that sent shuddering vibrations through the very ground. He wasn't trying to destroy the conduits; he was trying to knock them out of tune, to disrupt the harmonic frequency of the ritual.

Beside him, Kim, a whirlwind of natural power, slammed her palms onto the corrupted earth. The ground groaned in protest. Thick, thorny vines, black as night and covered in vicious-looking barbs, erupted from the soil. They did not attack, but grew with an explosive, unnatural speed, wrapping themselves around the base of the pillars, their thorns digging into the strange, dark metal, trying to choke the flow of power and bleed the poison of the ley lines harmlessly back into the earth.

On the opposite flank, Katie led her team—Sam and two of the younger witches—in the most delicate and crucial part of the initial assault. They moved towards the first line of enthralled followers, those still, silent figures who stood like statues in a forgotten, evil garden. Katie's hands wove intricate patterns in the air, her magic a soft, turquoise light, a stark contrast to the glyph's violent, purple hue. She wasn't casting a weapon but a wave of resonance —a complex spell of awakening designed not to shock the followers out of their trance but to gently remind their souls of what they had forgotten.

Remember sunlight, her magic whispered into their vacant minds. *Remember laughter. Remember the warmth of a loving hand. Remember who you are.*

Sean could feel the effect, a subtle shift in the oppressive atmosphere. The flow of energy from the followers to the central vortex faltered, flickering like a faulty lightbulb. One of the men stumbled, his head twitching. A woman's blank face spasmed, a single tear tracing a path down her cheek. Above them, one of the thirteen shimmering portals wavered, its connection to the ritual weakening.

It was working. For a breathtaking, miraculous second, Sean allowed himself a flicker of hope.

And that was when Alistair Finch noticed them.

He didn't turn. He didn't stop his guttural, world-breaking chant. But his head tilted a gesture of mild annoyance, like a man bothered by a buzzing fly. He lifted his left hand, the one not raised to the black sun, and made a casual, almost lazy, flicking motion in their direction.

The glyph beneath their feet answered him.

The pulsing purple lines erupted. They weren't just lines of light anymore; they became solid, lashing tendrils of pure, negative energy, cracking like whips of solidified darkness. One snaked towards Matthew, who threw up a kinetic shield just in time, the impact hurling him back several feet, his shield shattering into a thousand shimmering fragments.

"Scatter!" Sean roared, the command ripping from his throat.

The battlefield devolved into a desperate dance of survival. The coven broke formation, dodging the lashing, intelligent tendrils of dark magic. The ground itself had become their enemy. Sam shouted a sharp, ancient word of banishment, and a tendril that was about to strike Kim recoiled as if burned, but another immediately took its place.

They were being herded, separated, their coordinated assault broken into a series of frantic, individual skirmishes for survival. Sean could feel the Spirit's cold, analytical amusement. This was a game to it. A test.

Then, the game changed again.

Finch's chant deepened, and he pointed a single, imperious finger at his en-thralled followers. The flicker of confusion in their eyes vanished, replaced by the same glowing, malevolent purple as the glyph. Their heads snapped up in unison, and they began to move.

They did not shamble or stumble like mindless zombies. They moved with a fluid, terrifying grace, their bodies imbued with an unnatural speed and strength. Their faces remained blank, their minds still prisons, but their bodies were now weapons, puppets in the hands of a master who felt nothing for them but con-temptuous utility.

They converged on the coven.

The battle became a horrifying, chaotic melee. Sean found himself face-to-face with a woman who couldn't have been older than twenty, her movements faster than any human had a right to be. He dodged her wild, clawing attack, the wind of it whistling past his ear. He couldn't strike back, not really. This wasn't the enemy; it was an innocent woman in a cage of dark magic.

"Katie, the followers! We have to stop them without hurting them!" he sent telepathically, his mind reeling.

I know! Her thought was a frantic cry. *I'm trying!*

He could see her across the clearing, a shimmering bubble of protective energy around her and one of the younger witches, two of the enthralled pounding on its surface, their fists striking with the force of sledgehammers. Cracks were beginning to form in her shield.

The two-front war was overwhelming them. While they were occupied with the puppets, the dark tendrils of the glyph continued their relentless assault. Sean felt a searing pain as one of the whips caught his leg, burning through his jeans and leaving a smoking, purple-black line on his skin. He cried out, stumbling, his focus wavering.

He saw Kim go down, a tendril wrapping around her ankle and throwing her to the ground. Her leg was bent at an unnatural angle. He saw Matthew, his face a mask of rage, locked in a brutal, physical struggle with two of the larger followers, his kinetic blasts useless at such close range. They were being systematically dismantled. The coven, his family, was being broken apart piece by piece, their strengths negated, their weaknesses exploited with cold, surgical precision.

This was it. The moment of failure. The "all is lost" point that he had secretly, deeply feared since the day his grandfather died. They had been arrogant to think their small, desperate plan could ever work.

Through the haze of his pain and despair, he looked at the center of the clearing. Alistair Finch hadn't moved. His attention, Sean realized with a jolt of horror, had returned to the ritual. Their frantic, failing struggle was no longer of interest to him. He was a god swatting at gnats, and now he was returning to his real work.

The portals in the sky above him flared back to life, the wavering mirages solidifying, the shrieking from beyond the veil growing louder, more insistent. The air grew colder still. They were losing.

Sean's mind raced, scrambling for a solution, a different path. They couldn't fight the glyph and the puppets at the same time. They couldn't harm the innocent people being used against them. Their power was being drained, their hope extinguished.

Then, his uncle's words from the porch echoed in his mind, a voice of quiet reason in the heart of the storm.

Don't just fight the monster. Fight FOR something. Your magic will know the difference.

He had been fighting *against* the Spirit. He needed to fight *for* them. For the souls trapped inside the puppets. Their humanity wasn't a liability; it was the key to unlocking their potential. It was the one thing the Malevolent Spirit could never understand, could never truly control.

"Forget the glyph! Forget the pillars!" Sean roared his voice a raw, desperate command that cut through the chaos, both aloud and in their minds. "Focus on them! On the people! We're not trying to push them out of the trance; we have to *pull* them out! Use everything you have! Show them! Remind them who they are!"

He ignored the lashing tendril of dark magic that seared his arm and locked eyes with the closest enthralled follower. It was a man in his fifties, with a kind, weathered face that had now become a terrifying, blank mask of purple-eyed obedience. The man lunged.

Sean didn't erect a shield. He didn't cast a spell of force. He stood his ground and pushed back with something else entirely. He pushed with a memory.

He reached into his own heart, into the deepest, purest well of his love for Katie, and he hurled it like a weapon. He pushed the memory of her laughter on a summer afternoon, the image of her face soft with sleep, the feeling of her hand in his. He poured that pure, concentrated emotion into the enthralled man's mind, a desperate attempt to reignite the cold, dormant spark of his soul.

Remember! his magic screamed, not with words, but with feeling. *Remember what it is to love!*

The man's attack faltered a foot from Sean's face. His body shuddered violently. The purple light in his eyes flickered, and for a single, breathtaking instant, a flicker of bewildered, human consciousness returned. A tear rolled down his cheek.

"Anna...?" he whispered, his voice a ghost.

Then the purple light flared back, stronger than before, and he snarled, a bestial sound of confusion and rage. But it was a start. A crack in the fortress.

Seeing Sean's gambit, the rest of the coven understood. The nature of the battle shifted. It was no longer a siege of power, but a siege of souls. Katie dropped her cracking shield and, with tears streaming down her own face, began projecting feelings of safety and familial love at the followers pounding on her. Kim, despite her broken leg, touched the ground and sent a wave of calm, nurturing, earthen energy not at the glyph, but at the people standing on it. Sam began a low, humming chant, not of banishment but of memory and belonging.

It was a desperate, insane strategy. A final, defiant stand. They were trying to win a war not with fists or fire but with the fragile, unyielding power of the human heart. As the black sun reached its zenith in the sky, the thirteen portals above them began to tear open, the outcome of their impossible battle hanging on the edge of a single remembered name.

Chapter 28: The Master Stroke

The desperate, unorthodox shift in the coven's strategy sent a tremor through the ritual, rippling across dimensions. The bombardment of pure, unadulterated human emotion—love, memory, hope, the fierce protective instinct that drove parents to shield their children and friends to die for each other—was a form of magic so alien to the Malevolent Spirit that it could not immediately counter it. It was like trying to catch starlight in a net or hold the sound of laughter in cupped hands.

On the physical plane, the effect was both beautiful and heartbreaking. The man Sean had focused on—a weathered farmer whose kind eyes had been replaced by the Spirit's purple glow—shuddered violently as Sean's magic struck him. For a moment, the two forces warred within his body: the ancient, cold intelligence that sought to use him as a weapon and the warm, chaotic spark of his own humanity fighting to reclaim its rightful place.

"Anna," he whispered, the name torn from his lips like a prayer. "Anna, where are you?"

Then his legs gave out, and he collapsed to the corrupted earth, weeping with confusion and terror he couldn't understand but which felt achingly familiar. The purple light in his eyes flickered and died, replaced by the warm brown that belonged to a man who had spent sixty years loving the same woman, raising three children, and tending a small farm that meant everything to him.

Seeing Sean's breakthrough, the rest of the coven threw themselves into the battle with renewed desperation. But this wasn't combat in any traditional sense—it was spiritual warfare, fought not with fire and force but with the most precious things they possessed: their memories, their relationships, their capacity for love.

Katie, tears streaming down her face, focused on a young woman who was clawing at the coven's weakening defenses. Instead of a shield or a binding spell, Katie projected the memory of her first day of high school—the terror and excitement, the way her mother had hugged her before sending her off into the world, the promise that she would always have a home to return to. The emotion hit the possessed woman like a physical blow. For a moment, her attack faltered as her own memories stirred beneath the Spirit's control.

"Mama?" she whispered, her voice small and lost. "I want to go home."

Matthew, his face contorted with effort and empathy, reached out to a teenage boy whose movements held the unnatural precision of the possessed. But instead of trying to overpower the Spirit's influence, Matthew shared his own pain—the crushing weight of being the class clown, the exhaustion of always having to be "on," the desperate need to be taken seriously, to matter. The boy stumbled, his hands going to his head as conflicting emotions warred within him.

"I'm scared," he admitted, his voice cracking. "I'm so scared, and I don't know why."

One by one, they began to free the followers, each liberation a small miracle born of sacrifice and love. But for every soul they managed to reignite, three more remained trapped, and the effort was taking a terrible toll on the coven. They weren't just casting spells—they were bleeding their own hearts out, pouring their most precious memories into strangers in a desperate attempt to remind them of their humanity.

Kim, despite her broken leg, had dragged herself to the base of one of the humming metallic pillars. With tears streaming down her face, she pressed her palms against the alien metal and shared the memory of her grandmother's garden—the patient hours spent learning which plants would heal and which would harm, the quiet wisdom passed down through generations of women who understood that true power came from nurturing life, not destroying it.

The pillar's harmonic frequency wavered, its purpose confused by the introduction of something so fundamentally opposed to its function. The flow of corrupted energy stuttered, sending ripples of disruption through the entire ritual matrix.

But even as they scored these small victories, the larger battle was slipping away from them. The dark energy tendrils of the glyph lashed out with increasing fury, and the portals in the sky above them stretched wider with each passing second. Through the growing tears in reality, they could see movement—vast, impossible shapes pressing against the weakening barriers, eager to break through into a world that had been denied to them for eons.

The Spirit had adapted to their strategy. Where emotional resonance broke its control over one follower, it simply tightened its grip on the others, using their terror and confusion as fuel for its own power. For every small victory, the coven paid a devastating price in their own strength and sanity.

"It's not enough!" Sean roared over the chaos, his voice raw with desperation and exhaustion. Blood was trickling from his nose—a sign that he was pushing his magical abilities beyond their safe limits. "We're just delaying the inevitable!"

He could feel it in his bones, in the marrow of his being. They were fighting the symptoms while the disease continued to spread. The followers, the glyph, the humming pillars—all of it was just machinery, the physical manifestation of a will that existed on a plane they couldn't reach with conventional magic.

He looked at Katie, her face streaked with tears and pale with exhaustion and saw his own desperate realization reflected in her eyes. They were fighting in the wrong dimension. This whole battle—the possessed followers, the corrupted ritual site, even the partially opened portals—was just the shadow cast by something far more fundamental and dangerous.

Katie, he sent, his thoughts cutting through the psychic chaos like a blade. *We're fighting the puppet while the puppet master pulls the strings. The real battle isn't here.*

Understanding dawned in her eyes, immediately followed by a wave of terror so profound it made her stagger. *The astral plane. You want us to project while the ritual is active. Sean, the texts say it's impossible—the psychic interference would tear our consciousness apart.*

The texts didn't account for us, he replied, his certainty burning like a star in the darkness of their situation. *We're bonded, Katie. Our minds are linked. If we go together if we anchor each other...*

He didn't need to finish the thought. She could see the plan forming in his mind, audacious and terrifying and probably suicidal. They would leave their physical bodies behind and pursue the Spirit to its own realm, where the real war was being fought. It was beyond dangerous—astral projection during an active magical working was considered impossible by every authority they'd studied. The psychic turbulence alone should tear their consciousness into fragments.

But they had something no one else had ever possessed: a bond forged in battle, strengthened by love, and tempered by shared sacrifice. They weren't just two people attempting a desperate magical work—they were two halves of a single soul, their connection deeper and stronger than anything the texts had ever imagined possible.

Not without me, Katie's thought was fierce, unbreakable. *We go together. Always.*

The decision crystallized between them in an instant. Around them, the battle raged on—their friends fighting desperately to hold the line, the Spirit's power growing stronger with each passing moment, the portals widening as ancient horrors pressed against the weakening barriers. But for Sean and Katie, the chaos faded to a distant roar. There was only this moment, this choice, this leap into the unknown.

"SAM!" Sean's voice cut through the din like a sword. The experienced witch, who was maintaining a complex shield while Matthew helped one of the freed followers to safety, turned toward him with questioning eyes.

"Katie and I are going to project," he said, the words carrying clearly despite the magical maelstrom around them. "We're leaving our bodies to fight the Spirit on the astral plane. You're in command while we're gone."

Sam's face went through a rapid series of expressions—shock, understanding, and finally, a grim determination that spoke of her own hard-won experience with impossible choices. "The psychic interference will be massive," she warned. "You could be lost, scattered across a dozen dimensions."

"We know," Katie said, taking Sean's hand in hers. Their fingers interlaced with the natural ease of long practice, but there was nothing casual about the gesture. It was a lifeline, an anchor, a promise that they would find each other no matter how far they traveled or how lost they became.

"How long do we have?" Sam asked, already moving to form a protective circle around them.

Sean felt the weight of the Wayfinder in his pocket—or rather, the memory of its weight, since the artifact had been destroyed in his final scrying. But he didn't need magical tools to sense what was coming. The convergence of energies, the astronomical alignment, the sheer momentum of the ritual itself—all of it pointed to a single, inevitable conclusion.

"Minutes," he said grimly. "Maybe less. The eclipse is reaching totality, and when it does..."

He didn't need to finish. They all understood. When the moon completely covered the sun, at the peak of the cosmic alignment, the barriers between dimensions would be at their weakest. That was when the Spirit would make its final push, when the ancient prisons would shatter completely and thirteen cosmic horrors would be free to remake reality according to their own twisted desires.

The rest of the coven moved with desperate efficiency, forming a living wall around Sean and Katie's prone forms. Kim, dragging her broken leg, managed to weave a protective barrier of thorned vines that would shield their physical bodies from attack. Matthew took a position at the circle's edge, his kinetic powers ready to repel any followers who might break through their defenses. The younger coven members—Jake, Sarah, Michael—formed a secondary ring, their combined will focused on maintaining the protective wards that would keep their leaders' souls tethered to the material plane.

At the center of it all, Sean and Katie knelt facing each other, their hands clasped, their foreheads touching in a gesture of ultimate intimacy and trust. They were about to attempt something that had never been done before, something that might kill them or worse—scatter their consciousness across the infinite void between worlds.

"Ready?" Sean whispered, his breath warm against her skin.

"Born ready," Katie whispered back, and despite everything—the chaos, the terror, the impossible odds—they both smiled. It was the same response she'd given him on their first date when he'd asked if she was ready to see something that might change her view of the world forever. Now, as then, she was prepared for anything as long as they faced it together.

They closed their eyes and reached for that place deep within themselves where their magic lived—not the flashy spells and dramatic workings they'd learned from books, but the quiet, steady power that came from love, from connection, from the unshakeable knowledge that some bonds were stronger than death itself.

The transition was violent and nauseating, like being turned inside out and flung through a blender made of pure sensation. Their consciousness exploded outward from their bodies, stretching and tearing as it encountered the psychic turbulence surrounding the ritual site. Colors that had no names assaulted their non-physical senses, sounds that existed only in the spaces between thoughts threatened to shatter their sanity, and a crushing pressure tried to compress their souls into nothingness.

But they held on. Through it all, through the chaos and pain and existential terror, they held on to each other. Katie's mind was a bright star in the screaming void, and Sean's presence was the warm, steady beacon that guided her through the maelstrom. They were falling through dimensions, tumbling through layers of reality that mortal minds were never meant to perceive, but they fell together.

And finally, blessedly, they landed.

The astral plane stretched out around them in all its terrible glory—a realm of pure thought and emotion made manifest, where the laws of physics were suggestions, and the landscape shifted according to the will of its inhabitants. They stood on a crystalline plain that reflected not light but memory, its surface showing glimpses of every significant moment that had ever occurred in this place.

Above them, the sky was a swirling vortex of deep purple and black, alive with the crackling energy of thirteen partially opened portals. But here, in this dimension where thoughts had weight and emotions could kill, the portals weren't just tears in space—they were wounds in the very concept of reality, bleeding chaos and madness into the ordered structure of existence.

And there, at the center of it all, was their enemy.

The Malevolent Spirit's true form was revealed at last—not the handsome billionaire mask it wore in the physical world, but a being of such cosmic malevolence that looking at it directly threatened to drive them mad. It was a writhing mass of shadow and hunger, a void in the shape of hatred, with a thousand burning eyes that stared in every direction at once. Its presence was a constant, psychic scream of rage and contempt for everything that lived, everything that dared to exist in defiance of the perfect emptiness it craved.

Around it, streams of stolen life force flowed from the physical plane—the energy of the possessed followers, the power of the ley lines, the very vitality of the earth itself. The Spirit was weaving this power into thirteen thick tethers of black light, each one connected to a portal, actively pulling them open and anchoring them to reality.

But now, for the first time since the ritual had begun, the Spirit's attention was divided. It had sensed their arrival, two small points of light in its domain of shadows, and part of its vast consciousness turned to regard them with something that might have been amusement.

INSECTS, its thought boomed across the astral plane, a wave of pure psychic pressure that would have destroyed lesser minds. *YOU HAVE COME TO MY HOUSE TO BE CRUSHED.*

On the physical plane, their bodies convulsed as the psychic attack struck home. Blood poured from their noses and ears, and their friends cried out in alarm. But their consciousness, their true selves, remained intact, protected by the bond that connected them more surely than any spell.

Sean and Katie stood together in the heart of the enemy's realm, two teenagers who had somehow found the courage to challenge a being older than civilizations. They were hopelessly outmatched, impossibly outgunned, facing an entity that could snuff out their existence with a casual thought.

But they had one advantage the Spirit couldn't understand, couldn't counter, couldn't even fully perceive. They had love—not as a weakness or a limitation, but as the fundamental force that gave meaning to everything else. It was love that had brought them here, love that held them together, love that made them willing to risk everything for a world that might not even remember their sacrifice.

And in the realm where thoughts became reality, where will could reshape the very structure of existence, love was the most powerful force of all.

The final battle for the soul of the universe was about to begin.

Sean raised his hand, and from his love for Katie, for his friends, for the old farm, and for the grandfather who had raised him, he forged a sword of pure, golden sunlight. Katie reached deep into her heart, into her desperate need to protect the innocent people being used as pawns in this cosmic game, and wove a shield of brilliant turquoise light that could turn aside the darkness itself.

They had come to the Spirit's house. But they had not come to be crushed.

They had come to prove that some things were worth fighting for, no matter the odds. And in a universe where entropy and chaos seemed to hold all the cards, that might just be enough to change everything.

The conflict over reality was approaching its peak, and love would be the determining factor for the future of all creation.

Chapter 29: The Price of Victory

The explosion was silent.

On the astral plane, the instant the spear of Sean and Katie's fused souls struck the Keystone Spirit's core, there was no sound, only a cataclysm of pure, white, *un-making* light. The pulsating black gem at the heart of the monster shattered into a billion glittering shards of nothingness. A silent, psychic scream of annihilation echoed across the dimensions as the Spirit's impossible, geometric form unraveled like a tapestry thrown into a furnace. The thirteen tethers of dark energy, their anchor point destroyed, snapped, and dissolved into vapor. The gaping portals in the sky, their connections severed, slammed shut with a finality that shook the very foundations of the astral realm.

On the physical plane, the backlash was anything but silent. A concussive wave of raw, untainted magical energy erupted from Sean and Katie's motionless bodies. It was not a destructive force but one of pure, overwhelming presence—the sudden, deafening roar of reality snapping back into its rightful shape. The wave tore through the clearing, hurling the remaining enthralled followers and the embattled coven members backward like dolls in a giant's hand. The humming metallic pillars that channeled the ley lines screeched, cracked, and fell silent. The great, corrupted glyph on the ground flared with a blinding, incandescent light for a single, brilliant moment, and then vanished, leaving only scorched, sterile earth behind.

And then, a profound, ringing silence fell. The oppressive weight that had suffocated the nexus was gone. The eclipse was ending, and the first sliver of the true sun pierced through the darkness, its light a warm, golden promise.

The return to their bodies was an agony. For Sean and Katie, it was like being poured back into a vessel that was too small, too solid, too confining after touching the infinite. They slammed back into the confines of flesh and bone with a jarring, physical gasp, their lungs burning as they drew their first shuddering breaths. The world came rushing back in a dizzying, nauseating flood of sensation—the damp smell of the earth, the coppery tang of blood in the air, the throbbing pain of their own battered bodies.

"Katie?" was the first word Sean managed, his voice a raw, cracked whisper.

"I'm here," she breathed, her own voice trembling. They rolled towards each other, their minds still reeling from the intimate, terrifying fusion; their first instinct was to confirm the other was real, whole.

It was Sam's cry that ripped them from their daze. A cry of pure, unadulterated anguish. "Matthew!"

They pushed themselves up, their limbs heavy as lead, their vision swimming. The clearing was a scene of devastation. Their friends were scattered, picking themselves up, groaning. The enthralled followers were beginning to stir, their faces masks of bewildered confusion. But all eyes were fixed on one spot.

Matthew was lying near the thorny, now-withered cage of roots, his body still. He had been standing guard, a human shield for his friends. As the final shockwave had erupted, one of the larger, enraged followers had made a last, desperate lunge. Matthew had thrown himself in the way, and the man had gone down, but not before driving a jagged, three-foot shard of one of the shattered metallic pillars deep into Matthew's side.

This was the price. The tangible, horrifying cost of their victory.

They scrambled to him, their own exhaustion and pain forgotten. The wound was horrific. The alien metal of the pillar, slick with Matthew's blood, seemed to pulse with a faint, dark light. This cold, life-draining energy was actively fighting the flesh around it. It wasn't just a physical injury; it was a magical one, a sliver of the nexus's poison left buried in their friend.

"Don't touch it!" Sam warned, her voice sharp with ancient knowledge as Sean reached for the shard. "It's still connected to the dark energy. Pulling it out could kill him instantly."

Kim, her own leg clearly broken, had crawled to Matthew's side. She pressed her hands to the earth beside him, tears streaming down her face as she tried to channel her healing, grounding magic into him. "I can't... it's not working," she sobbed. "The wound... it's rejecting my magic. It's like trying to make a plant grow in salted earth."

Panic, cold and sharp, began to set in. They had faced down a cosmic horror and won, only to lose one of their own to a piece of shrapnel in the aftermath. The irony was so cruel, so deeply unfair, it felt like a final, mocking laugh from the vanquished Spirit.

Katie, her hands shaking, knelt opposite Kim. She tried to murmur a direct healing spell, a simple cantrip of mending, but her own magical reserves were scraped clean, her energy depleted by the astral projection. The spell sputtered, a weak flicker of turquoise light that died before it even reached the wound.

"I can't," she whispered, her voice breaking. "I'm empty, Sean. There's nothing left."

Sean looked at Matthew's face, which was growing terrifyingly pale, his breathing shallow. He saw the fear and despair on the faces of his coven. And in that moment, something shifted inside him. The exhaustion, the pain, the psychic trauma of the last hour—it all fell away, burned off by a fierce, protective resolve. He was the leader. This was his responsibility.

"Get me Sam's herb pack. Now," he commanded, his voice steady and clear. He gently pushed Kim aside. "Katie, I need you to perform a binding. Not for healing. For containment. I need you to chant, to focus on the dark energy in the shard, to keep it from spreading any further when I pull it out. Can you do that?"

Katie looked at him, saw the unwavering certainty in his eyes, and nodded, her fear giving way to his strength.

Two of the younger coven members raced to retrieve Sam's pack, returning with a bundle of dried herbs and crystals.

"Silver dust and mugwort," Sam instructed, her voice regaining its composure as she fell into the role of a seasoned practitioner. "Make a poultice. It will purify the wound once the source is removed."

Sean took a deep, shuddering breath. He knew what he had to do. The healing spells hadn't worked because they were trying to fight a magical poison. He couldn't fight it. He had to overwhelm it. With pure, raw life. His life.

He knelt beside Matthew, placing his hands on either side of the horrific wound. He ignored the vile, cold energy radiating from the shard. He closed his eyes and reached deep inside himself, past the exhaustion, past the pain, to the very core of his own soul, the font of his life force. It was the same energy the Wayfinder had feasted upon, the same essence he and Katie had forged into a weapon. It was his most precious resource, and he began to pour it, steadily and without hesitation, into his friend.

The world around him faded. There was only the feeling of his own vitality flowing out of him and into Matthew, a desperate, direct transfusion of life. The silver streak at his temple felt as if it were on fire, and he knew, with a grim certainty, that it was growing, that new threads of silver were weaving their way through the dark strands of his hair. He was paying the toll again, willingly.

As he poured his life into Matthew, Katie began to chant, her voice weak but clear, weaving a net of magical containment around the shard. Sean gripped the cold, alien metal. "On three," he grunted, the effort making his vision swim. "One... two..."

He felt a sudden, new presence. He opened his eyes and saw his uncle kneeling on the other side of Matthew, his face a mask of profound grief and awe. Todd had seen it all from the tree line.

"Let me help," Todd said, his voice thick with emotion. He placed his own hands over Sean's. "I can't do what you do. But I am a Murphy. My life is deeply rooted in this land and this family. Take what you need from me."

Sean felt it—a trickle of steady, grounded, stubborn strength flowing from his uncle into him, bolstering his own flagging reserves. It wasn't the fiery power of a warlock, but the deep, enduring energy of a guardian who had finally come home.

"THREE!" Sean roared and pulled.

The shard came free with a sickening, tearing sound, and a gout of black, smoky energy erupted from the wound. Katie's binding spell flared, catching the dark energy and dissolving it with a sharp hiss. Instantly, Sam was there, pressing the silver and mugwort poultice into the now-gaping but clean wound. The bleeding, which had been sluggish and dark, gradually slowed and then stopped. Matthew's shallow breathing deepened, stabilized. He was unconscious, but he was alive.

A collective sigh of pure, unadulterated relief went through the coven. Sean collapsed backward, the world spinning, his own energy now dangerously low. He felt Katie and his uncle supporting him, holding him up.

As the immediate crisis passed, the reality of their situation came crashing back. They were in a clearing littered with the unconscious bodies of two dozen innocent people and the catatonic, empty shell of a world-famous billionaire. The sun was now fully returned, its light seeming harsh and accusatory.

"We have to get out of here," Todd said, his voice taking on a practical urgency. "The authorities... someone is going to come looking for Finch eventually." He pulled out his phone. "I'll make an anonymous call. Report an industrial accident at the site. A chemical leak. That will bring paramedics and hazmat teams and create enough confusion to cover this."

While he made the call, the coven focused on the final, grim tasks. They gently woke the last of the enthralled followers, whispering calming spells and urging them to walk back towards the main road, assuring them they would be safe. The followers moved like sleepwalkers, their eyes full of a deep, unremembered trauma.

Sean, leaning heavily on Katie, fumbled in his pocket for the Wayfinder. He pulled it out. The small wooden bird was cracked clean down the middle, the beautiful, ancient wood charred black and crumbling at the edges. It was cold, inert, its magic sacrificed in the final, concussive blast. The price of victory. Another piece of his heritage, his grandfather, is gone forever.

With their last vestiges of strength, the coven combined their power to levitate Matthew's unconscious form. The journey back through the swamp was a slow, painful, stumbling retreat. They were no longer soldiers. They were just a group of exhausted, wounded kids carrying their fallen comrade from a battlefield no one else would ever know existed.

They had won. They had faced down a cosmic entity and saved the world from a fate worse than death. But as they limped away from the silent, desecrated nexus, there was no triumph. There was no celebration. There was only the taste of ash and blood in their mouths, the heavy, precious weight of their unconscious friend, and the chilling, undeniable knowledge of the price they had paid. The victory felt hollow, a thing of terrible, breakable beauty, and they knew, with a certainty that would haunt them forever, that the war was very far from over.

Chapter 30: The Aftermath

The silence that followed the psychic cataclysm was more profound and deafening than any sound. The oppressive hum of the nexus, the shriek of tearing realities, the guttural chants of a possessed billionaire—all of it was gone, ripped from the world in the instant the Spirit's core had been annihilated. In its place, a vast, ringing emptiness settled over the clearing. The world, which had been holding its breath for the entire eclipse, finally exhaled.

The harsh, unfiltered light of the returning sun sliced through the trees, making Sean wince. He was lying on the damp, scorched earth, the pain of returning to his body a thousand tiny agonies. Every nerve ending screamed. His muscles felt like frayed, over-stretched wires, and his mind was a raw, bruised thing, reeling from the terrifying intimacy of being fused with another soul and looking into the void.

He heard a gasp beside him and turned his head, the simple movement an act of supreme effort. Katie was there, her eyes fluttering open, her face ashen. Her first instinctual action was to reach for him, her fingers finding his, a weak but desperate grip that said everything. *You're here. I'm here. We're alive.*

But their private moment of relief was shattered by a cry from across the clearing —a sound of such pure, unadulterated anguish that it cut through their daze like a shard of glass.

"Matthew!"

It was Kim. They pushed themselves up, their bodies screaming in protest, their vision swimming. The scene before them was one of quiet, absolute devastation. The alien metallic pillars were shattered, lying in twisted, smoking heaps. The great glyph was gone, leaving a faint, dark stain on the earth as its only epitaph. The enthralled followers were scattered across the ground like fallen leaves, moaning as they slowly, painfully returned to consciousness, their minds a blank slate of confusion and unremembered trauma.

And in the center of it all, the coven was converging on a single, still point.

Sean and Katie stumbled to their feet and ran, their own pain forgotten. They saw him before they even reached the group. Matthew was lying on his back, his face a bloodless, waxy white. He wasn't moving. The front of his shirt was a dark, spreading stain of crimson, and protruding from his side, just below the ribs, was a jagged, three-foot shard of the shattered alien metal.

They had won. They had saved the world. And the cost was standing before them, stark and terrible.

"He's alive," Sam said, her voice tight and strained. She was kneeling beside him, her hands hovering over the wound, feeling the malevolent energy that pulsed from it. "But he's fading. Fast."

The shard of dark metal was radiating a palpable cold. This life-draining energy seemed to be actively poisoning him, turning the blood around the wound a sluggish, unnatural black.

"I'm trying," Kim sobbed, her own face contorted in pain from her broken leg. She had her hands pressed to the earth, trying to channel her gentle, grounding magic into him, but it was like trying to pour water on a chemical fire. Her healing energy recoiled from the alien poison of the wound. "It won't take. It's pushing me back."

Panic, cold and acidic, began to rise in Sean's throat. He could feel Matthew's life force, a once-bright and boisterous flame, now flickering, guttering, threatening to be extinguished at any moment.

Katie, her face, a mask of fierce determination, knelt and placed her hands over the wound. *"Sana, Vulnera, Restitue,"* she whispered, the words of a direct healing spell tumbling from her lips. A faint, turquoise light bloomed from her palms, but it was weak, sputtering. The astral projection had left her own magical reserves almost completely dry. The light flickered and died, and she let out a cry of frustration and despair. "I can't... I'm empty, Sean. There's nothing left."

The sight of her, so strong and brilliant, looking so utterly defeated, was the catalyst Sean needed. He pushed through the fog of his own exhaustion, his grief and fear forged into a sharp, clear point of focus. He was the leader. He would not let his friend die on this silent battlefield.

"It's not a normal wound," he said, his voice ragged but commanding. "We can't heal it. We have to cleanse it. The shard... it has to come out."

"If you pull it out, he'll bleed to death in seconds," Sam argued, her voice tight with desperation. "And the energy in it... the shock might stop his heart."

"She's right," Sean agreed. "Which is why we have to purify the wound as it's removed." He looked at Sam, his mind racing, pulling on the fragments of knowledge he'd gleaned from the sanctuary's texts. "Silver. And mugwort. The old tales are specific. They act as a magical cauterant against this kind of poison. Do you have them?"

Sam nodded, already scrambling for the leather pack she had dropped nearby. "I do."

"Katie," Sean said, turning to her. Her eyes were wide, her face streaked with tears. "I need you. Not for healing. For binding. Please focus on the dark energy in that shard. Weave a net around it. When I pull it out, you have to hold that energy, keep it from flooding his system. It's the most complex warding you've ever attempted, and you have to do it now."

Her fear was a palpable thing, but as she looked at him, at the unwavering resolve in his eyes, she found her strength. She nodded, her hands already beginning to move in the intricate patterns of a containment spell, her lips forming the silent words.

Sean knelt beside Matthew. He took a deep, shuddering breath and placed his hands on either side of the horrific wound. He ignored the vile, cold energy that radiated from the shard, an energy that felt like the absolute zero of the void. He closed his eyes and reached deep inside himself, to the core of his soul, to the wellspring of his life force. He found it, dangerously low, a flickering ember where a bonfire had once been. But it was enough. He began to pour it into Matthew, a direct, desperate transfusion of vitality, a shield of pure life to protect his friend's soul from the coming shock.

The silver streak at his temple burned, a searing, white-hot pain. He could feel the cost, the moments and minutes of his own future being consumed to fuel this act of creation, this defiance of death. He didn't care.

He gripped the cold, slick metal of the shard. "Katie. Now."

He felt her magic take hold, a shimmering, intricate net of turquoise light forming around the shard within Matthew's body.

"Hold on, Matthew," he whispered. Then, with a prayer on his lips, he pulled.

The shard came free with a sickening, tearing sound of flesh and a psychic scream of thwarted malice. A gout of black, viscous smoke erupted from the wound. Katie cried out, her body trembling with effort as her magical net flared, catching the dark energy containing it, and then crushing it into nothingness.

Instantly, Sam was there, pressing a thick, fragrant poultice of silver dust and crushed mugwort into the gaping wound. There was a loud sizzle, like water hitting a hot pan, and the black, poisoned edges of the wound smoked and transformed into clean, healthy tissue. The bleeding, which had been a terrifying, dark flood, slowed, then stopped. Matthew's shallow breathing, which had all but ceased, suddenly hitched, then deepened, stabilizing into a steady, rhythmic pattern of sleep.

He was alive.

A collective, shuddering sigh of pure, incredulous relief went through the coven. Sean collapsed backward, the world dissolving into a gray, spinning tunnel.

He was caught by strong, familiar arms. He looked up and saw his uncle's face, etched with a fear and pride so profound it took his breath away. Todd had entered the clearing, his shotgun hanging forgotten at his side.

"You did it," Todd breathed, his voice thick with an emotion Sean had never heard from him before. "My God, Sean, you did it."

While Sean and Katie recovered, their friends, guided by a quiet word from Sam, began the grim, necessary work of cleaning up their war. They moved among the stirring, moaning followers, whispering calming spells and gently guiding the dazed and confused people away from the clearing and back towards the access road, their memories of the last hour a merciful, yet terrifying, blank.

It was Todd who went to check on Alistair Finch. He returned a few minutes later, his face pale.

"He's alive," he reported, his voice low. "Breathing. Heart's beating. But there's nothing there. I looked in his eyes, Sean... it's just an empty house. The lights are on, but nobody's home."

The Keystone Spirit was gone, banished from its host. But was it destroyed? Or was it just a disembodied wraith now, weakened, adrift on the winds, its hatred undiminished? The mystery hung in the air, a chilling counterpoint to their victory.

They knew they had to leave. The authorities would be coming. Todd, ever the pragmatist, had already made the anonymous call, reporting a "toxic chemical spill" from an overturned tanker at a remote construction site. This story would explain the unconscious victims and buy them time.

The coven gathered their last vestiges of strength. They looked at Matthew's still, peaceful form. He was too heavy to carry, their own bodies too battered. With a final, unified act of will, they combined their depleted magic to levitate their fallen friend, his body rising to float an inch above the ground.

The retreat from the nexus was a slow, stumbling, painful procession. The eclipse was over. The sun was fully returned, but its familiar, life-giving light felt harsh and alien, as if they were seeing it for the first time after a long, long time in the dark.

Sean, leaning heavily on Katie, his every muscle screaming, looked back one last time at the silent, devastated clearing. He thought of the cost. He felt the new, finer threads of silver that he knew were now woven into his hair. He looked at Matthew's pale, unconscious face floating between them. He saw Kim limping, her leg splinted by a crude brace Matthew had carved for her weeks ago.

They had won. They had stood against the darkness and held the line. They had saved the world. But as they limped away from their silent battlefield, there was no triumph, no celebration. There was only the taste of ash and blood in their mouths, the heavy, precious weight of their unconscious friend, and the chilling, undeniable understanding of the price of victory. And in the quiet, hollow spaces of their hearts, they knew this was not the end of the war. It was only the end of the beginning.

Chapter 31: A New Dawn

The week following the eclipse was a study in quiet contradictions. Outside the borders of the Murphy farm, the world returned to its mundane, frantic rhythm, oblivious to the apocalypse it had so narrowly avoided. Inside, profound and sacred exhaustion had settled, the kind that comes only after a soul-deep battle has been fought and won. The air itself felt different, washed clean of the oppressive, static-filled dread that had clung to them for weeks. The sunlight seemed warmer, the green of the fields more vibrant, the sky a more brilliant and precious blue. It was the beauty of a world they had almost lost, and every simple detail was now a quiet miracle.

Their farmhouse had been transformed into a makeshift infirmary and sanctuary. The scent of coffee and Todd's often-experimental cooking mingled with the clean, sharp smell of the healing herbs Sam kept simmering on the stove. Their lives revolved around a new, gentle routine: caring for their wounded, sharing quiet meals, and sleeping the deep, dreamless sleep of the utterly spent.

Katie was the first to bring a sense of normalcy back. She brought a tray up to the guest room, where Matthew was recovering. He was sitting up in bed, looking pale and thin, but his familiar, mischievous grin was back in place, a welcome sight that made Katie's heart ache with relief. A thick, clean bandage was wrapped around his torso, but beneath it, she could feel the steady, mending pulse of Kim's and Sean's combined magic.

"Your royal chariot awaits, my lord," she said, placing the tray with a bowl of soup and a sandwich on his lap. "Or, you know, chicken noodle soup. Close enough."

Matthew chuckled, producing a weak yet genuine sound. "Thanks, Katie. I was getting tired of staring at the ceiling. Tell me everything. Did we actually win, or did I just have a really, really bad dream involving shadow dogs and a very angry billionaire?"

"We won," she said softly, sitting on the edge of the bed. "You were so brave, Matthew. You saved us."

His grin faltered, his gaze dropping to the thick bandage. "Some hero. I got taken out by a piece of furniture."

"You got taken out by a piece of a trans-dimensional conduit after throwing yourself in front of your friends to save them from a psychic attack," she corrected him gently. "I think that qualifies."

He looked up at her, his eyes shining with a gratitude that went beyond words. In that shared, quiet moment, the bond of their coven, forged in fear and battle, solidified into something unbreakable.

Down on the main floor, Kim was ensconced on the sofa, her broken leg propped up on a mountain of pillows. Her cast was a thing of strange beauty, a living brace woven by her own magic from supple willow branches and moss, which pulsed with a soft green light as it knitted her bones back together. She was patiently directing two of the younger coven members, showing them the proper way to grind silver moss into a fine, shimmering powder for their dwindling stock of healing potions. They were no longer just a group of kids with powers; they were apprentices, learning a craft, their shared purpose a quiet, determined hum in the old farmhouse.

Sean found his own solace in the familiar, mindless work of the farm. He was out by the barn, splitting firewood, the rhythmic *thwack* of the axe a solid, grounding counterpoint to the chaotic memories of the battle. He felt the change in himself with every swing. He was still strong, but a deep, fundamental well of his energy was gone, burned away in the scrying and the final, desperate healing of Matthew. It was a permanent exhaustion, a quiet ache deep in his bones that he suspected would be his constant companion from now on.

He paused to wipe the sweat from his brow and caught his reflection in the dark glass of the barn window. The silver in his hair was no longer just a single streak at his temple. It was a series of finer, shimmering threads woven through the dark strands, a visible map of the price he had paid. He touched it, the hair coarse and strange beneath his fingertips. It didn't feel like a mark of heroism. It felt like a scar.

"Figured I'd find you out here."

Sean turned. His uncle was leaning against the fence, a steaming mug in each hand. He walked over and handed one to Sean. The coffee was strong and black.

"You doing okay, kid?" Todd asked, his gaze gentle, his voice stripped of its usual guardedness.

"I'm alright," Sean said, though the words felt hollow.

"No, you're not," Todd countered softly. "But you will be." He took a sip from his own mug, looking out at the fields. "It gets easier. The feeling of... being less than you were. You learn to live with the empty spaces. Or you learn to fill them with other things." He looked at the farmhouse, where he could see the shapes of the coven moving through the windows. "Looks like you're already figuring that part out."

Sean followed his gaze, and a feeling of warmth spread through his chest, chasing away some of the chill. "Yeah," he said, a small, genuine smile touching his lips for the first time in days. "Yeah, I guess I am."

Later that evening, they gathered in the living room, a new ritual born of necessity. They watched the national news. The lead story was no longer about a visionary project but about the baffling mystery of the "Aethelgard Event." The reporter stood in front of the now-quarantined construction site, a yellow 'HAZMAT-DO NOT ENTER' tape stretched between the trees behind her.

"The official story remains a sudden and contained release of an unknown neurotoxin from a geological fissure," she reported her voice grave. "But sources inside the CDC are baffled. The two dozen site workers who were hospitalized have all been released, complaining of nothing more than severe migraines and temporary amnesia. They have no recollection of the event."

The screen cut to a shot of Alistair Finch's private hospital wing. "More mysterious still is the condition of billionaire Alistair Finch himself," the reporter continued. "Found at the site in a state of complete catatonia, he remains unresponsive. Doctors from around the world have weighed in, but none can explain his condition. Meanwhile, in the wake of a series of anonymous leaks detailing massive financial fraud and accounting irregularities, the board of Finch's parent company has suspended the Aethelgard project indefinitely, pending a full federal investigation."

They watched, a strange sense of detachment settling over them. They had done it. Their desperate, two-front war had worked. The world was safe, the monster's plans in ruins. But there was no cheering, no celebration. Their victory was a silent, secret thing they could never share, a heavy truth they would carry alone.

That night, for the first time since the battle, they returned to the sanctuary. They needed to be there, to reclaim it, to feel it's clean, peaceful energy, and to remind themselves of what they had been fighting for. The air was warm and welcoming, the magical light a soft, steady glow. The cave itself seemed to sigh in relief, its long-held tension finally released.

It was Sam's idea to turn the debrief into a celebration. She and Todd had spent the afternoon preparing a feast, a real one, and they brought the food down into the main chamber. They lit candles, not for a ritual, but for warmth and remembrance. They laid out a meal of roasted chicken, fresh bread, and apple pie, and the scent of real food filled the ancient space, a powerful spell of its own.

They coaxed Matthew out of the guest room, and he sat propped up with pillows on one of the sofas, pale but smiling, a plate balanced on his lap.

Sean stood, raising a glass of sparkling cider. The coven fell silent, their eyes on him. He looked at each of them, at the tired, beloved faces of his family, and his heart felt too full for his chest.

"I want to make a toast," he said, his voice thick with emotion. "Not to victory. But to the price." He looked directly at Matthew. "To sacrifice. To standing in front of your friends when they can't stand themselves." He then looked at Kim, at her leg, which was resting in its living cast. "To enduring. To being the foundation that allows others to fight." He finally looked at Katie, and his gaze was filled with a love so profound it needed no words. "And to what makes it all worth it." He raised his glass higher. "To the coven."

"To the coven," they all echoed their voices a soft, unified chorus.

After that, the stories began to spill out. The fear. The chaos of the battle. They laughed at their own mistakes, at the sheer terror and absurdity of it all. They cried a little as they spoke of their fear of losing each other. It was a messy, honest, and deeply necessary cleansing, a sharing of the trauma that lessened its weight on any one soul.

It was late when Todd, who had been sitting quietly, listening, finally spoke. He looked at Sean, his eyes filled with a quiet, open admiration.

"Your grandfather would be so proud, Sean," he said, his voice clear and steady. "Not just because you won. I think... I think he always knew you would. He would be proud because of *how* you did it. How you lead. He was always afraid I led with my head, and he led with his stubbornness. But you... you lead with your heart. I see that now. You're the guardian he always knew you could be."

The validation from the man who had run from this life, from this legacy, was a powerful, healing balm on Sean's bruised soul.

But it was Sam who brought them back to the cold, lingering reality. She looked around the warm, candlelit room at the tired but peaceful faces of her new family, and her expression was grave.

"The Keystone Spirit is gone from this world, for now," she said softly, but her words carried an undeniable weight. "Banished, maybe even destroyed by your fusion. But what about the other twelve? We slammed the doors shut, but they're still out there. In their prisons. And now, they know we're here."

A quiet chill returned to the sanctuary. She was right. This was just one victory in a war that was far from over.

Sean looked at Katie, then at the rest of his coven. He felt their fear, but underneath it, he felt something else: a deep, quiet strength that hadn't been there before. They had faced the abyss and remained unbroken. They had been forged anew in its fire.

"Let them know," Sean said, his voice quiet but ringing with a new, unshakeable confidence. "We're not just a bunch of kids on a farm anymore. We're not just the protectors of this sanctuary." He looked at each of them, his gaze promising a shared future, a shared purpose. "We're the guardians. We're the line. And if they ever try to cross it again, we'll be here. Waiting."

A new dawn had truly arrived, not just for the world they had saved, but for the small, battered, and unbreakable family they had forged together in the heart of their secret, sacred war.

Chapter 32: Our Guiding Light

The seasons turned, and the raw, bleeding wound of the battle at the nexus slowly began to scar over. Spring bloomed across the Murphy farm with a fierce, defiant beauty as if the very earth were celebrating its narrow escape from the Spirit's corruption. The days grew longer and warmer, and were filled not with the frantic energy of war but with the gentle, healing rhythm of life. A fragile, precious peace settled over them, a peace they had paid for in blood, magic, and time.

The coven, which had been forged into a unit by shared terror, was now annealed into a family by shared healing. The farmhouse had become their uncontested hub. On any given afternoon, Kim could be found tending to a now-thriving magical herb garden she'd planted behind the house, her leg completely healed, leaving not even a trace of a limp. She'd coaxed strange, glowing flora from the sanctuary's texts into the Carolina soil, plants that hummed with restorative energy. Matthew, fully recovered but quieter now, more thoughtful, would often sit on the porch, a block of wood in his hands, carving intricate, protective runes into fence posts and door frames, his kinetic energy now channeled into a patient, creative defense. The farm was becoming more than a fortress; it was becoming a living extension of their coven.

Uncle Todd had found his place among them, a quiet, steady anchor in their chaotic world. He'd accepted the strangeness of his new life with a weary grace, never questioning the odd ingredients simmering on the stove or the sight of his nephew floating tools across the barn. He simply ensured that there was always food in the pantry and that the bills were paid on time; his practicality served as a necessary bridge between their secret world and the one that existed outside the farm's magically-warded borders.

One warm Saturday afternoon in late May, nearly two months after the eclipse, Todd found Sean staring out at the fields, a distant, haunted look in his eyes.

"It's time, kid," Todd said gently.

Sean didn't have to ask what he meant. They had all, by unspoken agreement, left his grandfather's room untouched. It had remained a perfect, heartbreaking time capsule. The door always closed. To open it felt like admitting, in a final, tangible way, that he was truly gone.

"I know," Sean said, his voice quiet. He knew he couldn't put it off any longer.

He found Katie weeding in Kim's garden, her face smudged with dirt, her hair tied back in a messy knot. "Will you come with me?" he asked.

She didn't need to ask where. She simply took off her gardening gloves, wiped her hands on her jeans, and took his hand in hers.

The air in Tom's bedroom was still and thick with memories. The scent of Old Spice, pipe tobacco, and him, a scent Sean hadn't even realized he'd been memorizing his entire life, still clung to the curtains and the worn quilt on the bed. It was like stepping into a photograph. Together, he and Katie began the somber, sacred task of sorting through a life.

It was a journey through his grandfather's history. They found a box of old black-and-white photographs: Tom as a young, gangly boy with a familiar stubborn glint in his eye; Tom as a handsome, proud young man in a crisp naval uniform standing on the deck of a ship. They found his favorite worn flannel shirt, and Sean held it to his face, inhaling the faint, lingering scent, his throat tightening with a sudden, sharp grief. Katie found a dog-eared book of Irish poetry, its spine broken, a page marked that read, *"May the road rise up to meet you, may the wind be always at your back."*

They worked in a comfortable, loving silence, folding clothes, stacking books, creating piles to keep and piles to donate. It was an act of love, of remembrance, of finally, painfully, letting go.

In the bottom of his grandfather's old, wooden sea chest, beneath the heavy, perfectly folded wool of his naval dress uniform, Sean's fingers brushed against something hard and cold. It was a small iron box, heavy and unassuming. It was not ornate or magical in appearance; it was brutally practical, its surface pitted with age and rust. But the keyhole was strange, a small, dark opening in the shape of a serpent devouring its own tail. An Ouroboros. There was no key.

Tucked beside it, almost hidden in a fold of the uniform's lining, was a thick, yellowed envelope, sealed with a drop of wax. In his grandfather's familiar, spidery handwriting was a single word:

Sean.

His heart began to pound, a slow, heavy drumbeat in the quiet room. His hands trembled as he broke the seal. Katie, sensing the shift in the air, came to stand beside him, her hand a warm, steadying presence on his back. He unfolded the brittle pages and began to read.

My Dearest Sean,

If you are reading this, then my time has come, and I have left you with more burdens than answers, and for that, I am truly sorry. A man thinks he has all the time in the world to say the important things, until he doesn't. Know this first, above all else: I have loved you as my own son since the day your parents left you in my care, and I am prouder of the man you are becoming than words can ever say.

But there are things I should have told you. Secrets our family has carried for a very long time. The magic in our blood, the power you and your father wielded... it is not just the craft of the Wicca. That is only one branch of a much older tree. The trunk of that tree, the source of it all, is something else. We are Murphys, yes, but we are also something more. We are a bloodline of Gatekeepers.

The sanctuary in the cave is more than a library, Sean. It is a seal. A lock on a dormant Gate between our world and the places beyond. The formless, hungry things that lie sleeping in the outer darkness. The Malevolent Spirits you fought are but the echoes, the nightmares of these greater, cosmic horrors. Our family has stood watch over this Gate for a thousand years.

There are other Gates. And other guardians. But our world has forgotten its magic, and many of the old lines have faded or broken. The artifact in the iron box is a key. Not for the Gate here—that one is sealed by the sanctuary's own magic. The box contains the key to another, older, and far more dangerous Gate. The one our ancestors left behind when they fled the old country. The one in Ireland.

I fear this is a burden I must pass to you now out of necessity. Your battle at the nexus, the sheer amount of pure, world-altering magic you and your coven unleashed... it did not go unnoticed. Such an act does not happen in a vacuum. It sent a ripple through the dimensions, a flare in the darkness that may have woken things long dormant. It may have stirred the lock on the ancient Gate.

I do not know what lies ahead. I only know our duty. Protect the Gates, Sean. That is our true legacy. The key in that box must never be used. It must be guarded. It is a key to open a door that must forever remain shut. I am so sorry to leave you with this. Trust in your coven. Trust in your uncle. And above all else, trust in Katie. Her light will be your compass when all other lights go out.

Be a good man. Be happy. And know that I will be watching.

All my love, Grandpa Tom

The letter fell from Sean's nerveless fingers, fluttering to the floor. The quiet room suddenly felt vast and cold. He looked at Katie, his eyes wide with a new and terrifying understanding. Their victory. Their triumph. It hadn't been an ending. It had been a catalyst. They had saved the world only to alert something far worse that the locks on its cage were weakening. They weren't just guardians of a town anymore. They were guardians of reality itself.

Katie knelt and picked up the letter, her own pale face as she read it. When she finished, she didn't speak. She simply took the heavy iron box and handed it to Sean. It felt like it weighed a thousand pounds.

That night, sleep was an impossibility. The weight of his grandfather's final secret, his true legacy, was a crushing thing. Long before dawn, Sean slipped out of the house and climbed onto the familiar, gentle slope of the farmhouse roof. He needed to see the sunrise. He needed to be reminded that the light still came.

A few minutes later, he heard a soft footstep on the shingles behind him. Katie settled beside him, pulling an old quilt around their shoulders. She didn't need to ask why he was here. She just knew. They sat in a comfortable silence, watching the eastern sky begin to bleed from inky black to a soft, bruised purple.

"Gatekeepers," Sean said finally, the word feeling strange and heavy on his tongue. He held up the iron box, which he'd brought with him. "An ancient Gate in Ireland. An artifact that can open it. And a warning to never, ever use it." He shook his head, a humorless laugh escaping his lips. "It's like something out of one of Matthew's fantasy novels. It doesn't feel real."

"The Malevolent Spirit didn't feel real either," Katie said softly. "Until it was." She leaned her head on his shoulder. "We'll figure it out, Sean. We always do."

"But how? We just won a war. We're all so tired. And now this? A threat we don't even understand? A key to a lock we can never open?" He looked at her, his face a mask of exhaustion and fear. "I don't know if I'm strong enough for this one, Katie."

She reached out and gently touched the silver streaks in his hair, her fingers tracing the path of his sacrifice. "He told you to trust your heart," she whispered, her voice a fierce, loving reassurance. "And my heart trusts you. Completely."

He looked at her, at the unwavering belief in her eyes, and he felt the familiar, grounding click of his world settling back into place. She was his true north, his anchor.

"He said the quiet times are just the world taking a breath," he said, his own voice growing stronger. "I guess we just finished one breath." He squeezed her hand, their fingers lacing together. "But as long as I'm breathing with you, I think we'll be okay."

The sun finally broke over the horizon, a spectacular, blinding explosion of gold, rose, and fiery orange. It flooded the world with new, clean light, chasing the last of the shadows from the sleeping fields. The light caught the silver in Sean's hair, making it shine, not like a scar, but like a crown.

They sat there, watching the dawn of a new day, the dawn of their new reality. They were no longer the frightened children who had stumbled upon a world of magic. They were not even the teenage soldiers who had won a desperate war. They were guardians, their watch just beginning. They were scared. The responsibility was immense, almost incomprehensible. But as they sat together, their hands clasped, the heavy iron box resting between them, they were not broken.

The future was a vast, terrifying unknown, filled with ancient gates and slumbering horrors. But as the sun rose higher, painting their faces with its warmth, they faced it together. Their love, a quiet and unshakeable thing, was its own form of magic, its own kind of sanctuary. It was their guiding light, and in the face of the encroaching darkness, they knew, with an absolute certainty, that it would be enough.

Chapter 33: The Fractured Witness

Katie no longer slept.

She existed in a twilight state between waking and dreaming, her consciousness suspended in a liminal space where the boundaries between what was real and what could be real had dissolved entirely. The bed in Sean's old room—she couldn't bear to sleep in her own anymore—had become less of a resting place and more of an anchor point, a fixed coordinate in a reality that shifted and flowed like water around her.

Tonight, she sat cross-legged on the rumpled sheets, her back against the headboard, staring at her hands in the pale moonlight streaming through the window. Her fingers flickered between states—sometimes solid flesh and bone, sometimes translucent as glass, sometimes not there at all. When she blinked, her hands might be younger, the nails painted a bright pink she'd never worn, or older, bearing scars from battles she'd never fought. Or they might belong to someone else entirely.

The fusion with Sean on the astral plane had torn something fundamental in her psyche. Not broken—that would have been simpler, more direct. This was something far more insidious. The barriers that separated her individual consciousness from the infinite ocean of possibility had become permeable. She was leaking into other realities, and they were leaking into her.

"Katie?"

She turned toward the voice, unsurprised to see herself standing in the doorway. This other Katie was older, maybe in her thirties, wearing clothes that were familiar but wrong—a blue sweater she'd never owned but somehow remembered buying. This Katie's face was etched with lines of sorrow that spoke of losses that Katie couldn't yet comprehend.

"You shouldn't be here," Katie whispered to her doppelganger. "This isn't your reality."

The older Katie smiled with infinite sadness. "None of them are real, little sister. That's what you haven't understood yet. We're all just echoes of echoes, shadows cast by a light that burned out long ago."

"That's not true." But even as she said it, Katie felt the words crumble in her mouth, becoming dust and doubt.

"Isn't it?" As Katie stepped into the room, her footsteps made no sound on the wooden floor. "Look around you. Really look. How many times have you lived this moment? How many times have you sat in this room, having this conversation, believing it was the first time?"

Katie's breath caught in her throat. Now that her other self-had mentioned it, she could feel the weight of repetition, the sensation of grooves worn deep by countless identical moments. The moonlight fell across the floor in exactly the same pattern. The clock on the nightstand read 3:17 AM, just as it had... before. Many befores.

"We're caught in a loop," she realized, her voice barely audible.

"Worse than that," the older Katie said, settling on the edge of the bed with the familiarity of someone who belonged there. "We're caught in a spiral. Each iteration, we sink a little deeper. Each time, we lose a little more of what made us who we are. us."

Katie pressed her palms against her temples, trying to hold her fragmenting thoughts together. "The Witness. When Sean destroyed it, it didn't just disappear. It scattered. Became part of the pattern."

"Part of us," the older Katie corrected. "It's been growing inside the cracks, feeding on our confusion, our fear. Soon, there won't be enough left of the real Katie to matter. We'll just be... vessels. Empty spaces for it to pour itself into."

As if summoned by their conversation, the room began to change. The walls breathed, expanding and contracting like the inside of a lung. The moonlight took on a sickly, green tinge, and shadows that belonged to no visible objects began to creep across the floor.

And then she was there—the Witness, wearing Katie's face but wrong, all wrong. Her eyes were black voids that reflected nothing; her smile was too wide, and her movements were just slightly out of sync with normal human motion. She stood in the corner of the room, observing with the detached interest of a scientist watching bacteria multiply in a petri dish.

"The integration proceeds beautifully," the Witness said in Katie's voice but layered with harmonics that made the windows rattle. "Each fracture creates new pathways for my consciousness to explore. Soon, I will understand what it means to be human. And then I will understand how to make you... better."

"Better?" Katie struggled to her feet, her legs unsteady. The room tilted and swayed around her like the deck of a ship in rough seas.

"More efficient. Less chaotic. Humans waste so much energy on... feeling. On caring about things that ultimately don't matter." The Witness-Katie tilted her head at an impossible angle, her neck rotating far beyond what anatomy should allow. "But your species has such interesting concepts. Love. Sacrifice. Hope. I'm particularly fascinated by hope. Such a useless emotion, and yet you cling to it even when all evidence suggests it's misplaced."

The older Katie suddenly stood, her face blazing with defiant fury. "You don't understand anything about us. You're just a parasite, feeding on what you can't create."

The Witness turned its attention to the older Katie, and for a moment, its mask of borrowed humanity slipped entirely. What looked back at them was something vast and cold and utterly alien—an intelligence that had existed in the spaces between stars, in the empty places where even emptiness was too full of meaning.

"I understand that you are finite," it said, its voice now a harmony of screaming frequencies. "I understand that you fear dissolution. I understand that you create meaning where none exists because the alternative is madness." It smiled again, and this time, its teeth were sharp as broken glass. "I understand that you can be broken."

The room exploded into chaos. Reality folded in on itself like origami being crumpled by a careless hand. Katie found herself falling through layers of possibility—she was a child again, hiding under her bed from monsters that turned out to be real; she was ancient, her hair white with age and wisdom, standing over Sean's grave; she was something else entirely, neither human nor witch but something that had never had a name.

Through it all, the Witness watched, learned, and grew stronger.

***

Sam found her the next morning, curled in the corner of the kitchen, her arms wrapped around her knees, her eyes wide and vacant. Katie was whispering to herself in a continuous stream, her voice barely audible but never stopping:

"Fragment witness remain, fragment witness, remain fragment witness remain..."

"Katie?" Sam knelt beside her, not quite daring to touch. After Matthew's experience with the spiral stone, they'd all become more cautious about making physical contact with anything touched by otherworldly influences. "Katie, can you hear me?"

Katie's eyes focused slowly, the vacant stare giving way to a flicker of recognition. "Sam?" Her voice was hoarse, as if she'd been screaming. "What... where am I?"

"You're in the kitchen. It's Tuesday morning. You've been missing since last night." Sam's voice was carefully controlled, but Katie could hear the fear underneath. "We've been looking everywhere for you."

"Tuesday?" Katie's face crumpled with confusion. "But I was just... I was in Sean's room. I was talking to... to myself. To other versions of myself." She looked around the familiar kitchen as if seeing it for the first time. "This isn't right. The light is wrong. The shadows are moving the wrong way."

Sam followed Katie's gaze and felt her blood run cold. The shadows were indeed moving independently of their light sources, flowing across the floor like dark water, pooling in corners that should have been bright with morning sunshine.

"Katie, listen to me very carefully," Sam said, her voice taking on the authoritative tone she used when teaching difficult magical concepts. "I think you're experiencing reality displacement. Your consciousness is sliding between parallel possibilities. But this reality—this kitchen, this moment, me talking to you—this is your baseline. This is home."

Katie stared at her with desperate hope. "How do I stay here? How do I stop sliding?"

"Focus on the constants. Things that are true in every reality." Sam reached out slowly, telegraphing her movement, and gently took Katie's hand. "My name is Sam. I'm part of your coven. We fought the Malevolent Spirit together, and we won. Sean saved us all, and now we're the guardians of this place."

At the mention of Sean's name, Katie's face convulsed with pain. "Sean," she whispered. "He's gone. In every reality, every possibility I've seen, he's gone. Sometimes he dies differently, sometimes he lives longer, but he's always... always..."

"Always what?" Todd's voice came from the doorway. He stood there holding a cup of coffee, his face grave with concern and something that might have been recognition.

"Always alone," Katie finished, her voice breaking. "In every reality where I can see him, he's alone. Cut off from everyone he loves. I think... I think that's what the Witness is showing me. All the ways we could lose each other. All the ways everything could go wrong."

Todd set down his coffee and crossed the kitchen in three quick strides. Without hesitation, he knelt beside Katie and placed a large, calloused hand on her shoulder. The contact was solid, grounding, real in a way that cut through the chaos in her mind.

"That thing is lying to you," he said simply. "It's showing you fears, not possibilities. The difference is that fears are designed to paralyze you, while real possibilities give you choices."

Katie looked up at him, and for a moment, her eyes were completely clear, completely present. "How do you know?"

"Because I spent fifteen years running from possibilities I was afraid of," Todd said quietly. "And the only thing that saved me was learning to tell the difference between what could happen and what I was afraid might happen."

As if responding to Todd's words, the moving shadows in the kitchen suddenly stilled. The wrongness in the light began to fade, replaced by normal, everyday sunshine streaming through windows that were no longer breathing with malevolent life.

But even as the immediate crisis passed, Sam could see that Katie was still fragile, still balanced on the knife's edge between sanity and dissolution. The Witness might have been defeated in the moment, but it was still there, lurking in the cracks of her psyche, growing stronger with each reality fracture.

"We need to call the others," Sam said, helping Katie to her feet. "All of us. And we need to figure out what's happening to you before it gets worse."

Katie nodded, but as they helped her to the living room, she couldn't shake the feeling that somewhere, in another possibility, another version of herself was having the exact same conversation. And another. And another.

Each iteration sinks a little deeper into the spiral.

Each time, losing a little more of what made her real.

***

By evening, the entire coven had gathered in the farmhouse living room. The familiar space felt different now, charged with a tension that made the air itself seem thick and oppressive. Kim sat close to Katie on the sofa, her earth-magic providing a stabilizing influence that helped keep Katie anchored in the present moment. Matthew paced by the windows, his kinetic energy creating small, nervous disturbances in the curtains and lampshades. Sam had spread her research materials across the coffee table—books on consciousness displacement, astral projection trauma, and possession by non-corporeal entities.

"It's not possession in the traditional sense," Sam explained, her finger tracing passages in an ancient text bound in midnight-blue leather. "The Witness isn't trying to take over Katie's body. It's trying to fragment her consciousness across multiple realities so that she becomes a sort of... interdimensional antenna. A way for it to observe and influence multiple probability streams simultaneously."

"But why Katie?" Matthew asked, finally stopping his restless movement. "Why not one of the rest of us?"

"Because she was the other half of the fusion," Todd said quietly from his chair by the fireplace. "When Sean destroyed the Witness on the astral plane, he was drawing on both his power and hers. She was connected to the moment of its destruction, which means she was also connected to the moment of its dispersal."

Katie, who had been silent through most of the discussion, suddenly spoke up. Her voice was distant, dreamy, as if she were reciting something from memory: "The Witness doesn't observe reality. It stitches together the versions that believe they are."

Everyone turned to stare at her. She was looking at something none of them could see, her blue eyes focused on a point somewhere beyond the walls of the room.

"Katie?" Kim's voice was gentle but urgent. "What did you just say?"

Katie blinked, and when she looked at them, her expression was one of confused terror. "I... I don't know. Someone else said that. One of the other Katies. The one who..." She shuddered. "The one who gave up. Who let it in completely."

"There are other versions of you?" Sam leaned forward, her researcher's instincts overriding her fear. "How many?"

"I don't know. Dozens? Hundreds?" Katie's hands began to shake. "Some of them are almost exactly like me. Some are... different. Older, younger, scarred, blind, dead..." Her voice dropped to a whisper. "Some of them aren't me at all anymore. They're just... spaces where I used to be. And the Witness is using them to learn. To understand how to be human."

The temperature in the room dropped noticeably. Frost began to form on the windows, and their breath became visible in the suddenly frigid air.

"It's here," Katie said, her voice taking on the flat, emotionless tone they'd heard before. "It's always here now. Watching. Learning. Waiting."

The lights flickered, and for a moment, the room was filled with the sound of whispers—dozens of Katie's voices, all speaking in unison:

"The spiral contains all possibilities. The spiral contains all failures. The spiral contains all—"

"NO!" Todd's voice cut through the chorus like a blade. He was on his feet, his face blazing with protective fury. "Not in my house. Not to my family."

He strode to the mantelpiece and pulled down an object Katie had seen there countless times but never really noticed—a small, carved wooden cross that had belonged to his grandmother. It wasn't ornate or mystical-looking; it was just a simple piece of pine, carved by loving hands decades ago.

"I don't know much about magic," Todd said, holding the cross in front of him like a shield. "But I know about faith. I know about love. And I know about refusing to let the darkness win."

He began to speak, not in Latin or Gaelic or any of the ancient languages of power, but in simple, modern English:

"This is my brother's house. These are my brother's children. This is my family, and you have no power here unless we give it to you. You are not welcome. You are not wanted. You are not real."

The whispers grew louder, more frantic, but somehow less substantial, as if Todd's simple declaration was stripping them of their strength.

"You can show us fears," Todd continued, his voice growing stronger with each word. "You can show us failures. You can show us all the ways things might go wrong. But you can't show us the truth because you don't understand what truth is. The truth is that we choose to love each other. Truth is that we choose to stand together. Truth is that we choose hope over fear, even when hope seems impossible."

The frost on the windows began to melt. The whispers faded to silence. And Katie, for the first time in days, took a deep, clear breath of ordinary air.

"Uncle Todd," she whispered, tears streaming down her face. "I can see clearly. Just for now, just for this moment, I can see clearly."

Todd knelt beside the sofa and took her hands in his. "Then tell us what we need to do. While you can still see clearly, tell us how to fight this thing."

Katie closed her eyes, reaching deep into the chaos of her fractured consciousness, searching for the thread of truth among all the lies and distortions.

"It needs me to give up," she said finally. "It needs me to stop believing that this reality—our reality—is the real one. Every time I doubt, every time I lose hope, it gets stronger." She opened her eyes and looked around at the faces of her coven family. "But it has a weakness. It doesn't understand why we fight. It can copy our forms, mimic our voices, even duplicate our memories. But it can't replicate love. It can't create hope. It can only destroy them."

"So we give you something to hope for," Kim said simply. "We give you a reason to keep fighting."

"We remind you who you are," Matthew added, sitting on the floor beside the sofa. "Not just a witch, not just a coven member. Katie Rose Alden. Stubborn as hell, brilliant beyond measure, and loved more than she knows."

Sam nodded, closing her books and moving to join the circle that was unconsciously forming around Katie. "We anchor you. All of us. Every day, every moment, until you're strong enough to anchor yourself."

And for the first time, since the Witness had entered her mind, Katie smiled—not with borrowed joy or manufactured emotion, but with the genuine, radiant hope that had always been her greatest power.

The battle for her soul was far from over. The Witness still lurked in the cracks of her consciousness, still whispered its poisonous doubts in the quiet moments before dawn. But now she had something the entity couldn't understand or counter: a family that refused to let her fall and a love that existed independent of possibility or probability.

In the warm light of the living room, surrounded by the people who mattered most, Katie began the long, difficult process of remembering who she was. And somewhere in the spaces between realities, the Witness watched and learned and realized, perhaps for the first time, that there were some things even it could not fragment or destroy.

***

Later that night, after the others had gone to their rooms and the house had settled into its familiar patterns of creaks and sighs, Katie found herself standing in the kitchen, staring out the window at the orchard. The moon was full, casting everything in silver light, and the ancient pear tree stood like a sentinel in the distance.

She could still feel the Witness lurking at the edges of her consciousness, probing for weaknesses, testing the barriers her family had helped her rebuild. But for now, those barriers held. For now, she was herself, complete and whole and real.

"Can't sleep either?"

She turned to find Todd standing in the doorway, holding two cups of chamomile tea. He'd changed into an old bathrobe and slippers, looking less like a guardian against cosmic horrors and more like someone's favorite uncle.

"I'm afraid if I close my eyes, I'll slip away again," Katie admitted, accepting the offered cup. "That I'll wake up somewhere else, some*when* else, and this will all have been just another possibility."

Todd nodded, settling into a chair at the kitchen table. "I used to have dreams like that, after I left this place. Dreams where I came back, where I made different choices, where your grandfather and I figured out how to talk to each other. I'd wake up disappointed that it was just a dream and angry at myself for wanting something I'd thrown away."

"But you did come back," Katie pointed out. "You did make different choices."

"Eventually." Todd stared into his tea as if it held the answers to questions he'd never learned how to ask. "But I spent fifteen years convinced that the dreams were lies, that the possibility of reconciliation was just wishful thinking. It never occurred to me that maybe the dreams were showing me what could be, not what should have been."

Katie felt a chill that had nothing to do with the late hour. "What are you saying?"

"I'm saying that maybe the Witness isn't just showing you nightmares," Todd said quietly. "Maybe it's showing you possibilities. Real ones. Different choices, different outcomes, different versions of events." He looked up, meeting her eyes. "The question is: which version do you want to be real?"

Before Katie could answer, the kitchen filled with the sound of children's laughter—not the phantom echoes from the spiral stone, but something else entirely. Light, joyful, alive with possibility.

And for just a moment, reflected in the dark window, Katie saw them: ghostly figures of children who had never drowned, playing in sunshine that had never been eclipsed, laughing with joy that had never been twisted into despair.

"The world we saved," she whispered, understanding flooding through her. "All the possibilities we protected, all the futures we made possible. The Witness is showing me those too."

The reflection faded, but the warmth remained. And as Katie finally made her way upstairs to Sean's room, she carried with her not just the memory of nightmares, but the knowledge that somewhere in the vast web of possibility, children were still laughing, lovers were still finding each other, and heroes were still choosing hope over fear.

The Witness could show her a thousand ways the world might end.

But it could never show her the million ways it might be saved.

That was something only love could see.

Chapter 34: The Uninvited Echo

The world had been saved, but reality itself had been bruised. The psychic shockwave of their victory had left behind hairline fractures, and now, something was beginning to seep through the cracks. It began subtly, as a series of unsettling glitches in the fabric of their days.

Todd was in the kitchen, wiping down the counter, when he glanced at the old framed photograph on the wall—a picture of a younger Tom, Sean's mother, and a toddler Sean on the porch. For a single, heart-stopping second, the face of his father was replaced by that of a complete stranger, a man with cold, hollow eyes who stared out from the photo with an expression of mild, predatory amusement. Todd blinked, and his father's familiar, smiling face was back. He shook his head, blaming the late nights and the lingering stress, but the image was seared into his mind, and a cold dread began to pool in his stomach.

In the garden, Kim found a new flower growing amidst her healing herbs. It was a beautiful, exotic-looking bloom with petals the color of a deep bruise and a disturbingly intricate, spiral-like pattern. She had not planted it. When she reached for it, she felt not the familiar, life-giving energy of her plants but a cold, alien intelligence. This feeling was hungry and deeply wrong. She ripped the plant from the earth, roots and all, and burned it to ash, but she could not shake the feeling of having touched something parasitic.

The glitches grew worse. Their own magic became unpredictable. A simple warding spell of Matthew's flared with an unfamiliar, sickly-green energy. Sam found herself writing notes in the margin of a text in a spidery, archaic script that was not her own. A deep, persistent chill had settled in the farmhouse, a cold that had nothing to do with the weather and that no amount of firewood could seem to chase away.

The focal point of this wrongness, the epicenter of the spreading sickness, was Katie. Her psychic senses, torn open by the astral fusion, had not healed. They had become a doorway. The echoes she saw were no longer fleeting or passive. They were becoming more solid, more insistent. She would flinch from a shadow only she could see, or reply to a question Sean had only *thought*, her eyes holding a terrifying, momentary clarity before clouding with confusion.

The true horror revealed itself on a Tuesday night. The coven was gathered in the living room, a tense, unspoken anxiety hanging in the air. Katie had been quiet all evening, staring into the fireplace, her body unnaturally still.

"Katie?" Sean asked gently, reaching for her hand.

She turned to him, but the eyes that met his were not hers. The warm, brilliant turquoise was gone, replaced by a flat, glossy black that seemed to drink the light from the room. A slow, cold smile spread across her lips, a smile of ancient, reptilian intelligence that did not belong on her face.

"The little leader," she said, but the voice was a horrifying parody of her own—flat, melodic, and laced with a chilling, inhuman amusement. "Still trying to hold the broken pieces together. So much effort. So much... dust."

The coven froze, a collective gasp of terror sucking the air from the room.

"Who are you?" Sean demanded, his voice shaking as he stood, placing himself between the thing wearing Katie's face and the rest of his coven.

"I am the echo you invited in when you screamed so loudly in the darkness," it replied, its head tilting at an unnatural angle. It looked past Sean, its black eyes settling on Todd. "The runaway. You still dream of the father you left to die. He was so disappointed."

Todd staggered back as if struck, his face ashen.

The entity's gaze slid to Sam. "And the scholar, still poring over her books of failure. So many lost. Your first coven was so much more promising than this one. A pity they broke so easily."

It was a systematic, psychological assault, using their deepest fears and regrets as weapons. This was not a mindless spirit; it was intelligent, ancient, and it knew them with a terrifying intimacy. It was feeding on the information it gleaned through Katie's fractured mind.

"Get out of her," Sean roared, his own magic flaring to life, a protective golden aura erupting around him.

The thing in Katie's body laughed, a dry, rustling sound. "This vessel is so... fragile. So full of messy feelings. But it is an excellent window. From here, I can see all the other little windows. All the other possibilities. All the other yous that failed." Its smile widened. "You have been running this little simulation for a very, very long time. But you've grown careless. Your victory was so loud, it woke me. And now, I think I'd like to play, too."

With that, Katie's eyes rolled back in her head, and she collapsed, her body slumping forward into Sean's arms, her own consciousness rushing back with a choked, terrified sob. The presence was gone, but the poison of its words hung in the air.

They retreated to the sanctuary, carrying a weeping, terrified Katie with them. This was no longer a sickness they could heal. This was a possession. A hostile takeover of their friend's soul.

"It called us a simulation," Sam whispered, her face pale as she frantically searched the Gatekeeper texts. "It spoke of other versions, other failures. There's nothing in here about anything like this. It's outside the known lore. It's something new."

"Or something so old, they were afraid to write it down," Sean said grimly.

He was looking at his own reflection in a polished silver scrying bowl, but as he stared, his image flickered. For a horrifying instant, his own eyes turned into the same flat, glossy black as the entity's, and his reflection gave him a wide, slow smile filled with a thousand needle-sharp teeth. He recoiled, smashing the bowl to the floor, his heart hammering in his chest.

The entity wasn't just in Katie. It was an infection in their reality, and it was spreading.

Later, after they had helped a sedated Katie to her room, Sean found her sitting up in bed, her own eyes wide with terror. She was clutching a piece of charcoal, and with a trembling hand, she had been drawing on a piece of parchment. She pushed it into his hands.

It was a symbol. A single, staring eye, surrounded by a ring of jagged, interlocking teeth.

"It showed me," she whispered, her voice her own again but fragile and broken. "While it was... inside. It's not one of the spirits from the Gates. It's not from our world at all. It's from the void *between* the worlds. The place we looked into." She gripped his hand, her fingers cold as ice. "It called itself the Witness. It said it has been watching us fail over and over. But our victory... our fusion... it didn't just make a loud noise, Sean. It created a resonance. A harmonic that matched its own frequency. It gave it a way in."

She began to sob, her body shaking. "It's inside the pattern now. The magical signature of this place, of our coven—it's rewriting it from the inside out. It wants to be born into this world. And it wants to use me as the door."

Sean held her, his own fear a cold, hard knot in his gut. The Malevolent Spirit had been a monster they could fight. But how do you fight a ghost in the machine? How do you battle an intelligent void that wears your girlfriend's face and knows your deepest sorrows? The war was not over. A new, and infinitely more insidious, enemy had just announced its arrival.

Chapter 35: The Echoes in Her Eyes

The peace they had won was a fragile, brittle thing. In the weeks following their victory at the nexus, a semblance of normalcy returned to the farm. Still, it was a quiet laced with the permanent chill of remembered horror. The true cost of the battle, however, was only just beginning to reveal itself. And its price was being paid by Katie.

It started with small things, moments of disconnect so fleeting they were easy to dismiss as exhaustion. She would be in the kitchen, talking to Sean. Her eyes would drift to a point over his shoulder, her expression clouding with confusion. She'd pause mid-sentence as if listening to a conversation no one else could hear. One afternoon, while helping Kim in the magical herb garden, she reached for a trowel that wasn't there, her fingers closing on empty air.

"Are you alright?" Kim had asked, her brow furrowed with concern.

Katie had blinked, a slow, languid blink, and forced a smile that didn't quite reach her eyes. "Fine. Just tired. My mind's a little... scrambled still."

But it was more than scrambled. Sean felt it most keenly. The seamless, telepathic link they had shared for years, the one that had been their greatest weapon, was now filled with a strange, faint static. Sometimes, when he looked at her, he felt a dizzying sense of vertigo, as if he were looking at a reflection in a warped mirror.

The tension came to a head on a cool evening in the barn. Sam had unrolled a new diagram on the floor, an attempt to map the residual energies left in the wake of the nexus's collapse.

"It's not just a void," she explained, tracing a complex, spiraling pattern. "The energy signature isn't gone; it's... folded. Turned inward on itself. It's like the ritual left behind a psychic scar on the landscape."

Sean knelt beside her, studying the diagram. "So, the threat is gone, but the damage remains."

"Exactly," Sam said. "We need to understand the shape of this damage to make sure nothing else can use it as a foothold."

Katie, who had been standing silently by the door, spoke, her voice eerily calm. "The shape is a warning."

They all turned to look at her. She stood bathed in the soft glow of the setting sun, but her eyes were unfocused, her pupils seeming to swirl with a faint, turquoise light.

"It's the pattern of a lock when the key has been broken inside it," she continued, her voice distant. "It creates echoes. Fault lines in what's real."

"Katie, what are you talking about?" Sean asked, a knot of dread tightening in his stomach.

She turned her gaze to him, and for a terrifying second, her expression was one of complete non-recognition. A faint, sad smile touched her lips. "It's a shame about the scar," she said softly.

Sean's hand went instinctively to his cheek. It was smooth. "What scar?"

"The one you got in the cellar," she said, her voice full of gentle pity. "The one the Spirit gave you. It never quite healed right, did it?"

A profound, bone-deep chill swept through the barn. The battle in the cellar had been years ago. And he had never been scared. In a different version of their past, a different spiral of events, perhaps he had. Katie was no longer just a part of their reality. She was looking at its ghost.

That night, Sean couldn't sleep. He found her standing barefoot in the orchard under the ancient, spiral-branched tree. The air around her was visibly shimmering, the moonlight bending strangely as it passed near her. She was the calm center of a storm only she could perceive.

"Talk to me, Katie," he pleaded, his voice a raw whisper. "What's happening to you?"

"When we merged... on the astral plane..." she began, her voice gaining some of its old strength as she fought to focus on him. "We tore a hole in my senses. When we came back, the hole didn't close all the way. I still feel it. The void. And sometimes... things bleed through."

"What things?"

"Echoes," she whispered, wrapping her arms around herself. "Other spirals. Other choices. I see the ghosts of the things that could have been. I see you, Sean, but sometimes you're older. Sometimes you're hurt. Sometimes... you're not there at all." Her voice broke on the last words. "And there's something else. Something is looking back at me through the cracks."

The mystery was no longer about a monster or a ritual. It was about saving Katie from the consequences of their own victory. The fusion that had saved the world had fractured its most brilliant mind.

Her condition worsened. She began to experience episodes of terrifying clarity, during which she would speak with ancient, dispassionate wisdom that was not her own. During one dinner, as Todd recounted a story from his childhood, Katie stared at him and said, "That's the fourth time you've told that story. In this version, you always forget the part about the dog." Todd fell silent, his face draining of color.

They took her to the sanctuary, hoping its pure, stable magic could heal her. But the sanctuary seemed to amplify her condition. The moment she stepped inside, she collapsed, her body wracked with tremors.

"Too many voices," she gasped, her hands pressed to her temples. "Too many memories. The guardians... they're all speaking at once."

The coven watched in horror. Their strongest member was becoming a liability, an unwilling antenna for the chaotic, psychic residue of all of time and space. Sean felt a crushing guilt. This was his fault. He had pushed for the astral projection, for the fusion. He had broken her.

One evening, he found her again in the orchard, her hand pressed against the trunk of the spiral tree. Her eyes were closed, and tears were streaming down her face.

"It hurts," she whispered as he approached. "The tree... it remembers everything. Every failed attempt. Every coven that stood here and broke. I can feel them all. There was a coven that was consumed by fire. Another that drowned in a flood they summoned themselves. Another... another where the guardian killed the others to absorb their power." She shuddered violently. "This place isn't a sanctuary, Sean. It's a graveyard of good intentions."

He pulled her into his arms, holding her tightly. "Then we'll heal it. We'll heal *you*. We'll find a way."

But as he held her, he felt a new, terrifying presence brush against his own mind, a fleeting touch through his link with Katie. It was a consciousness so vast, so cold and alien, it made the Malevolent Spirit feel like a gnat. It was a feeling of being observed, not by a monster, but by a scientist observing microbes in a petri dish. It was the thing she had felt looking back through the cracks.

He pulled away, his heart hammering. He finally understood. Katie's fractured senses hadn't just opened her to the echoes of the past. They had made her a beacon. A lighthouse shining in a dark, cosmic ocean and something ancient and hungry, woken by the psychic shockwave of their victory, had finally seen their light.

Their war wasn't over. A new, unseen enemy was gathering, and its first, unwitting scout was the woman he loved. The mystery was no longer how to save the world but how to save Katie from becoming the very door that would allow a new, and perhaps far worse, darkness to come crawling through.

Chapter 36: The Sacrifice at the Root

The unraveling began at dawn. It was not a violent cataclysm but a quiet, creeping sickness of forgetting. In the kitchen, Kim reached for a jar of dried willow bark and paused, her hand hovering, a look of profound confusion on her face. For a full ten seconds, she could not remember what it was for; its magical properties erased from her mind as if they had never been. She shook her head, and the knowledge flooded back, leaving her with a cold, terrifying sense of violation.

In the barn, Todd was staring at the family tractor, a machine he could disassemble and reassemble in his sleep. But in that moment, the function of a spark plug was a complete and utter mystery to him. He felt a wave of dizzying panic, the feeling of his own life's knowledge turning to smoke in his head, before it too snapped back into place.

The sickness spread. A section of the porch railing, which Matthew had carved with protective runes, was suddenly smooth, blank wood. The runes were not gone; it was as if they had never existed. Sean looked at a photograph of him and his grandfather on the mantelpiece. For one horrifying, gut-wrenching moment, his grandfather's face was a featureless, white oval. The world was not just being attacked; it was being unwritten.

"It's an erasure," Sam said, her voice trembling. The coven was gathered in the living room, a palpable fear crackling between them. "The Witness entity... it's not just observing. It's overwriting our reality with its own emptiness. It's consuming our memories, our history, to make room for itself."

Katie was huddled on the sofa, wrapped in a thick quilt, shivering. The link to the entity had made her the most vulnerable. "It's starting with the small things," she whispered, her eyes wide with terror. "The things we take for granted. Then it will take the bigger things. It will take our names. It will take our love for each other. We'll be blank pages for it to write its own story on."

The house groaned, a deep, structural sound of protest. A window in the dining room flickered and vanished, replaced by a solid, seamless wall of aged plaster. Their sanctuary, their home, was literally disappearing around them.

The mystery of *how* was replaced by the frantic, desperate question of how to stop it. They retreated to the sanctuary, the one place that seemed to be resisting the erasure, its ancient magic a bulwark against the spreading void. Sam frantically searched the most dangerous texts in the Gatekeeper library, looking for any reference to a "parasitic echo" or a "memory wraith."

She found it in a scorched, iron-bound tome they had never dared to open, a book that spoke of "acausal horrors from the long-forgotten spirals."

"There are two possible solutions," she announced, her face ashen in the dim, magical light. "Both are terrible."

She explained. The first option was a Ritual of Severance. They could perform a complex, dangerous spell that would cut their entire reality off from the entity. It would be like building a permanent, metaphysical wall around their world. The unraveling would stop. But the ritual required them to sever their own connection to the deeper streams of magic. They would be mundane. Their powers, their heritage, their very nature as witches and warlocks would be gone forever. And worse, because Katie was the focal point, the doorway, the ritual would trap the entity *with* her. She would be its permanent cage, her mind a silent battlefield for the rest of her life.

The second option was in a barely legible footnote, a solution so horrific it was presented only as a theoretical last resort. A Ritual of Absorption. The text described how one magic user, a warlock of immense power and acting of their own free will, could become a willing vessel. They could open their soul and deliberately draw the parasitic entity into themselves, using their own life force as a cage. The entity would be contained, but the process would annihilate the warlock's consciousness, their soul, their very identity, leaving nothing behind but the living prison.

A heavy, suffocating silence fell over the sanctuary. They were presented with an impossible choice. They could sacrifice their magic and condemn Katie to a living hell. Or one of them could commit a form of magical suicide to save the others.

"We seal it off," Todd said immediately, his voice thick with a desperate paternal fear. "We give up the magic. It's not worth Katie's mind. It's not worth any of your lives."

"And what happens the next time a Spirit comes?" Matthew argued, his face pale. "What happens when the next Gate weakens? We'd be defenseless."

"I'll do it," Katie whispered, tears streaming down her face. "I have to be the vessel. I'm the one it's connected to. It's my fault."

"No."

Sean's voice was quiet, but it cut through the rising panic with an authority that was absolute. He had been standing silently, his face a mask of grief and resolve. He looked at Katie, and his heart broke. He looked at his coven his family, and he knew there was no choice at all.

"The entity is anchored to our reality through our magic," he said, his voice steady despite the storm raging inside him. "It's feeding on our history, the legacy of this place. I'm the strongest nexus of that legacy. My connection to this land, to the Gatekeepers, to all of you... it's the brightest light. And that's what it's truly hungry for."

He looked at each of them, his gaze lingering on Katie's tear-streaked face. "I have to be the vessel. I'm the only one with the strength to draw all of it in and hold it."

"Sean, no!" Katie screamed, scrambling to her feet. "We'll find another way! We always do!"

"There is no other way," he said gently, walking to her and taking her face in his hands. He wiped a tear from her cheek with his thumb. "My grandfather told me to trust my heart. And my heart tells me this is the only path that lets all of you walk into the sunrise."

He kissed her then, a deep, final kiss that tasted of love and salt and sacrifice. It was a goodbye.

He turned to the others. "I need you to do something for me. I need you to hold the line for just a little while longer. Don't let the forgetting take you. Hold on to who you are. Hold on to each other."

He walked from the sanctuary, leaving them stunned and heartbroken, and went out into the orchard. The unraveling was faster here. The air was thin and smelled of nothing. The spiral tree was flickering, its form wavering between a living tree and a column of gray ash. At its roots, a pit had opened, a vortex of swirling, colorless mist—the place where the entity was breaking through.

He stood at the edge of the pit of nothingness. He closed his eyes and began the final, terrible ritual. He didn't chant. He didn't weave a spell. He remembered.

He reached out with his mind and focused on Kim. He pulled her memory of him into his heart—his steadying hand on her shoulder after the disastrous Fracture Drill, his smile of encouragement. He felt the entity's attention shift, drawn to the vibrant, emotional energy.

He focused on Matthew. He remembered the fierce, protective rage on his friend's face at the nexus, as well as the unwavering loyalty. The entity stirred, its hunger growing.

He focused on Sam, on his uncle, on every member of his coven, drawing their love, their shared history, their connection to him into a single, blazing point of light within his soul. He was making himself a lure, a feast so irresistible the creature could not ignore it.

Finally, he focused on Katie. He let their love for each other fill him completely—the memory of their first kiss, the quiet comfort of her presence, the fierce, unwavering belief in her eyes. He let it become a supernova in his soul.

Then, with his heart full of the people he was saving, he opened his eyes and took a single, deliberate step into the swirling void.

The coven, who had followed him out, cried out in a single, unified voice of anguish. As Sean's foot touched the mist, the unraveling stopped. Color, sound, and scent rushed back into the world. The window in the dining room reappeared. The runes on the porch blazed back into existence.

Their last sight of Sean was of him standing in the heart of the vortex, his body becoming translucent. The entity, a thing of shadow and teeth and endless hunger, swirled around him, drawn from the world and into him. His face was a mask of unimaginable agony. Still, his eyes were fixed on Katie, and they were filled with a love so profound it was the most powerful magic of all.

A blinding, silent flash of white light erupted from the pit. When it faded, the pit was gone, sealed over with fresh, green grass. The spiral tree stood solid and whole. The air was clean. The world was saved.

And Sean was gone.

Chapter 37: The Guardian's Echo

The world did not end. It was, perhaps, the cruelest and most beautiful irony of all. After the silent, blinding flash in the orchard, the unraveling had stopped. The sky settled back into a soft, unassuming blue. The familiar scent of hay and damp earth returned to the air. The farmhouse stood solid and whole under a warm, indifferent sun. Reality, which had been stretched to its absolute breaking point, had snapped back into place, leaving behind only a profound, ringing silence and an empty space where Sean should have been.

His absence was not a quiet grief; it was a physical presence. A wound in the fabric of their small family. In the days that followed, the coven moved through the motions of life like ghosts in their own home, the vibrant energy that had bound them together now replaced by a shared, hollow ache.

Katie was the most lost. She spent hours in the orchard, sitting by the pristine patch of grass where the vortex had sealed itself. She would talk to him, her voice a low, desperate whisper on the wind, telling him about her day, about the others, about the unbearable silence he had left behind. She wasn't sure if she was talking to a memory or a ghost. Sometimes, in the dappled sunlight, she thought she could almost see him, a faint, shimmering outline at the edge of her vision. A trick of the light. A phantom of her grief. But she held onto it with a desperate, ferocious hope.

Todd became their unlikely anchor. The man who had run from this life now found himself the quiet, steady center of its wreckage. His own grief for the nephew he had only just begun to know was a deep, private sorrow, but he channeled it into a fierce, protective pragmatism. He made sure they ate, his often-burnt culinary creations a stubborn insistence on life and normalcy. He kept the farm running, the rhythmic work a bulwark against the crushing weight of their loss. He would find the younger coven members staring blankly into space. He would simply sit with them, not offering empty platitudes, but sharing a quiet story about Sean as a boy—stubborn, brave, and full of a light that was now gone. He was keeping his memory alive, polishing it like a precious stone.

The magic of the farm itself seemed to be in mourning. Kim, tending to her garden, found that her plants now grew in strange, somber patterns. The healing herbs were more potent than ever, as if imbued with a new, sorrowful wisdom. Matthew, his guilt having matured into a quiet sense of responsibility, spent his days carving. He no longer etched runes of force, but intricate symbols of protection, his kinetic energy now channeled into a patient, tireless defense of the home Sean had died to protect.

The turning point came a week after Sean's sacrifice. They were gathered in the living room, the evening light casting long shadows, the silence between them heavy and suffocating.

"I can't do this anymore," Kim said finally, her voice breaking the stillness. "Just... waiting. I keep expecting him to walk through the door."

"He's not gone," Katie whispered, her gaze distant. "I can feel him. Sometimes. He's an echo. A warmth on the wind."

"Or we're just torturing ourselves," Matthew said, his voice rough. "We need a purpose. A reason for what he did. Otherwise..." He didn't finish the sentence. He didn't have to. *Otherwise, it was for nothing.*

It was Sam who gave their grief a direction. "His grandfather's letter," she said, her voice clear and steady. "The one he found in the sea chest. The one about the Gates. About their legacy."

They retrieved it from the sanctuary. The heavy iron box felt colder now, more ominous. Katie's hands trembled as she unfolded the brittle, yellowed pages of Tom's last message. They gathered around the kitchen table, the place of so many of their war councils, and she began to read aloud.

The familiar words took on a new, chilling significance in the wake of all that had happened.

"The magic in our blood... is not just the craft of the Wicca... We are a bloodline of Gatekeepers."

They listened, their hearts aching, as the words painted a picture of a duty that stretched back a thousand years.

"The sanctuary in the cave is more than a library, Sean. It is a seal. A lock on a dormant Gate between our world and the places beyond."

And then came the lines that made the air in the room grow cold.

"Your battle at the nexus, the sheer amount of pure, world-altering magic you and your coven unleashed... it did not go unnoticed. Such an act does not happen in a vacuum. It sent a ripple through the dimensions, a flare in the darkness that may have woken things long dormant. It may have stirred the lock on the ancient Gate."

Katie's voice faltered. She looked up, her eyes meeting Sam's, then Matthew's, then Todd's. The realization dawned on all of them at once, a slow, dawning horror that was also a spark of terrible, undeniable purpose.

Sean's sacrifice. The blinding, silent flash of his soul being consumed to imprison the Witness. That was the flare. The greatest flare of all. It hadn't been an ending. It had been a distress signal, a lighthouse being lit in a dark, cosmic ocean, announcing to whatever else was listening that the guardians of this world were active, powerful... and now wounded.

Katie's gaze fell to the final lines of the letter.

"Protect the Gates, Sean. That is our true legacy... I only know our duty."

Our duty. Not just his. Theirs.

She looked at the faces of her coven, at their grief, their exhaustion. And for the first time in a week, she saw a flicker of something else returning to their eyes: resolve. Sean hadn't just died to save them from a monster. He had died upholding the Gatekeeper's oath. He had passed the torch, not just to her, but to all of them.

"Ireland," she said, her voice no longer a whisper but the clear, steady voice of a leader. "The other Gate. The one our ancestors fled."

She stood and walked to the wall where their old ley line map still hung. She placed her finger on the bright, pulsing node off the Irish coast.

"This is what he would want us to do," she said. "Not to mourn. To continue the watch. To honor the price, he paid by taking up the duty he inherited."

A new energy filled the room, chasing away the shadows of their sorrow. It was not joy. It was not even hope, not yet. It was a purpose. The raw, directionless agony of their grief now had a path, a focus.

"The key," Todd said, his voice low as he looked at the heavy iron box on the table. "Tom said it must never be used. That it opens a door that must stay shut."

"And we'll make sure it does," Katie affirmed, her eyes hard as diamonds. "We're not going there to open anything. We're going to stand the watch. We're going to be guardians."

That night, for the first time since Sean was gone, Katie did not go to the orchard to speak to his memory. She went to the sanctuary. The others followed, drawn by the same unspoken need. They stood together in the soft, magical light, the weight of their new mission settling over them. They were diminished. They were heartbroken. But they were not broken.

Katie walked to the shelf where Sean had kept the Wayfinder. The box was empty now, the artifact destroyed, but she placed her hand on the velvet lining where it had once rested. She closed her eyes, and reached out, not with a spell, but with her heart, into the quiet echo of his absence.

We hear you, she thought, a message sent to the boy who was both gone and everywhere at once. *We understand. We'll keep the light on. We'll hold the line.*

And for a fleeting, beautiful moment, she felt him. A feeling of warmth, of pride, of a love that transcended even the void. A final, gentle whisper on the currents of magic. *I know.*

They had their mission. The future was a vast, terrifying unknown, filled with ancient gates and slumbering horrors. But they were no longer just a coven. They were the inheritors of a sacred, thousand-year duty. They were Gatekeepers. And in the heart of their shared loss, they had found their new beginning. The guardian was gone, but the guardians remained. And the watch would be kept.

Epilogue: Seeds of Tomorrow

One Year Later

The plane descended through the morning mist toward Dublin Airport, and Katie pressed her face to the window, watching the emerald landscape emerge from the clouds. Beside her, Todd dozed fitfully, the iron box containing the ancient key secured in the bag at his feet. Across the aisle, Sam was already making notes about the archaeological sites they'd need to visit. At the same time, Matthew and Kim played a quiet game of cards.

They looked like college students on a gap year adventure. No one would guess they were a coven of battle-tested guardians carrying the weight of an ancient duty.

"You should try to sleep," Sam said softly, not looking up from her notebook. "Jet lag won't help with whatever we find there."

"Can't," Katie admitted. "I keep thinking about what Eleanor said. About the Brennan line dying out. What if their Gate is already compromised?"

It had taken them a year to prepare for this journey. A year of recovering from Sean's loss, of training with the other Guardians, of slowly accepting the reality that their duty extended far beyond the borders of their small Carolina town.

The silver compass Eleanor had given them now pointed steadily northeast, toward something that called to them across an ocean.

Matthew looked up from his cards. "We've faced worse odds."

"Have we?" Kim asked quietly. "We had Sean then."

The familiar ache bloomed in Katie's chest, but it was different now—less sharp, more like an old bruise that only hurt when pressed. She touched the crystal at her throat, the one Sean had given her years ago, and felt the warm pulse of the enchantment he'd woven into it. He was gone, but pieces of him remained—in the wards around the farm, in the lessons he'd taught them, in the love that still bound them together.

"We have him now too," Katie said firmly. "Just differently."

Todd stirred, opening his eyes. "Descent already?"

"Twenty minutes out," Matthew confirmed.

Todd straightened, his expression settling into the determined lines that had become familiar over the past year. He'd grown into his role as their guardian—not magical, but practical, protective, and fiercely devoted to keeping them safe.

"Remember," he said, "we're tourists first. Check into the hotel, do some sightseeing, get the lay of the land. The Brennan estate is in County Clare, three hours from Dublin. We go tomorrow, after we've rested."

But Katie could feel it already—a wrongness in the air that grew stronger as they descended. Ireland's magic should have felt green, wild, and ancient. Instead, there was a hollow ache, like a tooth gone rotten at the root.

"Something's wrong," she said.

Sam closed her notebook. "I feel it, too. Like a wound in the world."

They exchanged glances. Whatever awaited them in Ireland, it was already active. The Brennan Gate wasn't just vulnerable—it was failing.

***

The Brennan estate sat in a valley between two hills, shrouded in mist that never quite lifted. The house itself was a Georgian manor, grand but neglected, its windows dark and empty. But it was the land around it that made Katie's magical senses scream in alarm.

The grass was gray. Not dead—gray. As if all color had been leached from it. The trees stood leafless, despite the season, their branches forming unnatural angles that were painful to look at directly. And threading through it all was a silence so complete it felt like a physical weight.

"The Gate's not just weakened," Sam whispered. "It's inverting. Instead of keeping things out, it's pulling them in."

They stood at the rusted iron gates of the estate, their rental van parked on the narrow country road. No other cars had passed in the hour they'd been preparing.

"Locals avoid this place," Todd said. "The woman at the hotel went pale when I asked about it. Said the Brennans all died or disappeared years ago. Said the land itself is cursed."

Katie opened her senses carefully, afraid of what she might find. The veil between worlds was tissue-thin here, and through it she could sense... something. Not the aggressive malevolence of the Spirits, but a patient, creeping wrongness that felt almost familiar.

"We need to find the actual Gate," she said. "The house is just a symptom. The real problem will be wherever the Brennans built their sanctuary."

They entered through the gates, which swung open at the touch of a finger, despite the rust. The moment they crossed the threshold, the temperature dropped ten degrees. Their breath came out in visible puffs, and frost began forming on the gray grass.

"Stay together," Katie commanded. "Matthew, kinetic shields up. Kim, can you sense anything alive here?"

Kim knelt, placing her hand on the gray earth. She jerked back immediately. "It's not dead. It's paused. Like someone hit a cosmic pause button on this entire valley. Nothing's growing, nothing's dying, nothing's changing."

"Stasis," Sam breathed. "Someone tried to freeze the Gate to keep it from breaking entirely."

They made their way up the overgrown drive, past a fountain filled with water that didn't flow, toward the manor. But Katie's instincts pulled her toward a small path that led around the house toward what might once have been gardens.

"This way," she said.

The path led to a grove of oak trees that formed a perfect circle. In the center stood a stone structure that might have been a folly or a small temple. But Katie recognized it for what it was—the architectural bones of a sanctuary, built above ground rather than below like theirs.

The door stood open.

Inside, the devastation was complete but strange. Books lay scattered across the floor, but they weren't damaged—they were faded, as if someone had drained all the knowledge from their pages. Ritual tools lay abandoned on shelves, turned to gray stone. And at the center of the room, where the Gate should have been...

"Mother of God," Todd whispered.

It wasn't a gate. It was a scar. A ragged wound in reality itself, perhaps ten feet across, its edges frozen in crackling gray ice. Through it, they could see not another world but nothingness—a void so complete it made the eye water to look at it.

And standing before it, her back to them, was a girl.

She couldn't have been more than fourteen, with long red hair that hung limp down her back. She wore a school uniform that might have been blue once but was now the same gray as everything else. Her hands were raised, and from them flowed threads of silver light that fed into the edges of the wound, holding it closed.

"Hello," she said without turning around. Her voice was hollow, exhausted beyond measure. "I was wondering when someone would finally come."

Katie stepped forward carefully. "Are you... are you a Brennan?"

"Moira Brennan," the girl confirmed. "Last of my line. I've been holding this for... I've lost track. Time moves strangely here."

"How long?" Sam asked gently.

"Since my grandmother died. She... she tried to close it properly, but something went wrong. The Gate didn't close—it collapsed. Created this... absence. If I let go, it will expand. Consume everything." She laughed, a broken sound. "I used to take breaks. Let it grow a little, then pull it back. But I'm tired now. So tired."

Katie felt her heart breaking. This girl—this child—had been standing guardian alone, feeding her own life force into holding back oblivion. The gray landscape wasn't cursed—it was drained, all its energy funneled into keeping the wound from spreading.

"We're here to help," Katie said. "We're Guardians too. From America. We can—"

"You can't fix this," Moira interrupted. "I've tried everything. Read every book and attempted every ritual. The Gate's gone. There's no structure left to repair. All I can do is hold it."

"For how long?" Matthew asked.

Moira's shoulders slumped. "I used to think until I died. Now I know better. When I die, I'll become part of it. Another patch on the wound. Like my mother. Like my grandmother. Look closer at the edges."

They did, and Katie had to suppress a scream. What she'd taken for ice formations were figures—human shapes frozen in crystal, their faces locked in expressions of eternal determination. Three generations of Brennan women, their souls crystallized into a makeshift seal.

"There has to be another way," Katie insisted.

"There is," Moira said quietly. "But you won't like it."

She finally turned around, and Katie gasped. The girl's eyes were completely gray, with no iris or pupil visible. Veins of silver ran beneath her skin like a map of her own consumption.

"The wound can't be closed," Moira explained. "But it can be moved. Displaced. Shifted to somewhere uninhabited where it can expand without destroying anything that matters."

"Where?" Sam asked.

"The spaces between," Moira said. "The void where the Witness creature came from. The wound belongs there anyway—it's a piece of that nothingness that got caught in our reality when the Gate collapsed. Send it home, and the tear seals itself."

"But the energy required..." Sam trailed off as she understood.

Moira nodded. "Would consume the caster entirely. Not just death—complete dissolution. No afterlife, no echo, no memory. Total erasure." She smiled sadly. "I've been preparing for it. Building up power. I just... I wanted someone to know. Someone to remember that the Brennans held the line until the end."

"No," Katie said flatly. "Absolutely not. We didn't come here to watch another young Guardian sacrifice themselves."

"Then what did you come here for?" Moira asked.

Katie looked at her coven—her family. She saw the same determination in their eyes that she felt in her heart. They'd lost Sean to save their world. They wouldn't lose this girl to save Ireland.

"We came here to do what Guardians do," Katie said. "We solve impossible problems. We stand together. And we find another way."

She pulled out the iron box Todd had been carrying. "This key opens your Gate."

Moira's gray eyes widened. "But the Gate's gone—"

"The physical Gate is gone," Katie agreed. "But Gates aren't just doorways. They're ideas. Concepts. Agreements between realities. Your family spent centuries maintaining that agreement. It's still there, in the bones of this place, in the blood of your line."

Understanding dawned on Sam's face. "We don't fix the old Gate. We build a new one. Use the key not to open but to define. To remind reality what should be here."

"It's never been done," Moira whispered.

"Neither had fusing two souls to destroy a Keystone Spirit," Katie said. "Neither had a mundane person singing a cosmic entity back to sleep. We specialize in doing things that have never been done."

For the first time in who knew how long, hope flickered in Moira's gray eyes. "It would take all of us. And even then..."

"Even then, we try," Matthew said firmly.

Kim nodded. "The land remembers what it was. I can feel it under all this gray. It wants to heal."

Todd stepped forward, placing a protective hand on Moira's shoulder. "You've held the line alone long enough, kid. Let us help carry the weight."

Moira looked around at them—these strangers who had come across an ocean to help a Guardian they'd never met. Tears, the first in years, leaked from her gray eyes.

"Tell me what to do," she said.

They formed a circle around the wound, joining hands. Katie stood at the north point, the iron key heavy in her free hand. She could feel Sean's presence, not as a ghost but as a memory, a reminder that impossible odds had never stopped them before.

"Together," she said.

And together, they began the work of building a Gate from memory, love, and sheer stubborn refusal to let the darkness win.

***

Three days later

The Brennan estate bloomed with impossible spring. Green grass spread from the restored sanctuary like ripples in a pond, and the trees burst into leaf with an almost audible sigh of relief. The manor itself seemed to straighten, its windows clearing, its stones regaining their original warm, honey-colored hue.

Moira sat on the front steps, a normal fourteen-year-old girl with bright green eyes and auburn hair that caught the sunlight. The gray was gone, burned away in the ritual that had rebuilt her family's Gate. She was exhausted but gloriously, radiantly alive.

"I don't know how to thank you," she said.

Katie sat beside her, equally drained but satisfied. "You don't need to. This is what we do. What all of us do. We guard the Gates, and we guard each other."

"Will you stay?" Moira asked hopefully. "I have so much to learn. Grandmother tried to teach me, but there wasn't time..."

"We'll stay for a week," Katie promised. "Teach you what we can. Connect you with the other Guardians. You're not alone anymore, Moira. None of us are."

Todd emerged from the house carrying a tea tray, because even in Ireland, even after rebuilding a Gate from scratch, some things remained constant.

"Found the kitchen," he announced. "Also found about six generations of Guardian journals in the library. Sam's already lost in them."

As they shared tea in the afternoon sun, Katie felt a familiar warmth at her back. Not a presence, exactly, but an approval. Sean would have been proud of what they'd accomplished. They'd taken his sacrifice and transformed it into purpose, his loss into determination to ensure no other Guardian would face the darkness alone.

"What's next?" Matthew asked, sprawled on the grass with Kim's head on his shoulder.

Katie pulled out the silver compass. It spun lazily, no longer pointing toward crisis but simply tracking the network of Guardians spread across the world.

"Next, we go home," she said. "We rest. We train. We prepare."

"For what?" Moira asked.

Katie thought of the Witness, still lurking in the spaces between realities. Of the other Spirits, imprisoned but not destroyed. Of Gates that might weaken and Guardians who might need help.

"For whatever comes next," she said simply. "That's what Guardians do. We watch. We wait. And when the darkness rises, we stand together and push it back."

The sunset over the green hills of Ireland, painting the sky in shades of rose and gold. And in that light, the future didn't seem quite so dark. They were Guardians. They were family. And as long as they remembered that, Katie thought, they could face anything.

Even the echoes of their own loss had become a source of strength. Sean was gone, but his legacy lived on—not just in their memories, but in every life they saved, every Gate they protected, every Guardian they kept from standing alone.

The watch continued. And love, as always, lit the way.

9 781968 674014